I0613921

THE EXPERTS AGREE

The Widow on the Ledge is terrific!

"In a style rarely seen in popular crime fiction, Spero Lappas provides a fascinating insight into how a multi-talented trial lawyer strategizes, prepares, and tries his cases. Get ready to be awed and intrigued, startled and fascinated by this amazing first novel by a truly great lawyer and author. Oh, and just wait until you meet Evan Wonder, the newest hero among crime fiction superstars."

— Joshua Lock, Esquire
prominent criminal defense lawyer,
past president, Pennsylvania Association of
Criminal Defense Lawyers

"The Widow on the Ledge is a suspenseful legal thriller about a master of the courtroom and the chess board who mysteriously agrees to defend a widow charged with murdering her husband. Spero Lappas gives the reader a thrilling story with a knockout ending!"

— William C. Costopoulos, Esquire
celebrated criminal defense lawyer,
bestselling author of The Price of Acquittal

"Highly recommended! An amazing who-done-it thriller. Cunningly designed, ingeniously laid out and suspenseful. A must-read."

— *Major Diane Stackhouse (retired),*
Pennsylvania State Police

"A marvelous murder mystery! The author's knowledge of chess and classical literature will capture the reader's interest immediately. You won't want to put it down!"

— *The Honorable Jeannine Turgeon,*
retired trial court judge

The
Widow
on the
Ledge

The
Widow
on the
Ledge

Spero T. Lappas

ALITHOS

Also by Spero T. Lappas

Conquer Life's Frontiers:
A Philosophy of Individual Fulfilment

The Seventh Name of Happiness

New Tricks for Old Dogs

Copyright © 2025 by Spero T. Lappas.

All characters appearing in this work are fictitious. Any resemblance to real persons, living or dead, is purely coincidental.

All rights reserved. Designed and printed in the United States of America. No part of this book may be used or reproduced in any manner whatsoever without written permission except in the case of brief quotations embodied in critical articles and reviews. For information, contact:

Alithos Media Group, LLC
P.O. Box 6065
Harrisburg, PA 17112

ISBN: 979-8-218-70174-1

Contact the author at Spero@SperoLappas.com

Dedication

To all the courageous defense lawyers whose examples taught me how to stand up against injustice.

And why.

Thank you.

*Chess is neither a science nor an art. It is
what human nature most delights in:
A fight.*

Emanuel Lasker

Prologue

Courtroom One
The Dauphin County Courthouse
Eight Years Ago

N o one knew better than Attorney Evan Wonder that courtrooms are dangerous places. Judges and other politicians might like to call them temples of justice. Scholars and law students who have never been inside one might think they are laboratories where experiments lead to truth. But Evan had spent the last twelve years of his life walking around witness stands, judges' benches, and jury boxes, and he knew better than that. Courtrooms are battlefields, quicksand pits, lions' dens, high wires. Life is lost there. Futures are destroyed. Fortunes are ruined. Catastrophe awaits the merest slip and sudden death lurks behind every word. He knew those things, but he was still expecting today to be different.

The judge looked down from his bench at Ian Stonebridge, the assistant district attorney in charge of the Commonwealth of Pennsylvania's prosecution of Ronnie Porter.

"Mr. District Attorney, do you care to present any more testimony?" It was more a rhetorical question than a genuine inquiry. Over the course of the last three weeks, eighteen trial days counting the unusual Saturday sessions, Stonebridge had called thirty-two witnesses in his effort to put Ronnie Porter in a cell on Pennsylvania's death row. Now, there were no names left on his witness list. After Ian's inevitable "No, your Honor" it would be Evan's turn.

Six months ago, when the county's president judge had called in a favor to make Evan defend Ronnie Porter, the smart money was betting on a short trial and an easy conviction. But the odds had changed since then. Ronnie had a rock-solid defense now, one that should rescue him from danger and seal his gratitude that fate and luck had delivered him into the hands of Evan Wonder. The Prince of Darkness.

Evan glanced over at Ian, waiting for him to announce that "The Prosecution rests," but instead he heard him say, "Just one more witness, Judge. The Commonwealth recalls Trooper Hank Foster."

Hank was the arresting officer and the lead investigator into the murder that had landed Ronnie in such peril. Last March 15th Hank had been called out on a Sunday night and ordered to respond to the scene of the Round the Clock convenience store at the corner of Main and Seventh Streets in uptown Harrisburg. The police were too late to interrupt the crime (well, weren't they always?) but just in time to discover the body of the storekeeper, Marcus Washington, in a pool of blood with three traumatized eyewitnesses shaking like a bunch of leaves. Hank separated the civilians from the crime scene and waited for the coroner to confirm what he could see for himself—the victim had been shot three times, once in the face while still standing and twice from above after he had fallen to the floor. As lead investigator, Hank stayed at the store to coordinate the forensics and evidence collection. Other troopers took the witnesses to the state police barracks for interviews. The first thing they wanted to know was the time of the murder. All of the witnesses said the same thing. Seven o'clock. Sharp. The storekeeper's television had been on when the robber burst in and the opening theme for *60 Minutes* had just begun. Tick, tock. Tick, tock. Bang. Bang. Bang.

The next day, Hank put together some photo-arrays, six mugshots on a sheet of paper, and showed them to each eyewitness. One of the witnesses had been looking at the potato chip rack and ducked down as soon as the shooting started. He hadn't seen a thing. The other two picked the same photo. A small-time thief and juvenile delinquent who lived near the store and was known to shop, and shoplift, there from time to time. His name was Ronnie Porter. Foster, two uniformed troopers, and a couple of detectives from the Harrisburg City police department were at Ronnie's house a few hours later. He and his mother were still awake, watching reruns of *Misery Loves Company*. Hank appreciated the irony. He turned Ronnie over to Harrisburg City for processing and commitment at the Dauphin County Prison. On the way home, he stopped at a cop bar to decompress and think about what was coming next. Murder during the course of a robbery was a capital offense in Pennsylvania and the Dauphin County District Attorney loved the death penalty. It would be Hank's first capital case and he wasn't sure how he felt about that. After a few shots of Jim Beam with Yuengling lagers to wash them down he came to a comfortable conclusion: He was just the cop. Whether the guy lived or died was somebody else's problem. And anyway, whenever he thought about Ronnie standing over the dying Marcus Washington and pumping two more unnecessary bullets into his helpless body, Hank got really pissed off.

Both of the identifying eyewitnesses testified at trial. One was a second-year medical student who had come out that night to recharge his supply of snacks before a long night of studying, and the other one was a retired minister who was inside the store to pay for his gas fill-up. To no one's surprise they both pointed to Ronnie in the courtroom, swearing that their terror during the robbery had burned his face into their consciousness and they would never forget it. Also, to no one's surprise, Evan had slaughtered them on cross-examination. They were scared. They were distracted. They were focused on the gun. They were too far away. The store's lighting was wrong. Their angle was off. The police had pressured them. They couldn't possibly be as sure as they pretended to be. Why had they come into court claiming to be so positive? Was it because Ronnie was black and they were white? It was a public humiliation that they didn't deserve and no doubt they would never again have the same confidence in courts or lawyers that they had brought with them into the trial. But Evan's job, his mission really, was to save whatever client was sitting next to him at the defense table on any particular day. He had sacrificed most of the other aspects of his life to that mission, and his one unbreakable professional mantra was this: Anybody who testified against his client was going to get hurt. Both eyewitnesses stuck to their identification of Ronnie, and the fact that there were two of them corroborated each other's testimony, but Evan had made at least some of the jurors wonder if either witness could have identified his own mother if she had been the one shooting up the Round the Clock.

As soon as the prosecution rested its case, Evan was ready to present a solid alibi defense that would prove that Ronnie safely at home, several blocks away from the store when the shots were fired. The Commonwealth's eyewitnesses would seem awfully weak and

5

inconclusive by comparison. Evan was confident of an acquittal. But what the hell did Ian have up his sleeve?

One of the prosecutor's assistants turned on the courtroom monitors and displayed a Pennsylvania Transportation Department map of the area of Harrisburg City surrounding Main and Seventh. Round the Clock was marked with a red circle. There was a blue circle a few inches away marking Ronnie's house. Hank Foster stood up from his seat at the prosecution table holding his case binder and a sheet of notes. He also had an old-fashioned stopwatch. Foster gave Evan a sideways glance and headed for the front of the courtroom while one of Ian's clerks set up an easel next to the witness stand. All of a sudden, Evan's heart sank and his pen slipped out of his hand, landing on his legal pad with a soft thud.

"Mr. Wonder, everything still gonna be okay. Right?" Ronnie was tugging at Evan's sleeve, needing reassurance. Evan waved him off so he could listen to Ian's first question.

"Trooper Foster. How many times have you been to the defendant's home at 1705 North Maple Street?" Ian was pointing at the blue circle on the map. Every juror was staring at the monitor, but Evan and Hank were staring straight into one another's eyes. Hank was trying not to telegraph the haymaker he had in store, but Evan had already figured it out.

"I've been there twice," he answered calmly. "The first time was the day I arrested him." He struggled not to smirk at Evan. "The second time was yesterday."

Evan's heart sank with the knowledge that he had made the classic rookie mistake. He hadn't been paying attention to all the pieces on the chessboard.

PART ONE

The Crime

On the chessboard,
lies and hypocrisy do not survive long.

Emanuel Lasker

Chapter 1

The Lasker Chess Club
Harrisburg, Pennsylvania
Eight Years Later

Broad-brimmed Smokey Bear hats. Gray shirts. Darker gray pants. Name tags but no badges. Black neckties. A ton of militaristic hardware dangling from their utility belts.

Pose and swagger were required courses at the State Police Academy and the two troopers who had just passed through the double doors were accustomed to becoming the center of attention whenever they entered a room. They stopped a few steps away from the tables and waited for all heads to turn and acknowledge their importance. They did get a few curious glances, but to the people in this room two armed men with looks of intention were a mere distraction from more authentic forms of conflict.

The Emanuel Lasker Memorial Chess Club met five nights a week in a historic Harrisburg townhouse about half a block from the Pennsylvania State Capitol. Players from all around Pennsylvania came for the chess and for the competition, but in one way or another everybody at the Lasker was there because of Evan. He owned the place, kept the doors open, financed the tournaments, and played the game with sparkling brilliance. He had named the club after his idol, the philosopher, math genius and chess champion Emanuel Lasker. Grandmaster Max Euwe once said of Lasker that he was so brilliant that normal humans couldn't learn anything from watching him play. Some players thought that Evan was a lot like that. He set traps that were so subtle, so invisible, that his opponents never saw their peril until it crushed them. In hindsight, of course, every move leading up to disaster seemed as obvious as the broad side of a barn; but Evan played chess like a magician. He always had his opponents looking somewhere else while the miracle happened over here.

The competition at the Lasker helped to draw the region's strongest players, so did the beautiful game room, and so did the prize money. World champions and a few elite masters could support themselves with tournament purses or, in some countries, state sponsorship. But in America, certainly in Pennsylvania, even a top player rarely made enough money to let them quit their day job at Starbucks or stop driving for Uber. At the Lasker, every Saturday was tournament day, all comers welcome. A thousand dollars to the winner. Evan never played on Saturday.

But tonight was Wednesday and on Wednesday Evan played simultaneous chess. Evan played twenty-four games all at once on twenty-four boards set up on two long tables. The first two dozen members to sign up would get a piece of the master's attention and a chance, small though it may be, to walk out with the bragging rights of having given Evan a run for his money.

The club's game room was long and carpeted with two fireplaces facing one another and mahogany walls all around. Evan walked slowly from board to board down the path between the tables. At the tenth board he pushed his dark square bishop next to white's king. The bishop was protected by a rook five rows back. Checkmate.

Evan shook hands with the staff secretary to the speaker of Pennsylvania's House of Representatives and smiled. "Good game." It hadn't been that good, really, but why not make the guy feel like he had accomplished something?

"Attorney Wonder?"

Uh-oh. No one called him that anymore. No one had called him that in eight years.

He turned to the sound of the voice but didn't say anything. Cops or no cops, his clocks were running and

11

he had moves to make so he just raised his hand in the universally recognized gesture for "Wait a fucking minute." In case anyone misunderstood his message, he verbalized it. Two steps took him to the eleventh board where a student from Dickinson College had just moved a bishop into a center square. Evan pushed his queen-side rook to F-4. Two more moves would produce a forced mate.

"Now listen, Counselor, we don't have all day. We need you to come with us." The one on the left was a head taller than the other one. They reminded Evan of a couple of Muppets. Bert and Ernie.

"Counselor?" Evan smiled and finally paid them some attention. "Sorry fellas, it's not 'counselor' anymore. It's 'Professor.' Professor Wonder. What can I do for you?"

Neither trooper had any stripes nor rank insignia on his sleeves, but Bert seemed to be the one in charge. "Okay then, have it your way—Professor. District Attorney Stonebridge sent us to bring you down to the courthouse. Our car is outside. You can ride with us."

Evan frowned. The twelfth board was a sixth-grade prodigy named Stella. She was probably the strongest player in the room tonight other than Evan. A little too aggressive at times, almost reckless. Evan respected that and he was always cautious of her attacks. He moved his queen to queen bishop six and walked to the thirteenth board where he put his king's rook pawn on its fourth square.

"Sorry. I'm not going anywhere with you guys unless you have a warrant." One thing Evan remembered very clearly from the days before he became Professor Wonder was that state troopers hated being called "you guys."

"Or, of course, you can always just shoot me." The accountant at the thirteenth board looked like he was about to duck under the table. But first he castled king-side.

The fourteenth board was a local psychiatrist named Brenda Taylor who wrongly believed that she had escaped the threat from Evan's last move. Brenda and Evan had become close friends in the three years since she had joined the Lasker and they often reconstructed her games over drinks or late-night snacks. She was too technical a player to be called great but she did have an edge. She could read her opponents' faces. She paid attention to the pieces their eyes darted to. She understood body language and grasped the meanings of even the slightest physical reaction. It gave her a big advantage.

"Listen, counselor. Professor. Whatever you are." Bert was getting impatient now. "The district attorney has a murder suspect in custody. A Rachel Pope. She's under arrest for murdering her husband and she started talking to our detectives but now she wants a lawyer. We

13

brought her the on-call public defender but she didn't want him. She said she wants you. Let's go."

Evan's step faltered for an instant when he heard Rachel Pope's name. He recovered right away but he saw that Brenda noticed something on his face, something that hadn't been there before.

"I hate to take a minute right now, Brenda, but those guys seem pretty determined. I'd better talk to them. You can keep my clock running." Brenda nodded and watched Evan as he walked away.

Evan put on his most insincere courtroom smile for the troopers. Bert took half a step forward and placed his hand on Evan's shoulder. Evan grimaced as if the hand was covered with shit.

"Come on Counselor, everybody is ..." Evan didn't let him finish.

"First of all, you don't ever come into my house and give me orders, not your own orders and certainly not the ones that you carry for some pain-in-the-ass downtown who thinks he runs the world.

"Second, you are not welcome in this room. Which means you are trespassers. Which means that if you don't leave right now you are both committing a civil rights violation for which I can sue you under section 1983 of the Federal Judicial Code. Not to mention the fact that I would be authorized to use physical force to repel your invasion." He smiled. "By the time you're finished filling out reports, attending trials, and explaining to the commissioner why you acted like a couple of shitheads, all of your academy classmates will have been promoted to sergeant while you spend your weekends explaining to your wives why you can't afford a pontoon boat.

"And third," he shrugged his shoulder free of Bert's grip. "If you ever put your hand on my shoulder again I'm going to take it off your wrist. Now blow."

Evan walked back to Brenda's board. "My knight was attacking your bishop and your pawn. A classic fork. You saved the bishop, but now..." He moved the knight along its familiar L-shaped path, scooped up Brenda's pawn and laid it down on the table next to the fourteenth board.

"Checkmate."

The two of them smiled at each other. "Let's have a drink later and you can tell me what I did wrong."

"Sorry, Doc. Duty calls." Evan hated the idea that he was going to miss an evening with Brenda for a trip to some jail somewhere. It reminded him why he had quit being a lawyer.

The two cops had retreated as far as the hallway on the other side of the double doors where they stopped to whisper to each other and gesture in confusion. Why hadn't the big hats, the guns, and the swagger intimidated Evan into the raw obedience that police officers always counted on?

Evan called to them without turning his head. "Tell Ian Stonebridge that I'll be in his office tomorrow morning. Until then no one is allowed to talk to Mrs. Pope." They looked at him for a moment and then walked down the stairs. Evan thought that Ernie may have actually tipped his hat.

"What was that all about, Maestro?" asked the homeless virtuoso at the fifteenth board.

Evan just shook his head as he slid his rook into enemy territory. "Mate in two," he said, but his mind wasn't really on the chess anymore.

Chapter 2

Rachel Pope.

Evan hadn't thought about that name since their last phone call after the fire. He expected that she would have left Harrisburg by now but according to Bert she was still here. Or had come back. Or someone had dragged her back. In any event, after the last game of the night was over he placed a few calls to old familiar numbers. It hadn't been hard to find her.

The weather was clear that evening, so Evan had driven his vintage Cadillac to the Lasker. Half a block long, lipstick red, white leather top, and it attracted a lot of attention when he parked it in the official lot at the Dauphin County Prison. He locked it up and got out, glancing up at the windowless concrete walls and the reinforced fences topped with razor wire. Evan had spent the last eight years trying to banish the knowledge of such places to the shadow world of crises he didn't know about and diseases he didn't have. He started blaming

Bert and Ernie for shattering that illusion when they walked into the club, but he quickly realized that the fault lines ran much deeper than that. They ran backward from the cops, to the district attorney's office, to Rachel Pope, through the manicured lawns of Crawford College, and ultimately at least as far back as Ted Pope who launched the first trembler when he got burned to death last Christmas Eve.

When Evan started teaching at Crawford College six years ago Ted was one of the first people he met. Everyone on the faculty knew Ted, he was an academic all-star: the guy who carried the banner in every faculty parade and the celebrity whom the dean seated with the major benefactors at fund-raising dinners. He was the world-famous Dr. Theodore Pope, the Franklin Davis Professor of Classical Studies. America's leading scholar of ancient poetry, particularly the works of Homer, the great poet of ancient Greece. On the last night of his life, he had decided to skip the faculty's traditional Christmas Eve party to stay home and work on his latest book. According to the obituaries, it was about something called "The Homeric Question," whatever that was. Rumors had circulated that Ted had made some great discovery, but there were always rumors like that about Ted Pope; and most of his research materials, manuscripts, and notes seemed to have burned up in the fire.

Evan had also skipped the faculty party that night. It had started snowing around lunchtime by

18

evening the roads and lawns were covered by an inch or two. He was home alone when he heard the fire department's sirens and he looked out his front door in time to see the engines roaring past and the glow of the fire a couple blocks away. He bundled into his parka and hat and followed the trucks on foot, getting as close as the secure perimeter that the fire police had established. Flames were already spilling out of most of the first- and second-floor windows and escaping through the roof. Nothing could be seen of the interior of the house and entry was out of the question even for the most well-protected firefighter. The report of the tragedy would later say in the official jargon of catastrophe that "the structure was fully involved upon the arrival of the first reporting units." Ted's wife Rachel was home when the fire started and she had somehow made it out of a second-floor window onto the ledge above the front porch. She had her shoes on and had wrapped a blanket around herself. Evan thought it was blue. From his vantage point across the street, Evan could see her shivering as she awaited rescue. He figured she was shaking with fear, because even on Christmas Eve there would not have been any chill so close to the blaze. Evan watched as the battalion chief, a career fireman named Mike Morrow, reached the ledge in a cherry-picker and pulled Rachel into the basket to safety. Paramedics loaded her into an ambulance while some other firefighters smashed through the front door, only to be forced back by the intensity of the blaze. The fire company spent the next few hours pouring water onto the burning structure from a safe distance. Surround and drown. Evan later found out that Rachel spent the night in the hospital for observation.

Ted Pope's earthly remains were burned so thoroughly that the coroner couldn't tell at first if his body was lying face up or face down when he found it on the front lawn where the firefighters had put him.

Rachel made the funeral a private ceremony, easing the consciences of distant classicists who wouldn't be able to have their schools spring for the high travel costs. The eulogist quoted Homer and life went on. Rachel's friends, Evan included, called her from time to time to ask how she was holding up. Now, three months later, as he walked from his parked car to the first security checkpoint on the prison's secure perimeter, Evan recalled being surprised that she had seemed to rebound so quickly. The last time they spoke she mainly complained about the delay in collecting her husband's life insurance. "After all," she told him with not a hint of irony, "I do have plans."

The lobby officer looked to be about twenty-two years old and he was already a sergeant. The correctional job market offered meteoric advancement for any warm body willing to work in a dungeon for civil service wages. Institutional sleeve patches, military stripes, a badge, sweat stains and old dirt adorned his light blue shirt; open to the fourth button over a once-white tee-shirt. His name tag said "Kramer." He tilted his head up and away from his crossword puzzle paperback when Evan reached his desk. His shoulders stayed stooped and he didn't say a word. A cheap Timex laid face up next to the book, ticking off another night in stir.

"I'm here to see a client."

"You a probation officer?" His pencil stayed poised at eight across.

Must be the jeans, he thought. "A lawyer."

"ID."

Evan had kept his law license active and he still carried the blue and white identification card issued by the Pennsylvania Supreme Court. He showed it along with his driver's license to Sergeant Kramer who opened the center desk drawer and grabbed a paper which he pushed across the desk. It was a printed form requesting an official visit. Evan partially filled it out, scrawling an illegible signature and ignoring the spaces for "address," "time in," and "print your name." He wrote Rachel's name in the space for "reason for visit" and pushed it back. Kramer copied Evan's lawyer identification number and his driver's license number onto the form, gave him back his cards, and picked up a telephone handset. He muttered a few words, put the phone down and reached without looking for a big red button mounted to an electrical box on the cinder-block wall next to his desk. When he pushed it, a loud metallic "click" disengaged the latch in the steel gate to his left. The whole process had taken forty-five seconds and thirteen words. The sergeant went back to the crossword puzzle, often glancing at the Timex with mixed emotions.

It was actually more of a "clang" than a "click." The gate was heavy to push open and the bar which Evan grabbed was cold. He pushed it far enough to walk through and then let its own weight swing it backward on its hinges until it slammed shut against the steel jamb with a crash. Evan was inside.

Rachel had been put in a small conference room for her legal visit. It was about the size of her bathroom at home with a round table and two metal chairs. The cement walls had once been painted an allegedly pleasant shade of yellow, but they were now as drab as dead flowers. The hallway smelled of disinfectant and ammonia. Evan watched Rachel through the chicken-wired window that connected that dingy little room to the hall. She was slumped low in her chair, her arms dangling and her shins pressed up against the edge of the table. Her eyes were pointed at the dirty tabletop, but she was focused elsewhere. Surrounded by the gloom, she stood out like the last glowing ember in a cold bed of ashes.

The jail had only had her for a few hours and she had not yet been diminished. Her body was lean and full. Her hair was black and long and iridescent. She parted it low on the right and brushed it up and across her head to the left, straight down on the right. She was not beautiful, exactly, and certainly not pretty. But Evan could feel her energy even here, even through the concrete. Carnal. Erotic. Simultaneously hot and cold and, like steam rising from dry ice, seething at contact with the outer world.

Evan opened the door and walked into the interview room. Rachel didn't say a word. She smiled at first, relief at the presence of someone from the outside world, but as they sat quietly her smile faded. Evan scanned the copies of the arrest papers which he had picked up at the jail's records office on the way to the interview room. Finally, Rachel couldn't stand the silence any longer.

"Someone has to tell them that I didn't start that fire."

"Is that why you asked for me?"

"Yes."

"Forget it."

"Evan, you have to make them—"

"It doesn't work that way Rachel."

23

"I didn't start that fire."

"And you think that if I walk in and tell them that they'll let you go. Listen Rachel, they think you burned your husband alive. They think that you did it for the insurance money. Something has convinced them that you're guilty and they're not going to forget the whole thing just because I go down to the courthouse and tell them they're full of shit."

She put her legs down, feet on the floor, leaned forward and grabbed his hand. "I don't belong here. You know that. You know it can't be true."

Evan shook his hand free of hers and scoffed. "Do I? Do I really know that?" She grimaced. "And even if I did, Rachel—so what? No one cares what I think or what you think or what I think I know. You are a different person than you were yesterday. You're not the upstanding citizen Mrs. Pope anymore. Faculty wife, pillar of the community. Now, you're the defendant. The accused. Everything you think or know is worthless. For me to tell the police or the district attorney or a judge, or even a jury, that you say you didn't do it would just be a silly waste of time."

"But—"

"Stop it."

"—that night—"

"Quiet!"

"Why won't you let me talk?" She shook her head and sulked back in her chair. "This is my life. I'm the one that they arrested. I should have a say in all this."

"Sure Rachel, you have a say. Once you get a lawyer you can say whatever you want to him. Or her. But I don't want to hear any more talk about who's guilty and who's not because that stuff just doesn't matter." Evan was surprised how easily he had fallen into the nonchalant cynicism which his years of defending criminal cases had cultivated. He skipped the preliminaries of his New Client Speech and got straight to the bad news. "The process which has attached to you is not interested in objective truth. Courts are not debating societies. They only do one thing: They assign blame. Somebody murdered Ted and society needs to see that somebody is punished for it. Once that's done, we can all go on to the next case. Your testimony, the testimony of your friends, your loved ones—"

"The police don't know everything, do they?"

"We don't yet know how much they know, but you probably don't have too many secrets left anymore. The point is, testimonials and friendly witnesses can't help you. If you are ever going to get out of here, somebody has to find a fundamental flaw in the prosecution theory, something completely incompatible with guilt. That's why you need a lawyer."

"You'll defend me."

"Ha!" Evan stood up and Rachel grinned. For one so close to the gallows she was pretty chipper.

"Please, Evan. I know you don't want to but, I mean, isn't it better if I have a lawyer who believes I'm innocent? Someone who knows I didn't do it?"

"Nobody's innocent, Rachel. Especially in this case. Anyway, I don't defend criminal cases anymore. No offense, but my days of puking up bile are behind me. I'm an academic now. I dispense knowledge. Sin and death hold no fascination for me anymore."

"Really?" Another grin, a fragment of the old Rachel, the pre-jailhouse Rachel. "Then what are you doing here?"

It was an excellent question. "Listen, if I was ever going to get back into criminal defense I sure as fuck would not start with this case. I don't want to scare you and maybe I shouldn't tell you this at all. But the way this complaint is drawn up it's clear that the prosecution is charging you with an intentional killing in the course of a felony, and that means that—"

"I know. The detective already told me. 'Mrs. Pope you should know that this crime carries the death penalty.' Son of a bitch. I think he enjoyed telling me that." She breathed deeply. "Who are these people, Evan? This whole thing scares the shit out of me. Evidence.

26

Procedure. Rules. Testimony. I'm not guilty. I didn't do it. Doesn't that matter?"

"No, not too much. No one is deliberately trying to frame you but murder is scary. When it happens, people remember that the fabric of civilization is not as sturdy as we pretend. The community has to regain control, to restore balance. That's where you come in. Does it matter if you're not guilty, not factually guilty? Sure. It matters to you. But to the law? Don't forget, Rachel, the fire is over. The cops didn't see who did it. Your jury will not have seen who did it. No one really knows—no one will *ever* really know—if you're guilty or innocent. If there is enough evidence to convict you—be it true or false, and the jury buys it, case closed. We can all believe in civilization again."

"It's crazy," she said.

Evan remembered something that he had once heard Ted Pope say. "Mythology is filled with stories about the sacrifice of innocents to the forces of chaos. Andromeda to the serpent. The children of Athens to the Minotaur. Your case is nothing new."

"But Perseus saved Andromeda." Rachel knew her mythology. "And Theseus slew the Minotaur."

Evan knew when he was beaten. "I'll talk to someone." He had her write out a note on a sheet of legal pad which authorized the prison to give him the personal effects she had with her when she was arrested—keys, clothing, wallet—and then he walked her to the guard station in the hallway. She started to say something else but Evan shook his head, turned around and walked away.

Rachel had told him that some of Ted's books and papers had survived the fire and were in storage now along with everything from his college office. In the morning, Evan would use Rachel's keys to move all of it into his house but first he would go to the district attorney's office to talk to Rachel's prosecutor. Evan recognized the name from the arrest papers.

Chapter 3

The Dauphin County Courthouse still stood proudly across the street from the Susquehanna River at the corner of Front and Market. Many counties had courthouses in the columns and arches style of old banks and the university administration buildings. Dauphin County used to have of those but had razed it long ago and sold the site to a dollar store. The current marble office building looked like any other headquarters of municipal bureaucracy, except for the statue. On the riverfront side of the building, at the top of the stairs, stood a huge marble statue of a naked hero crushing a serpent under his heel. His right hand was raised triumphantly skyward and in his left hand he held a bunch of fourteen arrows. He and the serpent faced the wall of a fountain which bore two slogans. "The law of the wise is the fountain of life" and "God gave law to the world, it is up to man to maintain its purity." One naked guy against a world of injustice, only fourteen arrows for the job, and a snake trying to eat him the whole time. Directly behind this monument to Law

Transcendent, buyers and sellers came and went through a bank of revolving doors.

Evan walked passed the elevators, took the stairs to the second floor, and opened the double glass doors that led to the district attorney's office. The outer office was still run by young, entry-level county secretaries who worked on documents about blame and condemnation as blithely as if they were last year's budget. Evan didn't recognize any of them and after all his years away he didn't expect any of them to remember him. He was right.

"I'd like to see Ian."

"Your name?" one of them spoke as she kept typing and didn't look up.

He told her.

"You can have a seat. I'll see if the district attorney has time to see you." The receptionist knew that everyone who came to her counter answered somehow to the authority of that office and she didn't have to worry about being nice to them. She picked up the phone, pushed a button, and whispered.

Pretty soon Ian Stonebridge walked up to the counter. He was not ugly, exactly, but his face seemed indifferent to the trivialities of good looks. He was groomed, clean-shaven, smooth-skinned, and flat. At rest, his features were as blank as empty space. He camouflaged this vacancy with a frequent smile which was always sincere though rarely benevolent. "Well, well, well. When Beth told me that Evan Wonder was here, I told her she must be making a mistake. *Professor* Wonder has gone on to bigger and better things." He held out his hand and Evan shook it. "I'm glad to see that the error was mine."

"It's good to see you too, Ian. I'm sorry I couldn't accept your invitation last night but it was simultaneous chess night at the club. I hope you understand."

Ian was the district attorney now, having been elected by the good people of Dauphin County six years ago. Now, as Evan knew from the yard signs all over town, he was running for judge. Ronnie Porter's verdict got him promoted and Evan figured that Ian counted on Rachel to pull off the same trick. Prosecutors made handy judicial candidates because the voting public believed that both jobs involved locking up the bad guys and protecting honest citizens. Ian's campaign was taking advantage of that mistake, pointing to his record of convictions without explaining that most of them were uncontested guilty pleas. He promised more hard-nosed tenacity from the bench. Because his campaign manager had been a little slow out of the gate, Ian's opponent got to use that favorite bit of meaningless judicial sloganizing: "A tough man for a tough job." Instead, Ian was stuck with the perennial runner-up which declared him to be "Firm, but fair." His posters featured a three-quarters shot of a thoughtful, well-practiced pose. The race was on, and if there was one thing voters loved more than a grisly murder, it was a juicy trial. If Ian could put Rachel on the front page, beautiful, somber, broken, being led away to death row in chains as he looked on firmly-but-fairly, well, they might as well just swear him in right then and there.

Evan followed Ian back into the non-public part of the second floor. When they reached Ian's office, Evan made his pitch.

"Ian, I don't actually practice anymore. You know that. I've been out of this game a long time and frankly, I don't miss it one bit. Normally, I wouldn't come back here on any case, let alone a capital murder except that Ted Pope was a friend of mine and a colleague. Rachel is still a friend, and I might have some valuable insights here because I know all the players and I'm far enough removed from the system to have no ax to grind. That's why I'm here. Ian, your case stinks. The suggestion that Rachel killed her husband is ludicrous; I don't care what your circumstantial evidence says. I was hoping we could talk about it before things get too far along and the case develops a life of its own."

"I don't remember you ever being so direct in the old days, Evan. Maybe that's what comes from being away for so long." Ian stood and walked around his desk. "If only life were that easy. Come with me."

They walked to the office suite's main conference room. The table was covered with rows of accordion files each one labeled "POPE MURDER" in large block letters on the side. So much paper so early after an arrest indicated a much more mature investigation than Evan was hoping for. Ian picked up one of the huge folders and handed it over.

"Evan, this is for you. It isn't technically open file discovery, I'm not going to let you have our whole investigation, but it's more than your client is entitled to. This isn't just a circumstantial evidence case. You will do Mrs. Pope a service if you help her understand just how bleak her future looks." Without meaning to, he smiled— a small, tight smile that came from the enjoyment of great power. He could, and he knew it, free Rachel with a nod. He could declare that the evidence was too thin, that the chances of a conviction did not warrant further prosecution, or that he didn't expect to be able to prove her guilty beyond reasonable doubt. That would be that. No one in the world had the authority to second guess his discretion. Or, and this was clearly the track he was on, he could turn this case into an extravaganza. Money, life insurance, greed, a dead scholar, a beautiful widow, a long trial, drama, the threat of the gallows. This case had everything. Evan looked at Ian's table full of files and thought that the case may indeed have a little too much.

The two of them walked out of the conference room and down the hallway toward the front lobby. "It really is good to see you again, Evan. Read this over. If you decide to reconsider getting involved with this case, no one in this office would ever think less of you. Hell, we still scare our new lawyers with war stories about your famous cross-examinations. You'll always be the Prince of Darkness around here, Professor." Ian emphasized the last word. No matter what Evan may once have been, Ian considered him a rank amateur now and he wanted him to know it. He had something else to say, too. "Ever since Rachel asked for you last night, the big question around the courthouse is why you would consider taking this case in the first place. No one believes it's a favor to a fallen colleague, protection of the wrongly accused widow, and all that shit. She can't have much money and she's never touching the life insurance. But you were never much interested in money anyway, were you?" He tilted his head to a confidential angle. "Personally, I don't normally get involved in that kind of speculation, but I am intrigued. This can't possibly be about Ronnie Porter, can it?" He had that smile again.

"You know me, Ian. I don't let my cats out of the bag until the closing argument. But you can put your mind at rest about my fee. I've already arranged to make a little something off this case." The two shook hands again while Evan held the thick file under his left arm. "You needn't walk me out, Mr. District Attorney. I still remember my way around."

Chapter 4

Why did Ian mention the Porter case? Was it regret or apology or nostalgia? Or was it just because Ronnie Porter was always going to be the three-hundred-pound gorilla in the room on whatever day Evan and Ian crossed paths again? Today was that day and one of them had to be the first one to mention Ronnie. That may have been it, but that didn't explain the smile on Ian's face. That smile carried a different message. Bad things happen in courtrooms, it said. Awful things, terrible things, people get destroyed there. Lawyers, clients, defendants, it doesn't matter. Ian's smile wasn't any kind of conciliation. It was a warning. Evan had been out of practice for a long time and Ian was reminding him that in courtrooms even nice guys and old friends throw acid at each other. "Protect yourself at all times," he was warning. "What happened to Ronnie Porter hasn't changed anything."

Or had it? After Evan was forced to withdraw Ronnie's appeal, there was no point going forward with it after all, he told his secretary to send all of his case files to the clients with nice goodbye notes and the names of other lawyers who could help them. He sold his office building to a partnership of three up-and-coming civil-trial lawyers and donated the furniture and equipment to the local school district. He spent a few months after that sleeping till noon, reading till midnight, drinking too much, worrying his friends, burning through his savings, and trying to forget all about the law.

He had convinced himself that he deserved a little convalescence, but the life of a self-indulgent hermit really didn't suit him and the chess club was becoming a serious cash drain. He needed to have a job of some sort but returning to the practice of law was out of the question. As for marketable skills, years of criminal defense had taught him how to thumb his nose at authority, rationalize evil, and tolerate the company of scoundrels and fools. He knew how to ignore public contempt and thrive in an atmosphere of moral ambiguity. None of those were easily transferrable skills. There were a few law-related options that didn't involve actual practice with clients and cases: government service, judicial administration, and politics. But none of them appealed to him. Law teaching? That seemed to be the best of the lot, but he couldn't bring himself to be a cheerleader for the legal profession to a bunch of super-charged, fee-chasing, egomaniac, hyper-achievers. So he started looking around.

Crawford College was one of the many small, liberal arts colleges sprinkled around Pennsylvania. When its political science department advertised for an adjunct professor to teach legal theory, he applied. The campus was pastoral with rolling hills, wide lawns, pergolas, and gardens. The students were polite, the professors were mostly smart, and if he tried hard he could avoid the faculty politics. The work demanded a certain amount of concentration and preparation, but nothing compared to a trial caseload; there was a little sweat, but no blood and not many tears. After three years he was promoted to full time. Four years after that he was still happy to be there.

Evan had come to appreciate his new life as nice and boring and the monotony of his schedule brought him peace of mind. His cell phone never rang urgently in the dark and he never had to rush to blood-splattered crime scenes. Like many other faculty members, indeed like Ted Pope, he lived in a big old house close to the edge of the campus. He had packed away the fancy suits and wore sweaters and jeans most days. He usually walked, strolled actually, to his classes and his office. He had held on to all his cars, though. He had a Subaru Outback for camping vacations, and an old gray F-150 four-by-four for hauling wood and driving in the snow. But he usually drove the Cadillac around town and especially to campus. Professor Wonder's current colleagues considered it too big and flashy for any legitimate purpose: a politically incorrect and socially

37

unsound ostentation. For Evan, that was the point. It was a little passive-aggressive, perhaps, but the big red Cadillac reminded everyone of something that Evan was okay with: He wasn't really one of them.

When he got home, Evan spread Rachel's file out on the round table in his den and started reading.

The fire department battalion chief Mike Morrow suspected arson right away and called the state police fire marshal before the last embers were extinguished. This fire had burned too fast, too hot, to be an accident, and Mike believed that there may have been multiple points of origin. If the fire started in more than one place simultaneously that was strong evidence in favor of someone walking around the place with a box of matches. Mike's job was fighting fires, not diagnosing them, but this one rubbed him the wrong way.

Accidental fires start in a variety of accidental ways. Old wiring goes bad, a forgotten cigarette falls onto a sofa cushion, a prematurely discarded match ignites a wastepaper basket. Sometimes the criminal firestarter tries to imitate such an accident, tossing the match onto the wastepaper or leaving a pan of hot oil boiling on the stove, and then waits for nature to take its course. The problem with this approach is that not all accidents, inadvertent or intentional, mature into full-blown catastrophes. Sometimes the fire dies out early without involving any other part of the structure, so the

38

determined arsonist usually adds some chemicals to the mix; liquid accelerants which can be counted on to produce an all-out conflagration. Amateurs tend to a false confidence, believing that a raging fire will erase all traces of evidence and they expect that incendiary fluids will just burn up leaving no one the wiser. Oops.

Roger Williamson was the fire marshal assigned to the Pope house, and once he and his crew shoveled the second-floor debris out of the living room he found the telltale signs of an accelerated arson. Burning liquid responds to gravity like any other liquid, flowing downhill, and seeping into permeable surfaces. No floor is perfectly level and the liquid will gather in puddles at the lowest points leaving behind it a thinner coating of fluid which identifies its path. These "flow patterns" carry the fire to its fuel once the arsonist lights the match. The flames burn hotter and longer at the places where the puddles are deepest, and on a wooden floor these gradations indelibly burn into a distinctive scaled charcoal known to investigators as "alligatoring."

Williamson found this proof in the Pope living room. A layout of black ribbons and patches appeared to concentrate by the front door and at the bottom of the staircase and then spread around the first floor. Whoever lit this house took no chances.

He took hundreds of photographs, all of which were in the file, and then called for technical assistance to cut out large sections of the remaining floorboards with power saws. The crime lab chemists tested these cutouts and discovered that the accelerant was a hydrocarbon solution called diethyl ether. It was an unusual arson accelerant but an inspired choice. Ferociously flammable, explosive, highly volatile, and easy to buy without leaving a trace. There was a chemical supply house in Camp Hill, right across the river from Harrisburg, that sold the stuff in hundred-milliliter bottles. Ten of those would make a quart, more than enough to get the job done. According to the chemist's report diethyl ether vapor was heavier than air so it tended to cling to the ground, and it had a distinctive but unusual sweet odor. If you wanted to burn a house down with somebody inside, this was the kind of stuff whose smell would be more likely to be overlooked than, say, gasoline. "Something smells a little funny in here," instead of "Holy shit; the house is ready to explode!"

Just to be thorough, Williamson ruled out every accidental cause and checked the rest of the house, the basement, the surrounding area, and the attached garage. Nothing.

It was Christmas morning when Marshal Williamson declared an arson which meant that the professor's death was murder. He called it in to state police headquarters and Hank Foster was assigned to do the homicide investigation.

40

By then, Rachel was about due to get out of the hospital and Foster didn't know where she would go next. She sure wasn't coming back home. She was his only surviving witness, her status having not yet changed, and there were some things he had to know. What woke her up last night? Did she hear anything before the fire started? Glass breaking? Footsteps? How did she get out the window? Why couldn't the professor follow her? Did they keep chemicals in their house? What the hell happened? Hank toured what was left of the Pope house with Williamson to be sure they both saw the same story burned into the wreckage. Then he peeled off his overalls, shook off as much soot as he could, and headed for the hospital, still smelling like a bag of raw charcoal.

Rachel was gone by the time he got there. The duty nurse was very helpful and told Trooper Foster that Mrs. Pope had left early this morning. No, they couldn't show him her hospital record but, confidentially, she was just fine thank goodness. She would have left last night but she needed to wait for a friend to bring her some new clothes and anyway, the doctor thought that it was best to ... Well yes, they did still have the clothes she was wearing when the ambulance brought her in. They were smoky and, you understand, they carried such bad memories that she wanted them thrown away. Can they help in any way? Foster wasn't sure, probably not. But he didn't know where this case was going and he wasn't going to turn down evidence. He took the clothes, put everything in an evidence bag, and tagged it. Underwear, a nightgown, and sneakers. Sneakers?

Rachel's presence in the burning house gave her a sort of qualified immunity from suspicion. Still, spouses are always natural suspects in murder cases, especially at first, and she did escape without her husband. Foster's interest in Rachel was obvious from the supplemental reports he filed almost every day. To his credit, he did not let this curiosity preoccupy his attention to the exclusion of other possibilities. Someone had deliberately set fire to the Pope house; that much was definite. That person would have probably expected that the professor and Rachel would both be sound asleep while he (or she) spread the accelerant and lit the fire. The working hypothesis was that Ted had been the target, but it certainly didn't have to stay that way. Neither of them had any obvious enemies but someone had killed Ted and nearly killed Rachel. Hank Foster set out to identify bearers of grudges, disgruntled students, enemies or rivals.

He got nowhere. He interviewed a couple of possibilities, one of whom remained under suspicion for a while until Hank realized that nothing solid connected him to the crime. So with a positive arson and no one to have done it, Foster circled back to the wife.

A few weeks had passed since the fire and Rachel Pope had not made any statements about that night.

When Foster finally tracked her down, she had rented another house not too far off campus, she put him off with a reluctance allegedly borne of mourning. Then later, she just didn't think that she had anything to contribute to the investigation and, anyway, couldn't he just talk to the firemen? They were at the fire. Until, finally, it had been so long ago now and she just wanted to forget it and what was the use of resurrecting all those disaster feelings. Fear and entrapment, panic, helplessness. No thank you, Officer. You'll just have to do this without my help.

So that's what he did. He already knew about the professor's life insurance. The college's employee group health plan had a small death benefit which was paid right after the funeral. But that wasn't all. A few weeks before the fire, Dr. and Mrs. Pope had visited a National Life Insurance agent who gladly sold them universal life policies—"more expensive than straight term coverage, that's true, but you're comparing apples and oranges with the investment features of this plan"—each in the amount of five hundred thousand dollars, each payable to the surviving spouse, each with a double indemnity clause in the event of accidental death. Like in a fire. Violent death so closely following the writing of a big policy led to the natural suspicion of foul play, and National had an investigator waiting when Foster returned to the state police barracks from the hospital carrying Rachel's clothes with him. Foster told the investigator what Williamson had found in the Popes' living room as the two

43

of them walked to the laboratory services section to drop off the bag of clothes. The insurance man called his home office to put a hold on payment. The company would have to pay off even in the event of murder, if not to Rachel then to whoever was the ultimate heir to Ted's estate, but they couldn't pay Rachel if she was the slayer. That was the law. And anyway, the longer they kept the money the greater the chance that they would never have to pay it at all. As for Foster, he now had proof of a crime and a motive. That was enough to make Rachel a person of interest in a capital murder. He was really getting somewhere.

Next, Hank began talking to the Popes' former neighbors, then to the professor's friends, then to Rachel's friends. He got a picture of a marriage of toleration and inertia without any arduous commitment. Professor Pope had his writing, his books, and his scholarship to give him the sustenance which other men seek from a nurturing marriage. He did not ignore Rachel, exactly, but neither did he devote any effort to the day-to-day work of connectedness. As a husband he was loyal and respectful but Rachel eventually got the point that their union was not in his top drawer.

This brought her more relief than sorrow as it excused her resignation from the role of faithful spouse. She had once loved Ted Pope, that was sure, but she was not cut out for domesticity and certainly not for the formal career of faculty spouse. The senior professors told

Hank that they thought she was frivolous and immature, but in deference to her husband's distinction they expressed their views only in his absence. Now that he was dead, they were happy to unload to Foster. While the professor was devoted to knowledge, Rachel was devoted to fun. As for her infidelities—long the subject of faculty gossip, but only now exposed to police scrutiny—they were breezy and fleeting. Emotional entanglement was never likely because Rachel relished the limits of casual adultery and her lovers, reluctantly, had to accept them.

Some of Rachel's friends thought though that right before Ted's death they had seen a change in her attitude, a new sobriety, almost alarm. She stayed more to herself. It was as if, some reckoned, she had accidentally invested one of her romances with some of the devotion that Ted was too distracted to accept—or notice. Whatever it was, she was quieter than usual and more thoughtful than ever before. "Like she had a decision ahead of her, something serious," one of her friends ventured. That didn't fit with what the community knew, or thought they knew, about Rachel but to Hank Foster it made perfect sense that a person who was planning a murder might get a little moody about it. Murder, a suspect, a motive, and now inclination.

Evan had seen enough murder files to understand that Hank Foster's excitement was growing every day that his case built itself brick by brick. A policeman's reasonable doubt, for his own cases, stands up to innuendo like dust before a hurricane. The slightest disbelief of perfect innocence, the first hint that a suspect's story doesn't "hold up," the most haphazard confluence of proof and suspicion and the average cop has his hand on your collar. Foster was a little more reserved than that, but not out of uncertainty. He was sure Rachel did it, but what he had so far didn't give him enough solid proof for an arrest much less a conviction. He knew that he had to wait. He also knew that the first piece of real evidence that came into his hands meant big trouble for Rachel Pope.

Weeks passed with nothing new happening. No new witnesses came forward and no new leads developed. And then one day, Monday last week, the answer to the case came to him in the state police inter-departmental email. The crime lab chemist finally got around to examining Rachel's clothes. Underwear: nothing. Nightgown: nothing. Sneakers: "tests for the presence of hydrocarbons were positive on the soles of both shoes. Further spectrographic analysis identifies the substance as diethyl ether."

Hank must have jumped for joy when he read those words. Rachel had an unusual, volatile, highly flammable, arson accelerant on soles of her shoes. But she was on the second floor. And the fire had started on the first floor. And to get from her bed to the window where the firemen found her she didn't walk on the first floor. So she must have gotten it on her shoes before the fire started. Rachel was a woman with a million dollars to gain from her husband's death, one who was notoriously unfaithful to him and recently preoccupied as if by the need to make an important decision. She had escaped alone from the second floor of a burning house wearing bedclothes and shoes, and on the shoes was the very stuff that started the fire. The idea that she had awakened during the fire, tried unsuccessfully to wake the professor, and luckily made it onto the ledge to wait for the firemen was proven wrong by those shoes. As far as Hank was concerned, the shoes proved that she had spread the ether on the first floor, walked through it, tossed the matches, rushed upstairs, waited long enough to create the illusion of late awakening and to explain why she didn't call in the alarm herself, and then gone to safety on the porch roof leaving Ted Pope to roast in his sleep. Foster had been in Ian Stonebridge's office that afternoon, ready to make them both famous.

Evan gathered up the reports and put them back into the file. He stared out the window for a long time, thinking about the next call he had to make.

Chapter 5

Evan locked the case file in his office safe and punched in a phone number from his contacts list.

"Clint, Evan Wonder. We need to talk."

"Professor Wonder, my man. Long time."

Evan interrupted him. He had no time for small talk. "Rachel was arrested last night and charged with murdering Ted. It looks like I may be defending her." There was more to say, but he paused a moment for that much to sink in.

After the silence, "Murder? Rachel? You'll be ... What? Evan, are you even a lawyer anymore?"

The question that was on everyone's mind. "Yes, Clint, I'm still a lawyer. Sort of. Look, I need some information. Can you help me out?"

"Information, huh? In that case, meet me at the Blockhouse. An hour?"

"Come on, Clint. I'm an old man. Can't I just come to your house? I really don't have time for a lot of fucking around. Anyway, I just left the courthouse. I'm not dressed for the Blockhouse."

"Wisdom comes at a price, Evan. That's a very common theme in the Greek world. Two hours then."

Evan let out a long sigh. "I'll be there in two hours. No rough stuff, okay?"

Two and a half hours later, the score was 13-12. Clint had the lead but it was Evan's serve and he sent a high lob into the front wall with enough spin to carry it past the service line where it died on the floor as if it had landed in a puddle of glue. Clint swept at the ball and got enough of a piece of it to bounce it weakly off the side wall and onto the floor, three feet short of the bumpers. 13-13.

"Nice try. Are you sure you wouldn't rather we just talk? Squash is a thinking man's game, after all." Evan grinned at the younger man as he picked up the ball and strode across the court for the next serve. He bounced the ball a couple of times and glanced back. "Ready?"

"Just hit the fucking ball and you'll see who's ready."

Evan dropped the ball and smashed it with a hard forehand before it reached the floor. The ball was invisible on the way to the front wall and didn't lose much velocity to the rebound. It headed to the far backhand court where Clint's racquet stopped it before it hit the floor. The ball wobbled safely to the front wall but Evan was waiting for it and put it cross court, just a hair above the bumper bouncing it off two walls to the corner directly opposite to where Clint was standing. He turned and leaped with his racquet outstretched, horizontal in the air, and missed the bounce by four feet. 14-13.

"Most serious players think the secret to this game is staying upright." Clint didn't appreciate the joke. He picked up the ball and tossed it to Evan underhand. Evan walked in silence to the forehand service line and without prologue hit a shot off the front wall that was no more than a blur until it bounced two inches from the back forehand corner and skittered to a quick second bounce while Clint helplessly fanned up a small breeze. 15-13. Clint watched the play for the instant that it took to assure him that the game was lost and straightened up to his full height. He walked to Evan without the hint of a smile, pocketed the little ball and said, "Come on, old man. Let's talk about the gods."

Crawford didn't graduate many classics majors of any color, and when Clint Jackson started his undergraduate career there he surprised everyone. He was an African American kid from inner-city Detroit with mediocre high school grades but a drawer full of track-and-field medals from four years as a state champion hurdler. It came as no surprise, therefore, when Crawford became the track powerhouse in the Presidents Athletic Conference. The real surprises came in the classrooms where Clint discovered a fast love and a true gift for the classics. He dabbled at Egyptology and ancient African culture. He read all of Homer his first semester, then Aeschylus, the tragedians, the philosophers, Aristotle, Plato, then the pre-Socratics like Isocrates, Anaxarchus. These ancient worlds were brand new to him and his curiosity was insatiable. He took every class taught by Ted Pope and Crawford's other distinguished classicist Hector Montgomery, always demonstrating a level of insight for antiquity which was unique, almost unprecedented, among undergraduates. Ted Pope pulled a few strings and Clint got a fellowship to Harvard which he followed up with a Rhodes scholarship.

After completing a distinguished Ph.D. and publishing a few well-received papers on *The Iliad*, Clint turned down a few more prestigious job offers from big name schools with large departments to return to Crawford. It was nice there, a nice quiet place to live and think and teach. And of course there was Ted. Evan knew from Ian's file that the police had dropped in to talk to Clint right after Ted Pope died. They were still looking suspects and hadn't yet ruled out a subtle motive grounded in academic politics or some professional disagreement. Maybe Clint didn't see eye-to-eye with Ted on Homer. Maybe one of them had been rooting for the Trojans to win the big war. Eventually, all of those ideas seemed pretty silly and the cops left him alone. But then a few weeks later, they came back and stayed longer. They had learned that Dr. Clint Jackson was one of Rachel's most recent lovers.

The Blockhouse sat next to Crawford's athletic complex. Its two squash courts were neither heated nor air-conditioned, so on a hot summer day a squash match was thirsty work. Evan and Clint sat under a shady elm passing back and forth the thermos of screwdrivers that Clint always brought along for after the game. He raised the jug in both hands and poured a pint or so down his throat. "You know, Evan, at first they thought that I killed Ted. I feel almost relieved to hear that they've arrested Rachel. I know that's awful, but ..."

"Well, there's awful and then there's awful. Sure, no one wants to see Rachel convicted but you dodged a pretty close bullet and you're entitled to feel some happiness mixed up with all of the survivor's guilt you've got. You were a pretty solid suspect. Maybe you still are."

"Bullshit, Evan. Don't get me wrong, I want to see her get off. How bad does it look for her, exactly? Did she do it?"

"Let me worry about that, Clint." Evan took a drink and backhanded some of the dribbled orange juice off his beard. "What I want from you is information about Ted's work, his writing. You know, background on the great man."

Clint got serious and studied Evan for a long minute before he answered. "I know you're speaking with your tongue in your cheek, Evan, but don't make fun of Ted Pope to me. He really was a great man. Not just a great professor, but a great and noble and wise and gentle man. I was closer to him than I had ever been to anyone in my life. Until—"

"Yes, I know about 'Until.'"

Clint had explained all about 'until' to Trooper Foster and Evan had read the transcript of his recorded statement. Ted Pope's first wife, Martha, died five years after Clint started teaching at Crawford. Colon cancer. Ted took it hard but he kept working through his grief and so it didn't seem odd that within seven months he went to a classicists' conference in Cambridge. Neither Clint nor Hector Montgomery went along and when the conference ended a week later, Ted emailed to ask them to cover his classes because he would be staying on for further study. "We were happy to do it," Clint had told

Foster. "Frankly, we all thought this was something positive. He had been acting strangely ever since his wife died and we figured that a change would do him good. I didn't mind taking over his classes for a few weeks. Neither did Montgomery.

"But then Ted comes back with Rachel, her name was Rachel Arno at that time, and he explained that she was a master's candidate at Harvard who had decided to continue her education at Crawford. 'Please make her feel welcome,' he said. The whole faculty knew that the story was a load of crap. We don't even have a master's program at Crawford, so what would she be studying? 'Individual tutorials' Ted called it. From the day they got back from Cambridge the two of them were always together. Rachel even moved into Ted's house. The guest room he said, as if anyone was going to buy that. He started missing classes. The dean had to talk to him. A lot of people thought that he had lost his mind. Sure, she was young and beautiful but it all just seemed so strange for someone like Ted Pope, *the* Ted Pope, to be carrying on with some graduate student he met at a convention. But, strange or not, three months later they were married."

"Did they seem to love each other?" Foster had asked.

"Yes. Yes it did. It did to me anyway," Clint had answered.

Until.

Clint had resisted Rachel for a long time. Not that she ever chased or provoked him. She was never like that. But Crawford was a small place and its faculty social circle was even smaller. Pot-luck dinners, award ceremonies, commencement receptions. Spouses came to these faculty events and once Ted and Rachel were married—well, there she was. Clint started to notice that the air tasted different in her presence. He noticed that her eyes became electric when she laughed. Clint held out for years trying to ignore those things until one orientation mixer as they were standing next to each other at the bar waiting for a drink. He finally gasped out the invitation that had gotten stuck in his throat a hundred times before. Rachel just nodded. She came to his house the next day while Ted was busy in the library.

It would be hard to say whose betrayal of Ted Pope was greater. Probably Clint's because it was so unprecedented. Rachel, like the possessor of any great power accepted the consequences of its exercise; but for Clint, the loss was exquisite. The discard of a friendship, a mentoring, which had shaped his career and his life, his profession and his success, in exchange for an occasional hour of her flesh now and then. When she was willing. And available. No one knew for sure if Ted would have ever suspected except for the fact that Clint couldn't speak to him anymore.

"Yeah, 'Until.' That detective, Foster, he said I had a motive. He had to check it out, he said. The thing was, I did go to the faculty party that night and a hundred distinguished members of the Crawford College community saw me there." He shook his head in disgust. "I have to tell you, though, it hasn't exactly helped my academic standing to have a bunch of state troopers interview all of my colleagues to find out if I left the party in time to murder Ted."

"Yeah, well, count your blessings," said Evan. "Alibis are slippery defenses, even good ones. You're lucky that Rachel was home by the time the fire started or else you'd still be under suspicion as a co-conspirator." He recalled the strategy notes in Ian's file. "Eventually Foster figured out that if you burned Ted to death to get his wife, your motive would have gone up in smoke, literally and figuratively, if Rachel burned up too." They sat quietly for a few minutes.

"I can still use some information."

"About Ted?"

"No not about Ted, exactly," Evan said. "About Homer."

Chapter 6

Homer, huh?" Clint took another long draw on the thermos. "Well, I can give you the broad strokes, but if you need the fine lines you should talk to my colleague Hector Montgomery. He's world-class on Homer. He may have some outdated ideas but aside from that he's the best. Better than Ted even. Hell, it's in his blood."

"How so?"

"His father was Pollard Montgomery. Reader at Oxford. Professor at Harvard. I took a couple of courses from him myself. He was the master. The don. His work on Homer and multiple authorship kept that theory legitimate for decades. He even named his son Hector because he thought that the Trojan general was the most interesting character in *The Iliad*.

"He died in the end."

"We all die in the end, my friend. But Hector's death was grand. Heroic. He died for his cause, for something great. Montgomery always respected that, Pollard Montgomery. Maybe Hector Montgomery too. Not that I ever talked to him about it."

"It might be interesting to ask him."

"Maybe so. Montgomery never struck me as being too interested in death though. Anyway, you wanted to talk about Ted's work on Homer. How can that help you with Rachel?"

"I don't know that it can. But in any murder case it's a good idea to learn as much about the victim as you can and I know that Homer was important to Ted."

"Well now, son, let's start at the beginning. Nowadays, when we talk about Homer, we're talking about two great poems: *The Iliad* and *The Odyssey*. Homer-the-man has largely disappeared from our sight. Most people, including me, including Ted, think that Homer was an actual historical person who lived about eight or nine hundred years before Christ. From what we do know, we believe him to have been a blind, itinerant singer of tales who composed and performed long epic poems about the Greek gods and heroes. In general terms, *The Iliad* deals with an episode of the Trojan War beginning with a dispute between Achilleus, the greatest Greek warrior—you remember, the guy who was invulnerable except for his heel—and Agamemnon, the commander of the Greek army. *The Iliad* ends with the death of Hector and the continuation of the war. The other surviving Homeric poem is *The Odyssey*. That one tells the story of the hero Odysseus, his travels home from Troy, his adventures along the way, and his ultimate slaughter of dozens of enemies back in Ithaka. Back in Troy, Odysseus had invented the Trojan Horse which gave the war to the Greeks after ten years of stalemate.

"These poems were not merely the greatest literature of their age; they were much more than that. Homeric thought about the gods, the virtue of heroes, and humanity's place in the universe influenced philosophy, religion and life in general for centuries. Most scholars agree that Homer took the raw material for his poems from old mythology and historical events. There really was a Trojan War, after all. It was his presentation of this material, and his compilation of the stories into the organic whole of his poems, that made Homer so important. He was the greatest genius of early antiquity, and, some would say, the creator of Western literature.

"For centuries—for millennia, really—knowledge of Homer was the hallmark of erudition. His work was studied and memorized, analyzed down to the letter. Throughout all the wars of antiquity, the spread of modern religions, the Dark Ages, the eventual backlash against ancient Greek thought as pagan, Homer survived all over the world. Scholars and thinkers who had nothing else in common and who came from different cultures and worlds met on common ground when it came to Homer. Ted followed Homer all over the world. He traveled to Greece, Western Europe, and the Middle East, He scoured libraries and monasteries and universities for a glimpse of Homer. Old translations, scraps of parchment, pieces of ancient scrolls. Anything that brought him closer to the man himself."

The sun was low in the sky and it was starting to get dark. Evan stood up and walked off some of his stiffness. "Why?" he asked. "We have the poems, don't we? *The Iliad* and *The Odyssey*. That's what Homer wrote. That's what students read and study and that's what's important, isn't it?"

"Well yeah, Evan, we have those poems. And yeah, they're important. But we have them from the vantage point of almost three thousand years. Remember that for all of those three thousand years Homer was being studied by the best minds of the ages. Aristotle wrote about Homer, Plato wrote about Homer. And those guys were a lot closer to him, culturally and timewise, than we are. Their views are enormously important to our understanding of the poems and the poet."

Evan sat back down and tucked his knees under his chin. He took another chug of screwdriver and passed the jug back to Clint. "Okay. Aristotle. Plato. You can read what they had to say in any library. Why did

Ted have to run around the world to read Aristotle and Plato?"

Clint shook his head and then drained the thermos. "Evan, no offense, but you're talking like a lawyer now. If you want to read what some judge had to say yesterday, or last year, or in 1826, what do you do?"

"I look online or maybe go to the courthouse if it's something very recent, or else to the law library and look up the case I want."

"Right. Well, antiquity is a little different. First of all, a lot of what we study comes from a pre-literate age. The original sources are all verbal. That's why they call it the 'oral tradition.' Remember, Homer himself *sang* his poems. He didn't write them down. He performed them over days and weeks to an audience which sat and listened. Then some of the listeners went off and performed them for other audiences, and so on and so on down through the ages. It was not till long after Homer's death that anyone wrote down a word of what he had to say.

"Homer worked from memory and so did hundreds of singers, rhapsodes is the technical term, after him. They memorized the whole poems and repeated them over and over again, and so before Homer was written down it's very likely that the poems changed from recitation to recitation. Maybe it's possible to remember twenty thousand lines of *The Odyssey* but it's probably impossible for dozens of singers, all independent of one another, to remember the whole thing the same way over and over again. So when the poems *were* written down there were a lot of different oral versions available for transcription, and the different scribes wrote down different versions of the same poems. One thing Ted did was search for the non-standard versions. Non-canonical transcriptions."

"That was *one* thing he did, huh?"

"Sure. And then as far as ancient criticism or commentary is concerned, he was looking for lost texts."

"Lost?"

"Lost. With Homer it's a little tricky, but consider Sophocles, the great Greek playwright who wrote in the fifth century before Christ. We now have seven plays which are reliably attributed to Sophocles. But by reading the work of other ancient authors who knew about Sophocles, we know that he really wrote at least a hundred and twenty plays. We have seven. The rest are lost."

"Lost how?"

"Lost lost. We don't have them. They existed once upon a time and now they don't. We don't have any copies of them; no one has ever found any copies of them. They've disappeared. Erased by the centuries."

Clint shook his head at the sadness of that thought. "A lot of the paper, parchment, and vellum that the text was written on was probably just destroyed by age, ruined and disintegrated by mold or moisture or rot. But a lot of it was destroyed. Up until the third century A.D., for example, there was a great library in Alexandria, Egypt. We believe that it contained nearly everything that had ever been written. Its librarians cataloged all those works and scholars translated them into all the known languages. But in the late third century the library was destroyed. It was wiped off the face of the Earth by civil wars and so were a hundred or so of Sophocles's plays and who knows what else. As far as Homer is concerned, we know that Aristotle mentions *four* Homeric poems, not two. A few other ancient commentators identify one of them as a poem called *The Margites*, a story about a crazy hero who wanders around and has adventures along the way. Kind of like an ancient Greek Don Quixote. Where is it? Where is the other poem that Aristotle knew about? Nobody knows. They may have burned up in Alexandria, but if somebody finds them someday they could answer a lot of questions about Homer."

"Did Ted ever find anything valuable?"

"Sure he did, lots of times. A few lines here, a scrap of parchment there. He had a knack for discovery, plus he had the best contacts in the world. Any scholar anywhere in the world with a possible Homeric artifact knew that Ted Pope would do credit to the find. His opinion of authenticity was the Good Archeology Seal of

Approval. No one would ever dispute Ted Pope on a bit of Homeric authentication."

"Look, Clint. I know that Ted was great guy and all that. One rung below the angels." Clint glared at me. "But he was human, after all. If no one could question him, then why couldn't he just dig up some old poems and call them Homer. Everybody would believe him, and the find would make him more famous than ever. He wouldn't even have to lie exactly. Just be a little too optimistic in his appraisal."

Clint looked at Evan as if that was stupidest thing he had ever heard. "I'm not sure about your profession anymore, Evan, but in my line of work we're interested in the truth. Ted would never exaggerate an opinion because it would have been dishonest, and because it would contaminate the Homeric canon. Right now, we have the two long poems, fifty thousand lines of verse, and experts continue to argue about whether or not the same person composed all of that by himself. Most experts believe that there was one and only one Homer, but it's not unanimous. There is a school of thought called deconstructionism that says that the poems were composed by several, maybe dozens, of different singers over a period of centuries. That's what Hector Montgomery believes. His father Pollard believed the same thing. Ted? He wasn't sure and so he looked wherever he thought he might find some evidence one way or the other. If Ted Pope or someone else came up with a new piece of Homer it could change the entire face of Homeric scholarship. What would it look like? What would it sound like? What would be the subject matter?

"The point of all this, Evan, is simply this: If Ted Pope started playing fast and loose with what-is-or-isn't-Homer the consequences would be far-reaching. Guys like Montgomery don't believe that the same poet could have written all of *The Iliad* and *The Odyssey*. Maybe each one is just a mash-up of a lot of earlier short poems. If Ted found something that proved that, the deconstructionists could celebrate. On the other hand, if he produced evidence that tied everything together—well, you see my point. Ted was not about to fuck around with Homer because he loved Homer. If he ever found something good, something certain, he'd come out with it." Clint stood, signaling that it was time to go. "Maybe that's what he had planned for the book he was writing when he died," he said. "If so, there's another example of an ancient script being lost, or lost again."

Evan nodded. "Maybe. The police believe that the only manuscript of the book burned up with him."

"So I heard." Clint smiled. "You know, knowing Ted, I think that's the way he would have wanted it."

PART TWO

Pre-Trial Motions

*The attack is that process by means of which
you remove obstructions.*

Emanuel Lasker

Chapter 7

The first move in a chess game is called the opening. The player with the white pieces goes first and can choose among twenty possible moves: two each for the eight pawns and the two knights. The black pieces answer white's first move with a response called the defense. The players take turns after that and in a very few exchanges there are more possible sequences and more possible board positions than the number of atoms existing throughout the known universe. Pawns and knights and rooks and bishops and even the mighty queens dance around the board with a single-minded purpose: inflicting upon the opponent's king a certain destruction from which he can't escape. "The king is sacred," wrote Lasker. "It perishes when no plausible recourse can save it from capture. Whenever that occurs the game is at an end."

The greatest players look into the future ten or twenty or fifty moves ahead, envisioning just the right mixture of strategy and insight, caution and daring, which will result in victory over their opponent's forces. They plan every move to lead to the next one and the next one after that until their opponent is helpless and defeated. That position, in which the king is mortally threatened and cannot escape, is called checkmate. It gives the white attacker or the black defender ultimate and total victory on the field of battle but it never happens until the very last move of the game. In chess as in the law, checkmate is the contest's final verdict.

In a criminal case, the prosecutor always plays the white pieces. The state gets to choose the game's opening move. Whom does it arrest? What crimes does it charge? When does it act?

After the opening move, the prosecution moves its pieces around the board: marshaling its evidence, selecting its witnesses, perfecting its theory of the case. The prosecutor has a thousand options, every move during the life of a criminal case opens new possibilities and brings new chances to attack the defendant's black king and prove guilt beyond a reasonable doubt. Checkmate.

The defender, on the other hand, plays his pieces to block white's attacks and protect the black king from destruction. Because the prosecution begins every case with an advantage, the goal of the defense is to treat the state's case with skepticism. With every move of every piece, the defense will try to drown the chessboard with doubt as to the defendant's guilt. Sometimes the defender tries to prove that no crime was committed, sometimes that someone else committed it. But often the best defense will simply sew distrust in the minds of the jurors about the prosecution's claims against this defendant. "Maybe a crime did happen and maybe we don't know who else could have done it," says the agnostic black king. "But it couldn't have been me." With the right moves, the defense can checkmate the state by showing that its case is phony. Counterfeit. A bluff. "The merciless fact," observed Lasker, "will contradict the hypocrite."

At least that's what Evan was hoping for as he sat in his study and read through the case file for the fifth time. He was trying to play the game in reverse from the not-guilty verdict he wanted for Rachel back to the moment of her arrest. Reasonable doubt, an attack on the certainty of the prosecution's theory, might be all that stood between Rachel and death row. He couldn't deny that a crime had happened because the accelerant proved arson. And he didn't have any alternate suspects with which to mount an effective SODDI defense: "Some other dude did it." The police had already looked for anyone with a grudge against the professor and their search came up empty. Sure, he wasn't universally beloved—who is? A few academic disputes. Some scholarly disagreements. A disgruntled student or two. But homicidal rage? Nothing. The closest they came to another suspect was Clint but his alibi held up and his motive didn't. So Evan was left with a case in which to save

Rachel he would have to expose a fatal flaw in the Commonwealth's case against her. And that meant that he would have to find one.

The block of North Second Street where Ted and Rachel Pope had lived together was a quiet old residential neighborhood of mature oak trees and brick houses. A few streets like that still strolled through Harrisburg, although they were outnumbered and surrounded by multiplex housing developments with their instant anonymity, smooth walls and urban tundra. Ted Pope had lived here for thirty-two years. He moved in when he first came to Crawford as a young assistant professor. Even then, as his well-known biography reported, he was a thoughtful student of the great epics. He combined a sharp insight with a youthful daring which allowed him to dash boldly toward new answers for great old questions, sometimes stepping over the stodgy old intellectuals who spent their lives reworking the same tired theories. He climbed the academic ladder rung by rung with steady scholarship and an occasional quantum burst of innovation. Good luck played a hand, too, as Ted would have been the first to admit. Once, when he was twenty-eight and a brand-new PhD, he spent a month in an obscure church library on Santorini and discovered a few lines of ancient writing from the fifth century before Christ which referred to a third, long-lost Homeric epic. The academic journal articles he was able to squeeze out of that scarp of parchment made him a full professor at twenty-nine, and the rising star of American letters.

Today, the familiar house at 9152 North Second Street was an ashen wreck. It would take a while for all the layers of municipal and insurance company bureaucracy to finalize the planned demolition, and with Rachel's ownership rights thrown into doubt by the prosecution the whole process was a confused mess. Certainly, nothing would happen for a long time because as attested to by dozens of lines of yellow "POLICE ONLY" tape which were strung around the place like party streamers, the wrecked house and its crumbling floors and walls were still evidence in a murder case, Exhibit A in the prosecution of Rachel Pope. Evan ignored the warnings on the tape, stepped over a strand of police ribbon and started to look around.

He didn't get too far before he heard a voice from behind. "Hello, Officer." The neighbor from 9154 was walking toward him. Evan knew from the police report that her name was Gladys Reynolds and she had been the one who called in the fire alarm on Christmas Eve. She was the widow of a Lutheran minister who had died about eleven years ago. The two of them had moved onto Second Street shortly after Ten Pope and his first wife. Neither family ever had children so, inevitably, they had bonded together as friends and neighbors. When Pastor Reynolds died, Gladys had become dependent on the Popes for society and human contact. Then Mrs. Pope died. Then Rachel entered the picture. Then the fire. It had been a tough few years for Gladys.

She was wearing a simple, but obviously expensive, blue dress and a white sweater buttoned only at the neck with a single strand of pearls over that. Her grey hair was stylish but conservative and it reflected the deliberate care she paid to her appearance. You never get a second chance to make a first impression, after all. She walked toward Evan with a deliberate, patrician, confidence but stopped on the legal side of the police tape.

"I don't believe we've met before, young man. Are you helping Trooper Foster with this awful case?" She addressed the presumed police officer with the courtesy due a servant, civil or otherwise.

"Not exactly, Mrs. Reynolds. But I am investigating Dr. Pope's death. May I ask you a few questions?"

He didn't wait for her to resolve her confusion about his identity. "I know from the police report that you called in the alarm to 911. Do you remember what time you first discovered that the Popes' house was on fire?" A simple question. Non-threatening. Start the interview with a question that the witness doesn't have to think about, something she will know by heart and answer automatically.

"Why, yes. Of course I do. It was 10:35. Exactly. I had left my cell phone in the kitchen so I used my bedroom's landline. I looked at my clock radio as I placed the call. 10:35. Sharp. But I have already told all this to Trooper Foster."

Evan only had time for another question or two before her suspicions stopped this conversation.

"Yes, I know. His report says that you were upstairs in bed before you called 911." Evan looked up at 2521 and pointed to the second-floor windows that faced the Pope house. "Is that your bedroom, Mrs. Reynolds.?"

"No." She involuntarily looked up at her own house. "That's the guest room. The master bedroom is on the other side. Facing north."

Mrs. Reynold's house at 9154 was north of 9152 which meant that the north-facing windows looked away from the Pope house. "Then, how did you see the fire from your bed?" It was a more direct question than interrogation manuals would recommend, but Evan knew he was running out of time.

"Why, I didn't actually see the fire at first. I had just come upstairs and gotten into bed a minute or two earlier. I hadn't even turned off my bedside lamp when I heard something. Not an explosion, exactly. Just a sound. Like wind, more like a tornado. It didn't last but a moment and I didn't know what it was, but I knew that something was very, very, wrong. I ran to the guest room window and I saw that Dr. Pope's house was—glowing. That's when I knew that a fire had started so I rushed for my phone and called 911. 10:35 p.m. On the dot."

She had her arms crossed now in the classic pose of the reluctant witness. "Maybe we had better wait for Trooper Foster to get here before we speak further. He said he would come right away when I told him that there was another officer looking around here."

Of course. Of course she would have called the police to report suspicious activity at a crime scene. Isn't that what law-abiding citizens were supposed to do? See something, say something? Evan might as well come clean now.

"But I'm not a police officer, Mrs. Reynolds. I'm Mrs. Pope's attorney. My name is Evan Wonder."

"Oh, then you're—." Her surprise made her stammer. "You mean you are—."

"Defending her? That's right. I'm glad that we've met. I would have needed to speak to you before the trial in any event."

"Well, I don't know if I should be talking to you Mr. ... Wonder? Yes, Wonder. I am a prosecution witness after all and, well, I suppose I should check with Trooper Foster before I speak to anyone from the other side."

"What side are you on exactly, Mrs. Reynolds?"

"Side?" She hadn't meant to say it, and she tried to take it back. "I'm not on any side really. I just think that it's a terrible thing that happened to the professor.

Such a fine man. Always just the finest man. Gentle, brilliant. And to think that she set the house on fire to kill him in his sleep. Well—." She shook her head as she looked at the ashes.

"Who did?"

"Did what? Burn the house down? Why the wife of course. Who else is there?"

"Did anyone tell you not to talk to me, Mrs. Reynolds? Anyone at all?"

"No, no. But I am a *prosecution* witness."

She emphasized the word with pride. Evan corrected her. "No, you're not. You are a witness to an event which may or may not be a crime. And you are free to talk to anyone you choose. If you are called to testify in court, you will have to testify truthfully no matter which side calls you to the courtroom. No doubt the prosecutor thinks that you have some valuable information about this case. You would be doing Mrs. Pope a great service if you would share that information with me."

She crossed her arms and her voice rose slightly. She had clearly had enough of this. "Young man, doing services for that woman is not my intention. I daresay she deserves the worst fate that could befall her."

"That's not a very neighborly attitude, Mrs. Reynolds." Evan stepped out over the police line. "In the two or three minutes that we have been talking, you've expressed partisanship with the prosecution, displayed reluctance to cooperate with the defense, shown personal animosity toward Rachel, and felt the need to clear your front yard conversations with the state police. You hardly know Rachel Pope. You have no special knowledge of the evidence against her and you don't know whether she's guilty or not—which, by the way, she isn't—so the source of this hostility must be your own relationship with Dr. Pope."

She had no talent for conflict and this direct challenge was beyond her experience. "What exactly are you suggesting? What lies has that woman been feeding you?"

"No lies, Mrs. Reynolds. And I'm not suggesting anything untoward. But Dr. Pope was your neighbor long before Rachel was in the picture. I know all that. He and his first wife were your contemporaries. You all had many years together to develop a valuable and close friendship. And Mr. Reynolds of course."

"Professor Pope and my husband were such good friends." As the warm memories washed over her, her demeanor softened. She looked past Evan at the burned-out house. "And Mrs. Pope. We were all so young. Just getting started. We grew up together. My husband and I watched Ted Pope as he became famous and distinguished. We were proud of him in the way we would have been for a brother. When Mr. Reynolds passed away," she flinched at the pang of the old but still sharp hurt, "the Popes were my family. And the night Mrs. Pope died, Ted and I sat at my kitchen table and cried together." She turned toward her own house and looked at the kitchen window. And at the past.

Evan was reluctant to bring her to the night on which she became the sole survivor of those decades of friendships but the mood would soon change and he needed some answers. "What about the night of the fire, Mrs. Reynolds. What else did you see that night?"

"She killed him."

"Please just tell me what you saw." She was still wistful and Evan tried to get another answer before her mood toughened again.

"That first glow that I saw erupted quickly. By the time the fire trucks got here the fire was huge, it spilled out of his house. It came out the roof. Heat rises you know."

"I know."

"And she—the wife—she just sat there. Waiting. Not at all afraid. Just waiting. Like a child really. Hugging her knees and rocking. Up on the roof over the front porch. Next to the window from the upstairs hall."

"Waiting?"

"Yes. Calm. Serene. The firemen took her off the roof and when they brought Ted out she just stared at the body. There was nothing left. It was like ... It was ... How could she stand to see it? To look at it? Then they took her to the hospital. But she was fine. She was just fine." Gladys was getting wound up with the memory of Rachel's undeserved survival. "She burned that man to a cinder and walked away without a blister."

"Why are you so sure she did it, Mrs. Reynolds?"

"If she's really your client then you must know what she was. She was unfaithful. She was not a wife to him at all. By the end, by that night, I suppose she saw murder as the easiest way out." Gladys returned her stare to Evan. Newly confrontational. "Let me tell you what I know about her, about your client. She was with another man that night. She had just come home from being with another man before she killed her husband."

"You saw that?"

"I did. I saw her get out of his car before I went upstairs to bed. I was disgusted that she that he would have the gall to have him drive her home. With her husband inside. And it wasn't the only time I had seen that car here. It was here some days when Dr. Pope was teaching, or away at a conference." She touched the strand of pearls. "She is a vicious woman. Cold. You'll see. I never doubted it for an instant."

There was nothing about another man or a strange car in the police reports. This could change everything. "The man, Mrs. Reynolds. Do you know who he was?"

"It doesn't matter who he was. Some cheap bum, I'm quite sure. Not the match of Ted Pope."

"Did you ever see his face? Clearly?" Evan hesitated. "Would you recognize him?"

"No. I don't think so. I'm not certain I would." She straightened up to her best authoritative height and re-folded her arms. The conversation was nearly over. "I will be telling the police that you asked me all these questions. I will certainly tell them that you came here and trespassed and deceived me into talking to you."

"You're free to tell them anything you'd like, Mrs. Reynolds." It was Evan's turn to get authoritative. "But none of that is true and it's a crime to lie to the police. Why didn't you tell the police about the other man and the car you saw on the night of the fire? You haven't told those things to anyone before, have you?"

"No. No I haven't. I don't expect you to understand this. But maybe you will. When that Trooper Foster came to see me, he had already spoken to people from the college. People who knew Ted and his wife. They had told him all about, we'll all about her activities. It was all so tawdry. Dr. Pope was such a good man. It's bad enough that he had to come to such an end. Victimized. Stripped of his dignity. His nobility. He's just an object now in some court case with a bunch of strangers poking around his life like it's a cheap riddle. I won't have his last night on earth become the source of further humiliation. I won't help them make him look stupid."

"Then why did you tell me?"

She paused and stared at Evan in a way that made him feel exposed. "I thought that you should know," she said finally. "I want you to tell that woman that someone saw everything."

She turned away and walked back to her house. Evan stepped back in, over the evidence tape.

Chapter 8

The layout of the house was just about as Evan remembered it. The front door opened into a large foyer which in turn led to the living room. From the living room there were doors to the kitchen, dining room, and hall and a staircase to the second floor. The staircase was walled on both sides, an enclosed tunnel leading upstairs. Pieces of the floor were missing at the places where the fire had started. The inside of the house was as dark as a cave. The walls were covered with ash and smoke as completely as if a ghoulish crew of house painters had rollered the whole interior with thick black oil base. Evan had brought a flashlight and pointed it up the stairs. The black walls continued up to the second floor. It was hard to see anything clearly with the blackness absorbing all the light.

Evan knew that the whole place was structurally unsound so after seeing what he had come to see he turned around and walked back out through the space where the front door had been. North Second Street was a safe enough neighborhood that some residents still left their doors unlocked, especially if someone was home, Rachel had told Evan that she and Ted often did that. But the firemen reported that the doors were all locked when they got there and they had to use their axes to break in. That was a point for the prosecution. If the house had been all locked up when the arsonist started the fire, then the case was a classic closed room mystery. The fire would have had to have been started *inside* the house by someone already inside, somebody who had a supply of diethyl ether. That fact was another plank in Rachel Pope's gallows.

When Evan turned to leave he saw the dark green Ford Crown Victoria pull up outside. Black wall tires. Rubber antenna on the rear deck for a radio repeater. No extra chrome. The ostentatious blandness of the un-marked state police car. Hank Foster got out the passen-ger's door. Some twenty-five-year-old crew-cutted white guy in a new cheap suit was driving. He was a step be-hind Foster.

"Hi, Hank." Evan was still inside the police line. He stepped over the tape as if that were no big deal. "What are you doing here? I would have thought you'd have seen enough of this place."

"We got a report that a police officer was here in-vestigating. Since we hadn't sent anyone we figured some non-police personnel was snooping around in a re-stricted area. What the fuck is going on here, Evan?"

"Snooping around. Investigating. The search for truth. You know."

"No joking, Evan. This is serious. You're not au-thorized to be inside the police line. I already called Ian. He'll be here in few minutes."

"Good idea. It's nice that he gets out of the court-house once in a while. See ya."

Evan headed for the Cadillac. Crew-cut, silent and still until now, took a step forward and put his hand on Evan's elbow. "Just a minute. You'll have to wait here until Mr. Stonebridge gets here and we get this situation all sorted out."

Evan pulled his elbow free and looked crew-cut straight in the eye. Hank didn't say or do anything. He would never have admitted it but he was delighted at his sidekick's youthful indiscretion.

"Am I under arrest?"

"No, sir. But you still have to wait here with us."

"If you're making me stay here with you, that's technically an arrest. If you aren't charging me with a crime, then it's an unlawful arrest. And pretty soon you're going to have to decide how far you want to play this game because I really am leaving. Right now."

"Just calm down, Counselor. We'll straighten all this out when the district attorney gets here."

"Fuck you." Crew-cut's eyes got a little wider. "If you think that I'm going to hang around here so that I can eat shit from Ian Stonebridge you're nuts. If you want to charge me with something, be my guest. If not, I'll see you later."

"How's tampering with evidence sound." Crew-cut.

"Actually, that sounds pretty stupid." He glanced over at the senior officer on the scene. "Who is this jerk-off anyway, Hank? Listen, son," Evan assumed a paternal air to which his ten or so years seniority hardly entitled him. "First, this crime scene hasn't been secured since shortly after the fire. There are no guards and I don't think you check it regularly or else a call from the neighbor wouldn't hustle you over here ready to flash your badges around. Any tampering you might find inside will be impossible to pin on me. Second, my client still owns this place and she has the right to have her representative look in on her property from time to time. Third, there damn well better not be any evidence left inside to tamper with or I'll be asking the court to throw this case out for police incompetence." A request like that would be total bullshit but crew-cut didn't know that. Hank did but he kept quiet. "And finally, what do you think I could do here anyway, even if I *wanted* to tamper with evidence? Rebuild the house behind your back? Bring back Ted Pope to say he isn't really dead? You know Hank, this kid is full or great ideas."

"Trooper Piper here may be little overly aggressive, Evan," Hank snickered, once and involuntarily, as he took a step forward. "But this is still a crime scene, Evan. It's roped off. You're not allowed in here, you know that."

Crew-cut hadn't made any effort to place hands on Evan again. "I heard you used to be a good lawyer once," he said. "No one told me you were such a pain in the ass."

"Same thing. Now look kid, settle down and watch your mouth before you find yourself spending the next few years explaining why you torpedoed a slam-dunk conviction by intimidating Mrs. Pope's defense attorney. If you get a warrant for me, I'll be at the college. Otherwise, you two should go back to work. Catch some bad guys. Solve some crimes."

Hank spoke up now. "We already solved one, Evan. This one." He turned his head toward crew-cut who met his stare and didn't break off. "Trooper Piper here is new to the criminal investigation division and maybe he gets a little bit too enthusiastic sometimes. He doesn't understand the system yet like we do." Hank looked back at Evan. "But no matter. This case is a lock. Rachel is as good as finished." He smiled, genuinely friendly. "Why don't you just get her to plead guilty?"

"Maybe I will, Hank. Nobody knows what the future holds. So long."

Chapter 9

The next few weeks saw little action in the case of *Commonwealth of Pennsylvania versus Rachel Pope* and Evan still had what he was now thinking of as his day job; so when Crawford College's classes started up again in early September, a crisp Tuesday afternoon found him walking to Anders Hall to teach his weekly session of Case Studies in Constitutional Criminal Law. That how the catalog described Political Science 304. The kids called it Great Moments in Courtroom History. By the time he arrived at the second-floor lecture hall where the class met the students were already there. He had looked at the class roster back at his office so he knew that the class was fully subscribed and that about half of the students were recidivists: repeaters from previous semesters who would take anything the college offered with Evan's name on it. He walked to the teacher's podium and looked around the class and smiled. Nearly everyone smiled back. Always a good sign with your basic jury. He found a familiar face in the third row.

"Good afternoon, Ms. Gabriel. Please give us the facts of *Commonwealth v. Moore*." Sarah Gabriel was a bright and energetic senior who had taken all of Evan's courses and had already applied early decision to seven law schools. She would probably get accepted by at least six of them. *Moore* was a hard case and Sarah was an easy call to be sure of a correct statement. Evan folded his hands behind his back and started wandering around the classroom while Sarah Gabriel described Martin Moore's tale of woe.

"Martin Moore was twenty years old when he was arrested for murdering a bank guard during a robbery attempt. Right here in Harrisburg. Moore walked into the bank, apparently high, and demanded money at gunpoint from the tellers. He left the bank with about three thousand dollars. A security guard caught up to him in the parking lot and was bringing him back inside when Moore shoved the gun in the guard's side and shot him point blank. The guard died instantly. Moore kept running and that afternoon he hopped a bus to Baltimore. He might have gotten away with it, but he was still messed up and he started a disturbance on the bus. Waving the gun around, threatening the other passengers. The driver radioed the Baltimore Port Authority and some police cars stopped the bus and took Moore to jail. His description matched the police reports about the Harrisburg bank robbery so the Baltimore police called Harrisburg. A couple of Harrisburg detectives went to Baltimore arrested Moore and extradited him back to

Pennsylvania. He was tried and convicted of first-degree murder and sentenced to death. After his first appeal was denied the case gets interesting."

"Interesting, huh? What was the prosecution's evidence at trial?"

"You name it. When the Baltimore police took him off the bus he still had the murder weapon. Ballistic testing confirmed that. There were security cameras inside the bank that recorded the robbery and cameras in the parking lot that got the murder. Plenty of eyewitnesses could identify him. Oh, and when the Harrisburg detectives got to the Baltimore jail, Moore gave them a full confession."

"Not a bad prosecution case." Evan raised his arms for emphasis. "Inculpatory statements, eyewitness identifications, scientific evidence, a confession, and the defendant's arrest while holding the murder weapon. No wonder his appeal was denied. It's an open-and-shut case."

The recidivists in the class recognized this banter as a forensic call to arms and a dozen hands rose. "Let's stay with Ms. Gabriel for a moment. What exactly got interesting after the first appeal?"

"Well, Moore didn't have a defense but he did have an issue," she continued. "The prosecution had Moore's confession and they wanted to use it against him. He objected and filed a pre-trial motion to suppress his confession. To have the court rule that it could not be used."

"Why? Hadn't they read him his Miranda warnings?" Evan looked around the room and saw a lot of hands waving. Everyone knew about Miranda warnings. "You have the right to remain silent. You have the right to an attorney." And on and on and on. All of the worthless advice that police are required to give a suspect before a custodial interrogation.

Gabriel again. "Yes. They read him his rights, and he understood them. Maybe a little better than they wanted him to. After the reading of rights, Moore said that he wanted to call his brother-in-law to get him a lawyer. The police admitted this at the suppression hearing."

Evan looked for another hand. "What did the brother-in-law do?" Jason Freres was next. A junior philosophy major, his interest in the law was purely academic. After much genuine reflection he had concluded that the law was a mighty sloppy way to order society. "Mr. Freres, what about the brother-in-law?"

"Well," Jason started slowly, "they never called the brother-in-law. Instead, the police officer asked Moore if that was what he really wanted to do. 'Why involve your family in this?' is the way the detective explained the conversation when he testified about it in court. Then he said 'Do you really think that a lawyer can change all this?' and he pointed at a surveillance photo that showed Moore shooting the guard. 'I guess not' Moore said and he gave the police his confession. Yes, that was him in the picture. Yes, he robbed the bank. Yes, he killed the security guard. Yes, this was the gun he used. The confession eliminated any possibility that Moore's lawyer could argue mistaken identity or accidental shooting or anything else. Moore was convicted and sentenced to life in prison. Then, of course, he appealed."

"Very good, Mr. Freres." Evan pointed to the back of the room.

"What did he do while his case was on appeal, Mr. Given?" Matt Given was a junior history major, another recidivist who struggled for every C plus despite a conscientious application to the coursework. Something about the law was indecipherable for him, but he waved his hand and this was an easy question. A fact question.

"Well his first appeal was turned down. But then he appealed again, to the Pennsylvania Supreme Court. His lawyer filed all the briefs that he had to and then there was a hearing on the appeal."

"Oral argument," Evan corrected.

"Oral argument," Matt continued. "The Supreme Court sat on Moore's case for a long time, two years almost, and then one day before they decided anything Moore escaped from prison. He was complaining of severe headaches so the prison doctor had him taken to a hospital for an MRI of his brain to see if he had a brain tumor. After the MRI, while he was being taken back to his hospital room, he shoved an orderly, rushed past the prison guards and ran. But then the moron steals a car from the parking lot and is caught up in a roadblock within an hour. He was on his way home to see his mother. Half the cops in Pennsylvania were looking for him and he heads right where they expected him to be. He was back in jail the same day." Given waited a beat and smiled, pleased with himself. Evan smiled back. "Right." Given was a good kid and Evan decided on the spot that he got a one-letter upgrade for the term. An arbitrary decision, but they were studying the law after all so what the hell.

"Okay." Evan summed up the facts. "His appeal gets turned down once, it's at the second level and he escapes for an hour. But Ms. Gabriel was right; he didn't really have any defense to the charges. The jury heard all the evidence and they nailed Mr. Moore for first degree." Evan kept walking around. "What's the point, Mr. Freres?"

"The point was the case that the jury heard."

"Why?"

"Moore claimed that his confession should have been suppressed. When he asked for his brother-in-law to get him an attorney, that was the same thing as asking for an attorney directly. He claimed, and he was right, that the police questioning should have stopped at that point. When the police detective kept at him with the evidence they had, that violated his constitutional rights and his confession should have been excluded. He was right. He wanted a new trial, and he should have gotten one."

Good. "Exactly right. That was the defense position. Let's hear the prosecutorial view on all this. Ms. Gabriel, isn't that rather a thin reed on which to challenge an entire conviction? And in a murder case at that. 'Let me call my brother-in-law?' So what if he asked for his brother-in-law?"

"Personally, I agree."

"Personally, I expected that you would."

"But Jason is technically right. The confession was illegally obtained and it should never have been used against him. The law says that once a defendant asks for a lawyer, no matter how he asks, the questioning has to stop. Here it didn't stop. The police asked him another question. Did he really want to involve his family? Then they asked him another one. Could a lawyer change the evidence against him? The detective who pointed to the security photograph was really asking him, 'Is that you in this picture?' Another question."

She was right. Time to move to the next stage. "But he appealed to the Pennsylvania Supreme Court. As we all know, they never wrote an opinion about the case but the transcript of the oral argument session is in your handouts. What impression did you get from the questions the justices asked at argument?" Evan looked around the room. "Did they agree with you, Mr. Freres?"

"I think so. The sense of the questioning seemed to be that the law was pretty clear on that point. Once a suspect is in custody and he asks for a lawyer, the police can't ask any more questions. The police violated Moore's rights. The trial judge violated the constitution by letting the D.A. use the confession as evidence at the trial. I think the Supreme Court was going to give Moore a new trial."

"Very good. I agree, the Supreme Court would have given Moore a new trial. But that never happened. Why not? Tell us again, Mr. Given."

"He escaped."

"So what? They caught him the same day."

"That's what I say. But after he was caught, the Supreme Court threw out his appeal."

"You mean they upheld his conviction. They affirmed the lower courts."

"No. At least I don't think so. I think they just said that because Moore escaped they didn't want anything more to do with him. Next case."

"Yes, Mr. Given, for the Supreme Court it was 'Next case' but for Moore it was a lifetime in the penitentiary for an hour of freedom. He didn't hurt anyone during his escape did he?" All heads shook. "Right. And likewise during his flight and his recapture. He just ran away from the hospital, drove around for an hour and surrendered as soon as he got caught. So why does he lose his appeal? Ms. Gabriel?"

"The Supreme Court said that when a person escapes from prison while his case is on appeal he is making an affirmative choice to abandon his appeal. He can't escape, stay a fugitive while his case is pending and then resurface if he's happy with the decision. He's litigating his appeal with his feet, so to speak. I think the Supreme Court decided that Moore was thumbing his nose at them and they returned the favor."

"But he was recaptured the same day." This was Jason. "His escape was stupid and impulsive. But here was a guy whose trial was unfair, he was facing a life sentence and he had no reason to trust the legal system. He saw his chance to run away from all of that and he took it. No one else would have done anything different.

He wasn't thinking about abandoning his appeal or anything like that. He probably wasn't thinking at all. He was desperate and scared, he wanted out and he left."

Evan nodded. "Desperate and scared" was a charitable way to excuse a robber, murderer, and fugitive from justice. But Jason didn't bat an eye. "Perhaps Mr. Freres is right and the Supreme Court is wrong. What do you say Ms. Radcliff?" Deborah Radcliff was a senior Classics major. Ted Pope had been her faculty advisor. Evan didn't know what she was doing in his class. "Was Moore intending to abandon his rights to have his appeal decided by the Supreme Court? Or did he simply want a fair trial?"

"Yes. Well, I think Jason is right. Moore was acting impulsively, and I think the Supreme Court was too. Moore's conviction was two years when he escaped. He probably was tired of waiting for the decision and worried that it wouldn't go his way. But the Court must have been worried too. They could have turned down his case or refused to hear it at all. But they stewed about it for two years."

She was on the right track. "Yes, I think you're getting close to the answer, Ms. Radcliff. 'The court must have been worried too.' About what?"

"That they would have to give him a new trial. He had gunned down an innocent man. While robbing a bank. At gunpoint. This guy did not deserve a break. And

I think that the Court was balking at the idea of giving him another chance just because some policeman asked him one too many questions. Their problem was that they didn't really have a choice. Moore was going to get a new a trial and the Court didn't like having to give it to him. That's why they were stalling. When they had a chance to wash their hands of the whole thing, they jumped at it."

"But that's not the way the courts are supposed to work." Jason again. "If there's going to be a law that says 'Everyone gets a fair trial except for people we don't like,' then let's write it down someplace and be honest about it. I agree with Deborah. The court screwed Moore because they didn't like him. No doubt he had committed an awful crime, but this kind of case makes the legal system look bad."

Deborah spoke up. "How arbitrary would it have looked if Moore got a new trial, maybe a reduced sentence, just because some cop told the truth for a change? He could have just lied at the hearing. 'Oh no, Your Honor. He never asked to call anybody.' I think the court did the right thing. The guy was guilty, he was convicted, and the Supreme Court found a way to avoid a second trial."

"But the trial's the thing, isn't it?" The period was almost over and Evan had to drive the point home. "What difference does it make if we give a defendant a trial if we admit illegal evidence?"

Deborah again. Evan let her finish. "What difference would it possibly have made if they didn't admit the illegal evidence? Let's say his appeal was never dismissed, let's say he got a new trial and the confession didn't come in. The prosecution still has the murder weapon, the camera footage, and the eyewitnesses. Moore would have been convicted all over again. The whole suppression issue was just a waste of time. A legal game. We can disagree about the way the courts reached the final result, but the result itself was correct. Moore deserved to be convicted and they saw to it that he stayed convicted." She sat back in her seat and smiled.

Evan's phone alarm beeped with a two-minute warning.

"Class is almost over and before we leave I have something to talk to you all about. You know, I assume, that I'm defending Mrs. Pope against the charge that she killed Professor Pope. Some of you knew Dr. Pope. All of you knew about him and probably admired him. There's a lot of gossip going around the campus about why I took this case. Everyone here knows that I've been retired from practicing law since before I started teaching at Crawford, and I swore I would never set foot in a courtroom again. Perhaps that tells you how strongly I feel about this case. Dr. Pope was a friend of mine. Mrs. Pope still is a friend of mine. This kind of consideration isn't supposed to affect a lawyer's decisions, but I'm sure that she's innocent. I don't have any more to say about it, but if anyone here feels uncomfortable with any part of what I've just said, I'll be glad to see you privately.

"In closing today's class, I'd like all of you to think about the concept of a fair trial. What if Moore hadn't escaped? Ms. Radcliff is quite correct, he would have gotten a new trial and been convicted all over again. Maybe. But what if an eyewitness died in the meanwhile? Or what if the films weren't clear enough for a positive identification? Or what if one of the jurors at the second trial simply took pity on him and deadlocked the deliberations? Then what?" Evan looked around the room. "Was it fair to deprive him of the chance, even a slight chance, that he might win his second trial?

"The right to have a trial conducted according to the rules that the law requires is the same thing as the right to have a lawyer who knows how to enforce those rules. The constitution guarantees both of those rights. Moore deserved that. Mrs. Pope deserves the same thing, and I intend to see that she gets it." He looked around the room. Lots of solemn and unconvinced faces. It really was unrealistic for him to expect his students to fully comprehend the gravity of what he was saying.

Evan dismissed class and the students rushed out the door. Only Deborah Radcliff lingered, one blue-jeaned leg dangling over the arm-tray of her chair, tapping her knee with a pencil eraser.

Chapter 10

Rose Miller, the administrative assistant for the Political Science Department, was waiting for Evan when he reached his office the following Monday. Rose was probably about forty years old, but she had the appearance and personality of a person who could be any age at all. If Evan learned that she was really thirty, he would have been only slightly surprised, and less still if she told him she was sixty. She was somewhere between five and six feet tall, weighed between one and two hundred pounds, and dressed in a style of casual frumpiness. She treated every professor in the department as a member of her family, but each one was a different member. Johnstone, the chairman, was her dictatorial father. Sally Morrow, who taught political thought and theory, was her twin sister. They actually did look a little bit alike, especially around the tweed skirts and Shaker sweaters. The rest were either cousins or aunts or uncles except for Evan and Dr. Rhinehart who taught international affairs. To Rose, Rhinehart was the black sheep nephew: the one who only visits you at

Thanksgiving to gorge himself on your turkey, each time with a different poodled-up floozy who calls you "Hon" and barks out compliments about the cooking with her mouth still full of sweet potatoes. Nobody liked Rhinehart.

But Evan, no matter what their age differential would or would not allow, was her favorite son. Not the son who brought home the perfect report card, got the lead in the high school musical, and was voted Most Likely to Succeed. No, that would have been Professor Markey, Public Administration and the American Presidency. Evan was the son who needed a little extra help getting along with his friends and who always stayed out too late. When he did get home there was a good chance that one of his car's bumpers would be in the back seat. She had not been the least bit surprised to find out that his lawyer nickname had been the Prince of Darkness.

There wasn't much secretarial work for her to do in the department, mostly scheduling and greeting the professors' visitors and students; but any work Evan gave her always got priority. And then there was the food, fruit and rolls for breakfast when he stopped at the office before an early class. Homemade something or other wrapped in foil for him to take home for dinner. She had even started buying the Blue Mountain coffee beans he liked and grinding them fresh for the department coffee pot. It didn't taste quite perfect when it wasn't French pressed, and no doubt Johnstone would hit the roof when he finally figured out what it cost. But Rose knew it was Evan's favorite and that was good enough for her. She was by far the nicest person in the department if not the whole college.

She gave Evan a moment to get settled in his office before tapping a couple of light knocks on his door and opening it without waiting for an answer. "Professor Wonder?" She sort of peeked her head into the crack, and then followed it through as if her entry were confidential, surreptitious. "We have to talk." Uh oh. She never called him "Professor." Something was going on. As if to confirm his suspicions, she looked out into the hall to make sure the coast was clear before she closed the door. And locked it.

"Sure, Rose. Let's talk." Evan knew that this could mean anything, from her latest feud with Rhinehart to her concern about the weight that Evan had lost lately. He took his feet off the desk, swiveled his chair around to face front and waited for her to sit down. Her face had a look of genuine uneasiness which would have worried Evan but for the fact that this was Rose after all.

"It's about that Miss Radcliff in your Great Moments class." Now she had his attention. "She's been calling for you. Every day. She keeps saying that needs to see you right away, that you've been ignoring her emails. The chairman was at my desk yesterday when I had her on speaker. He heard the conversation so I had to give her an appointment. She'll be here any minute. She wants to talk about Dr. Pope."

Fucking Johnstone. "Well, she is a student, Rose. Part of my job is talking to students, you know."

"You have fifty-seven students registered to your classes." Trust Rose to know the exact number, unlike Evan. "They don't all call you every day. No one else calls you every day. When Dr. Johnstone heard her say that you've been avoiding her, he said he was going to talk to you about it."

"No he isn't," Evan said with an emphasis borne of true confidence. Howard Johnstone was a full professor, he had an endowed chair. He was two years away from a much-anticipated and long-awaited retirement. And he hated Evan. He viewed him as an impostor to authentic academia. A dilettante. A poser. Worse still: a lawyer with a JD and no PhD. Christ. If Evan had been Dracula or Godzilla he would be no less welcome in Johnstone's world of elite scholasticism. He had been looking for some way to make trouble for Evan ever since the chancellor overruled his objections and gave Evan this job seven years ago. Whatever obligation Johnstone felt toward running an efficient department would take a backseat to the pleasure he would get from making things uncomfortable for Evan about the Rachel Pope case. There was nothing unusual about teachers dodging student calls and Johnstone wouldn't give a damn about it under normal circumstances. But one professor defending a faculty wife who is charged with murdering another professor? That was pretty unusual and Johnstone had been chomping at the bit for some way to confront Evan. He couldn't simply forbid it because outside work didn't violate Evan's contract with the college. But once students started to complain he could accuse Evan of "pedagogical inefficiency." If your students resent you, you can't teach them effectively. Allegedly.

Deborah Radcliff would be Johnstone's opening move.

Evan had anticipated such a gambit and he was ready with his countermove. "Bring Ms. Radcliff in here as soon as she arrives. Leave the door open. Then ask the chairman if he can give me a few minutes in about an hour."

Rose leaned forward. "It's just that, well, with this Pope case and all the pressure you've been under I was afraid that ..." Evan knew what Rose was afraid of and she stopped her in mid-hunch.

"Don't worry, Rose. Everything is fine."

"I know, Evan; I mean, I'm sure it is. Or will be. It's just that Professor Johnstone resents you. You know that. And he's such a sneaky bastard."

Rose never swore and her outburst made Evan realize how truly afraid for him she was. "Come on, Rose, you know what I did before I came to Crawford. I've spent half my life dealing with murderers, thieves, and scoundrels of every kind. Not to mention every cop in Pennsylvania who wanted a piece of me, the FBI and the Treasury, and once or twice Cosa Nostra. I think I'll be able to handle one more sneaky bastard, especially an over-the hill globalization geek." That made Rose smile. "Johnstone won't lay a glove on me," Evan assured her.

Deborah Radcliff arrived at the political science department ten minutes later and Rose ushered her into Evan's office.

"Ms. Radcliff, I understand you have a newly found interest in murder."

"Not murder generally," she was relaxed and direct. "Just this one. The Pope murder. I'd like to understand why you're representing the woman who murdered my advisor. And one of your colleagues. I thought, everybody thought, that you retired from practicing law before you started teaching here."

"Then everybody was right. I did. But now I'm back."

"Why?"

Evan considered her carefully. Even in a modern atmosphere of student-faculty familiarity, it was unusual for a student to challenge a professor so directly, at least before final grades were recorded. Maybe she had some agenda. But maybe she was just curious. Either way, Ted Pope had been her advisor and his students loved him. Deborah was probably no different and since she was stuck with Evan for the rest of the semester in Great Moments she probably just wanted to decide how much she should hate him.

"I quit practicing law because one of my clients, an innocent man, was wrongly convicted of murder and I could no longer stand to be around that kind of injustice. I came back because Rachel Pope is innocent of this murder and I am determined that I won't just sit on the sidelines while another injustice like that happens again. Not if I can help it."

"Can you? Help it, I mean?"

"You don't know much about chess, do you Ms. Radcliff?"

"A little. Enough to know to stay away from your club."

Evan smiled at that. "Well, if you knew a little more you'd realize that this contest hasn't reached the endgame yet and it's still impossible to predict the outcome. But you must have some interest in criminal law or else you wouldn't have taken my course." She nodded. "So maybe you'd like to see what it's like to be involved in a big case. Grunt work, really. Errands. Note taking. Maybe read and summarize some police reports. You might find it interesting. Maybe I can even talk the registrar into giving you some independent study credits."

Extra credit. Every student's dream. Evan could let her write up her experiences as a term paper and accept it as a research project. It would all be totally legit, and as his research assistant, she couldn't complain about him defending Rachel and Johnstone would have to quit his bitching. It was the perfect counter-gambit.

"In fact, if you sign this confidentiality agreement," he slid a document across the desk, "you can get started now."

She scrawled her signature and returned the form to Evan. "What do I do first?"

He walked over to his filing cabinet, filed her agreement, and retrieved the accordion file that Ian had given him on their first visit. "You can take this home with you and read it. Don't lose anything. Don't show it to anybody else."

Evan's desk phone buzzed and he picked up the handset. It was Rose. "The chairman says he can see you right now for five minutes."

"Thanks Rose." Evan stood up. To Deborah, "Come back tomorrow morning at ten o'clock and we'll talk about the case." He marked one page with a paper clip before handing her the file. "I think you'll probably want to start here." He walked Deborah to the door and headed down the hallway.

Chairman Johnstone was waiting for him. The chairman's office was about five times as large as the cubby holes assigned to the normal faculty members. The furnishings were old and rich. Real wood and leather, no particle board or sheet metal. There were large windows looking out on a broad lawn, meticulously landscaped with hydrangea bushes, ornamental grasses, and fieldstone. It was nowhere near as nice as Evan's law office had been, but in the world of small college academia it was pretty sweet. Evan took a chair and waited for Johnstone to sit down.

"Harold, I thought that we should clear the air. Obviously you know that I've been retained to defend Rachel Pope, and ..."

"Yes, Evan, and I have to tell you that ..."

"Stop. You don't like it. I know that already. Most of the administrators on this campus don't like it and I bet none of the faculty like it very much either. You all liked Ted, you believe that Rachel is guilty, and you want to see her get convicted. Well, Harold, my job is to see that she doesn't, and I'm going to do that job and I don't care what you or anybody else thinks or says. You want to fire me for standing up for a citizen's constitutional right to a fair trial? Go ahead. Now that I am re-learning my way around the courthouse again it wouldn't be too much of a chore to file a wrongful termination lawsuit against Crawford, this department, and you personally."

"Evan, you can't talk that way to me. I am your superior, don't forget."

That made Evan laugh out loud. "Harold, you may be my supervisor but my *superior?* Not on the best day you ever lived. I have some advice for you. Stay away from the media glare. Keep your mouth shut when reporters come calling. Stop slandering Rachel to the faculty. And most of all, stay the fuck out of my way or I promise that you will be very, very sorry."

Johnstone was dumbstruck. When he regained the power of speech he said, "I could fire you for that Radcliff girl alone. Don't think I haven't noticed her."

"We've all noticed her, Harold. Everybody notices her. But she works for me now. She's interning as a legal assistant at the newly reconstituted Wonder Law Firm. By the way, she'll be applying for three credits of independent study and I'll be approving her application at the end of the semester."

When Evan left the room, Johnstone was still gasping for air.

114

Chapter 11

Evan got up early the next morning and went down to the storage room in his basement where he had stashed all of the paraphernalia of running a law office. He found a box of three-ring binders and a hole punch, boxes of colored markers and highlighters, file folders, legal pads, index cards, and sticky notes. He would organize the file in a series of searchable digital files on his laptop, but there was still a lot of paper that had to be available at his fingertips whenever a cross-examination question or legal argument required it. He carried everything up to his dining room which he had converted into his war room. He started labeling the first few binders: "court documents," "witness statements," "medical records," "police reports." The process made the case feel very tangible and real. It made him a little bit sick to his stomach.

At ten o'clock sharp, Deborah was sitting in Evan's Crawford College office. She was pissed. "You didn't tell me she failed a polygraph test."

"Yeah. Before she had the good sense to ask for a lawyer, the police convinced her that taking the test was in her best interests. When they told her she failed it, that's when she quit talking and that's when Stonebridge sent the police to get me.

Deborah read from the polygraph examiner's report. "In response to relevant question number 6: 'Were you in any way responsible for the death of Dr. Pope in the fire at 9152 North Second Street?' The subject Rachel Pope answered 'No.' It is this examiner's conclusion that the subject's physiological responses to question six and its answer are consistent with deception and that the subject was untruthful in her answer to question six."

Deborah lifted her head and stared at Evan. "She lied! How could you say that she's innocent when you knew about this?"

"That report doesn't prove anything. It's not admissible in court and ..."

"So what if it's not admissible. You know about it and you still think ..."

"I still *know* that Mrs. Pope didn't start the fire. That test means nothing to me. A polygraph test is just someone's subjective interpretation of some of the physiological changes that can occur while a person is answering questions. Some of those changes may or may

116

not be relevant to psychological stress and psychological stress may or may not indicate falsehood. None of the connections which would be required to make polygraphy reliable have ever been proven and no one outside law enforcement really takes it too seriously." Evan took the report out of her hands. "But *inside* law enforcement, they love it."

"How come?"

"Mainly because it pretends to be the Holy Grail of criminal investigation. A foolproof way of knowing for sure if a suspect committed the crime and that can come in handy if the difference between truth and lies is a trip to death row. Some people just want to believe it so much that they convince themselves that it's true." Deborah pushed up her round horn-rimmed glasses until they were propped just below her hairline, the yellow bangs falling around and in front. "Don't you have mysteries like that in Classics?

"Well, there are few questions about Homer," she answered.

"Are there indeed?"

"Never mind Homer, what about Mrs. Pope. How can you possibly be so sure she didn't do it? This Trooper Foster has put together a pretty solid case against her." She put the eyeglasses back on her nose and thumbed through the pages of the file.

"Never mind all that. You're right, Foster has a good case, and he's got a couple of strong motives. For one, there's the million dollars of insurance money. And then," he looked right at her so he could gauge her reaction, "she was fucking around on Professor Pope. With other faculty at this college. Maybe even someone you know."

Deborah shrugged but didn't fall out of her chair. "I saw that in the file. Is that why Trooper Foster interviewed Dr. Jackson?"

"I think so," said Evan. "He's got an alibi though and Rachel made a better suspect so she's the one in jail. The case against her is circumstantial but still plenty strong enough to send her to death row if we don't save her. Now that you've read the file maybe you can tell me how we do that."

She grimaced. "*We* don't save her. I knew Dr. Pope. He was a great teacher and I liked him. I'm not sure I can do this. Helping you defend Mrs. Pope."

Evan understood. Abject horror usually trumps academic curiosity. "Tell you what. The preliminary hearing is tomorrow. Come and watch, then make up your mind. Okay?"

Deborah nodded slowly. Evan took back the discovery file and locked it in his desk.

Chapter 12

After the Ronnie Porter case, Evan took all of his lawyer suits, French-cuff shirts, fancy shoes, and ties and stashed them away in the closet of his guest room. His wardrobe was mainly sweaters and jeans nowadays. For special faculty events or important tournaments at the Lasker he had a few sportscoats and some chinos and that was about as dressed up as he had gotten in seven years. But then the day of Rachel's preliminary hearing arrived and he had to open the closet. He picked a solid blue suit, a white shirt and the Jerry Garcia painted tie. Black belt, wingtips, grey socks. He laid out the clothes on his king-sized bed and stared at them with dread. He knew that a few minutes later he would feel like he had never left.

The preliminary hearing under Pennsylvania's criminal law was a strange beast. Its official purpose was to allow an impartial judicial officer an early opportunity to decide whether the prosecution had enough evidence to force a defendant to stand trial. The Commonwealth's burden was to convince a judge that a crime had taken place and that the defendant may have done it. In that way, the system could get rid of frivolous cases where the evidence was so weak that the defendant's innocence was obvious or, more to the point, where a future conviction just wasn't in the cards. Otherwise, the judge would decide that the prosecution had presented a *prima facie* case, one that looked good "at first glance," and bind over the defendant to stand trial in the Court of Common Pleas: the Pennsylvania county courts.

That was the idea, anyway. In practice, preliminary hearing judges didn't find too many weeds in the garden of criminal arrests. They couldn't toss a case that they found to be incredible, contradictory or absurd. They were not allowed to reject the testimony of obvious liars. If there was any evidence that a crime had been committed and that the defendant was somehow implicated then she was headed downtown. Prosecutors loved this standard. It was easy to meet and it allowed for long pre-trial incarceration of innocent citizens who could ever be proved guilty beyond a reasonable doubt. Many guilty pleas were extorted from defendants who were being bound over for trial and just wanted to cut their losses and get out of jail. For those on bail, the need to eliminate the personal uncertainty and risk of an unresolved arrest often had the same result.

The preliminary hearing was not a total waste of time for the defense, though, because a smart lawyer could use it to learn more about the prosecution. A criminal case, unlike a civil lawsuit, doesn't involve a lot of pre-trial exchanges of the evidence. In a lawsuit over a five-dollar debt, the defendant can make the plaintiff come to his lawyer's office and testify under oath until the lawyer runs out of questions. He can subpoena independent witnesses and hear their stories. He can demand, and get, any documents or records he wants—indeed anything which even piques his interest—from anyone within the court's subpoena jurisdiction. Trial by ambush has become a thing of the past. Information flowed smoothly because the civil courts had come to believe that settlements grow out of complete knowledge instead of fearful uncertainty and risk.

But the same citizen who could learn all about his opponent's five-dollar claim can learn almost nothing about a case where the state tries to lock her up or kill her. In a criminal case the defendant usually begs for scraps of information from the prosecutor's file. Some rules do exist for the disclosure of certain categories of evidence. But those categories are narrow and the rules are self-enforcing. Ian had given Evan a lot of documents but he never suggested it was everything he had nor had he promised to have turned over the most important parts of the file. Evidence which proved that the defendant might be innocent has to be disclosed, but nobody really checks to make sure that happens. Sometimes somebody just forgets to hand something over and sometimes the police report is misleading because the investigation was sloppy. But sometimes there is pure fraud. Evidence of innocence, payments to prosecution witnesses, proof of misidentification have all gotten buried or shredded or lost to help the fight against crime.

But there *was* the preliminary hearing. The D.A. didn't have to put on all his witnesses; he didn't even have to put on many. But he needed some. A *prima facie* case was still *some* case and *some* evidence was required. That meant witnesses and that meant cross-examination. A skillful cross-examiner could work a preliminary hearing witness to get the kind of pre-trial discovery which the law did not theoretically allow. The prosecutor could scream objections at every question but the fact remained that every area raised by the direct examination was fair game for cross. And many judges got frustrated by the rules which required them to act like stooges for the prosecution and so they gave the defendant a lot of latitude.

The judicial officers assigned to conduct preliminary hearings were called magisterial district judges. Most of them were not lawyers and the supreme courts of both the United States and Pennsylvania had agreed that they didn't have to be. They usually did not have courthouses of their own so Rachel's hearing was held in a medium-sized suite of rooms in an uptown professional office park, sandwiched between a dentist and a real-estate agent. The prosecution was usually represented by the arresting officer who could read from their reports of witness interviews. The near certainty of the result—"I find that the prosecution has made out a *prima facie* case and bind the defendant to court on all charges" —made most preliminary hearings uninteresting yawners.

This one, of course, was different.

All three local TV stations had reporters and cameras in the parking lot awaiting the players' arrivals. By the time Evan parked the Cadillac, Ian had already been interviewed in the parking lot and was waiting inside. Evan smiled as he walked through the media gauntlet.

"Is Rachel guilty?" one reporter shouted.

"Do you expect the case to go to court?" yelled another one.

"What about the death penalty? Doesn't she deserve it if she's convicted?" asked the third.

Evan always thought it best to say nothing on the way into a courtroom. If his case collapsed into a disastrous humiliation, there would be less shit to eat on the way out.

"I do have a statement for the record." He stopped at the office door and the cameras made a semi-circle in front of him. Some of the reporters pushed their microphones in his face. The print guys had hand-held recorders.

He paused, looked down, and then up at the crowd. Look directly at the lens in the middle, he remembered, so the video doesn't make you look shifty or evasive.

"I just want to say," he hesitated for emphasis, "that I am grateful for the beautiful weather we are having today in Dauphin County and just as soon as this hearing is over I plan to go hiking on the Susquehanna Trail. Thank you." He turned away from the pissed-off crowd and walked inside.

The preliminary hearing courtroom would have made a medium-sized executive office. The judge's bench was a small desk behind a wall of fake wood paneling and cheap molding. The judge had a high-back chair but not enough room to swivel or rock it, lest he bang into the back wall and leave more of the black smudges which already marked up the white plaster. Most of the molded plastic chairs in the gallery went to the reporters who had followed him in and they sat chatting and joking while they waited for the action to start. Ian sat comfortably in a straight-backed chair at one of the plain wooden counsel tables. He was at the eye of a storm of activity as subordinate attorneys, legal assistants, cops, and other helpers scurried around to find folders, to re-read already worn-out witness statements and generally just to enjoy the excitement that goes along with being part of a major prosecution.

Evan stood at the back of the room for a few minutes taking in the atmosphere. A courtroom artist with long dirty hair balanced her sketchpad on her lap and started to fill in the background for her first drawing. The freelance court stenographer who had been hired to record the testimony unpacked her equipment. A dozen or so deputy sheriffs repeatedly exchanged the joke of the day which involved an offer to do the prisoner's next body cavity search. Such was the carnival atmosphere of the big case. Thrills, danger, humor, surprises, and high stakes. There really was nothing like it. And, like it or not, the search for complete truth rose no higher than second or third place in the consideration of anyone involved.

Rachel had been seated at the other table, three feet away from Ian and his crowd but in another reality entirely. She still wore handcuffs and as near as she sat to the tumult, her oblivion to it was as complete as if she were in a different dimension. The jail had finally caught up with her and she sat stone still, disoriented in her panic. She mostly looked down at the few sheets of court papers which all inmates carry around like talismans. They were part of the magic which now controlled her life and she stared at them almost prayerfully. Every now and then she raised her head gingerly, as if her neck hurt or she was facing a painfully bright light, and squinted around at the attendants to this strange liturgy. They had gathered here to work on her, to do things to her. To sacrifice her. The formality of the ritual, though, invested her with a rough importance. The cops, the lawyers, the judge, the reporters, even the spectators, were all here because of her. But, strangely, she had no identity to them, she was just the person (had they left her even that much, really?) upon whom they would practice their professions today. Not the subject of the sacrament but its object. In the midst of public commotion she was solitary. Detached, cut off, magnified. Not a surgical patient, but a dissection specimen. A bug in a bell jar.

At ten o'clock on the nose a wooden door opened behind the judge's bench and a bald head craned out. "Where's the defense attorney? We have to stay on schedule."

"Right here, Judge." Ian and Rachel turned simultaneously at the sound of Evan's voice, but only Ian smiled.

"Well, get down here and sit down. Is everybody ready to proceed? We have to stay on schedule." The efficiency expert assigned to this case was the Honorable Dan Blasko, the district magistrate for northeast Harrisburg. He had held office for just over six years, not long enough to remember Evan's once illustrious career. Like many of his colleagues, Dan's legal education amounted to an eight-week course, taught by cops and assistant district attorneys, which covered the basics of the Pennsylvania Crimes Code, the motor vehicle laws, and the need to always rule in favor of the Commonwealth. He was not a lawyer, but he knew that the slightest evidence would likely satisfy the *prima facie* standard and he knew which table the prosecutor sat at. Those pieces of knowledge were sufficient to his function. He could have run for re-election on the motto "Firm but fast."

Evan walked to the defendant's table and put down his briefcase. Ian's entourage had eight bulging file boxes. Evan had a pad, a copy of the criminal complaint, a few sheets of the discovery materials and two pens, one red and one blue. Rachel was shivering, trembling. Evan looked over at her and patted her hand as the matron unchained her for court. She gave him the kind of mechanical smile with which a terminal patient thanks the doctor for confirming the diagnosis.

"Ready for the Commonwealth, Your Honor," Ian obliged.

"Ready for the defense." Evan followed suit.

"What is your name, sir?" the judge asked. Evan told him.

"Are you an attorney?" he asked condescendingly. A few of the sheriff's deputies snickered. Evan turned to his left and spoke softly to Rachel about the weather and asked her when her birthday was. There was not a chance in the world that Blasko would dismiss the charges against Rachel, so as long as Evan stayed on the safe side of the minimum allowable courtroom decorum he was okay and he wanted everyone to understand that he wasn't there to be made sport of.

"I asked you if you were an attorney." Judge Blasko resented losing a valuable thirty seconds repeating the question.

Evan casually turned away from Rachel. "Me? Oh, my apologies. I assumed you were speaking to Mr. Stonebridge. Yes, I'm an attorney. Ian, you're an attorney too, aren't you?"

Ian didn't answer, but the judge followed up with "Where is your office," clearly ungrateful for Evan's help with the license check.

"Madison Hall at Crawford College."

"What?" He must not have been aware of Evan's return from the grove of academia. Ian waded into the thick of this confrontation in the making.

"Mr. Wonder is one of the most distinguished law professors in all of Harrisburg." He damned Evan with the sort of faint praise usually reserved for the juiciest pork chop in a kosher kitchen. "And he appears on behalf of the defendant."

128

"Well let's get on with the hearing," the judge called a truce. "How does your client plead?" Technically an irrelevant question since guilt or innocence was never the subject of a preliminary hearing but it was never too early for a defendant to deny the case against her. "Not guilty," said Evan to no one's surprise, and they were off. Ian called his first witness: Battalion Chief Mike Morrow, the first firefighter on the scene.

Chapter 13

I n any other profession, where the metaphor wouldn't have seemed so contrived, Mike Morrow would have been called a fireplug of a man. He was short and squat, with the sort of physique usually found on powerlifters and beer kegs. He had bright red hair, closely cropped, and wore the white shirt of his office over a pair of blue twill work pants. His stride to the witness stand showed the easy competence of a man who plied a trade in which there was no margin for error. Firefighters, like submariners, learn to survive in strange and unnatural surroundings by developing zero tolerance for failure. No mistake is innocent to a man who might die for it. In the relatively cool air of the courtroom his smile was ready and sincere, and as he passed the defense table he patted Evan on the shoulder to let him know that someone here remembered the old days. Mike would be a complete non-partisan, until the verdict. If Rachel had set this fire—and Mike would accept the verdict as proof positive one way or the other—he would be in favor of roasting her alive at the next threealarmer. He stuck his chief's cap under the crook of his left elbow as he raised his right hand and stood at attention for the oath. Then he settled himself into the witness chair, looked around and waited. Ian had him give his name and occupation for the record and then directed his attention to the night of the fire. Evan picked up his blue pen.

"Tell us, Chief, what time did you receive the alarm for 9152 North Second Street and what you did as a result of that alarm?"

Mike didn't have or need notes. He could have testified accurately about a fire that was twenty years old. Firemen remember fires. "The alarm came into the station at 10:35 p.m., a fire at 9152 North Second Street. A report of flames sighted. I took the chief's car and arrived first. The engines were right behind me. I arrived at 10:47. I located the closest hydrant and got ready to hook up some lines. The house was already fully involved. Flames were coming out of all windows and the fire had burned a hole up through the roof. The whole inside of the house was filled with flame and smoke. We poured water on the house from outside, but even by the time I got there anyone who was still in that house was not coming out alive. Unfortunately."

"Had anyone come out alive?"

"Mrs. Pope there." He gestured at Rachel. "As soon as I arrived I saw her sitting up on an overhang,

132

kind of a ledge over the front porch. There was a window right behind her that she had escaped through. The first truck was there within less than a minute after I got there, and they had a ladder so we went right up and got her down."

"Tell us what her condition was when you brought her down."

"She was safe and away from the fire." First thing's first for Mike.

"Her physical condition, Chief. How did she appear? What was she wearing, what was her demeanor?"

"Well she looked healthy. Unhurt. No burns. I think she got a little smoke so we had the ambulance take her to the hospital."

"Cross-examine."

Mike had told us what he knew, and Evan knew better than to ask questions that would elicit stories about the heroic firemen. But there was something he needed to know, and with a little luck he could get it out of Mike today. "Did you visit her at the hospital, Chief?"

"Yes. We needed some information from her and the nurses said it was alright to speak to her, so we did."

"And how did she seem to you there?"

"The same. Shaken up, but uninjured."

"Did she understand your questions and answer them?"

"Pretty much, I think the doctor had given her something to quiet her down so we didn't spend much time with her. We just got what we needed and then we left."

"Chief, did the doctor tell you what Mrs. Pope's condition was, whether he had identified any injuries to her?"

Ian was on his feet to make the hearsay objection, but Evan spoke up before he could finish. "Your Honor, hearsay is admissible at these hearings, as Mr. Stonebridge well knows, and the answer to this question will save us all the trouble, not to mention the extra time, of calling the doctor to the stand." That was good enough for Dan.

"That objection is overruled. Chief, you may answer the question."

"We asked the doctor how she was and he told us that aside from her nerves he hadn't found a thing wrong with her."

"Not a single thing?"

"That's right. She was perfectly fine."

"Had they examined her thoroughly?"

"Well, they said they had. Gave her a complete going over. Checked her whole body: her eyes, her nose, her lungs, anything that could have been injured by the fire or the smoke."

"Thank you, Chief. No further questions."

Ian called the fire marshal, Roger Williamson, to explain the fire scene investigation. He took the court through the basics of his inspection of the premises, clearing the floor, photographing the scene, finding the flow patterns, and then got to his findings.

"Your Honor," he needlessly addressed his remarks to Dan. "I found evidence that a large amount of a liquid accelerant had been around the first floor of the home. That accelerant was ignited and it carried the fire throughout the living room, dining room, and hallway areas. The fire then spread to the second floor which was the condition of the house when the firefighters arrived."

"Do you have an opinion, Marshal, as to the manner of origin of this fire?"

"I do."

"Please give us your opinion."

"In my opinion the fire started by the deliberate act of a person who distributed the accelerant, in this case diethyl ether, and then lit it for the purpose of igniting the structure."

"Do you have an opinion as to when the fire started?"

"Yes. Based on the flow patterns which I discovered, a large amount of accelerant was used in this particular fire. Once that accelerant was lit, the fire would have spread very rapidly, and in this type of structure, the fire would have involved the entire home in a very short time. Therefore, I believe that the fire would have started very shortly before the first alarm was called in to the fire department."

"Thank you. Cross-examine."

Evan stood up. "Thank you. Marshal Williamson, can you tell us how much accelerant was used to start this fire?"

"Not exactly, but there was enough. The fire burned very hot and it spread very quickly. Probably a quart or more."

"You found it on the first floor of the house?"

"We did; and the flow patterns we found indicated that it had been spread throughout the hallway at the bottom of the stairs, in the foyer directly inside the front door." Experts were supposed to be non-partisan but Roger was a Commonwealth employee after all and he couldn't resist tossing in a zinger. "Incidentally, that would be precisely where a person who was headed up the stairs to the bedroom which the defendant shared with her husband would accidentally get some of it on her shoes."

Thanks, Roger. "So you believe that my client either spilled some ether on her shoes or she poured it in front of her and then walked through it?"

"That's what the evidence suggests, Counselor." He frowned. "If arsonists didn't make mistakes we'd never catch them."

"Thank you for that criminology lesson, Marshal, but let's get back to this particular case. Did you find any vessels for the ether? Containers, bottles, cans?"

"No. That chemical is often sold in glass bottles. The defendant probably brought the bottles upstairs with her and they were destroyed when the second floor collapsed."

"So you believe that someone spread some quantity of this highly flammable and volatile chemical on the first floor of the Pope house?"

"That's my opinion. The arsonist probably hoped that the fire would be ruled accidental."

"Then what?"

"Then?"

"Yes. What did the arsonist do after walking around the first floor pouring out the ether?"

"Well, then she used a match or some other ignition source to light the fire."

"That's what you think happened? In your expert opinion?"

"Well sure. Someone had to start the fire."

"That's all. Thank you." Evan reached for a pad and made a note about glass bottles.

The rest of the hearing went as Evan expected. Ian called Hank Foster to testify that Rachel was the beneficiary of Ted's life-insurance policy and that she had made a claim for benefits. Once he introduced the lab report proving that Rachel's shoes had tested positive for diethyl ether, Evan didn't have a prayer of getting the charges dismissed. He just shook his head when Blasko asked if the defense had anything to present. The courtroom listened in silence as the judge bound Rachel Pope over for action by the Court of Common Pleas on the charges of arson and first-degree capital murder.

Rachel sat stone straight as Blasko announced his decision. Stonebridge and Foster exchanged smiles of satisfaction, shook hands with perfunctory formality, and walked out of the courtroom to bask in the glory of the press that awaited them.

Rachel had recovered from her shock and now she was angry and belligerent. "You didn't say a fucking word. You didn't even try to talk him out of it. Whose fucking side are you on anyway?"

"You figured me out, Rachel. I've decided to throw the case."

She leaned toward Evan as much as she dared with the warders standing right behind them. "Come on, Evan. I've got to know something. Give me a clue. What's our plan? What do we do next? You've only come to see me one time at the jail, one fucking time, and since then nothing. I don't know what they've got against me. I don't know who their witnesses are. I have to hear the evidence in court for the first time. I've got a right to know these things. I'm getting nothing from you, and then this hearing. You didn't even put up a fight."

Evan let her rant and rave for a couple more minutes and then stood up without a word and walked away. She forgot herself for an instant and started after him, but a deputy sheriff kept her in her chair. "You through with her, Counselor?"

"Yeah, for now."

"Evan!" Rachel called out as he left. The one advantage of having Rachel in jail was that it was easy for him to walk away from her complaints.

Hank and Ian were standing in the parking lot shoulder to shoulder, giving the usual answers to the reporters' usual questions.

"Judge Blasko's ruling today means that Rachel Pope will receive a trial by a jury of her peers which will hear all the evidence and decide her fate." Ian.

"We believe that the evidence of Mrs. Pope's guilt is overwhelming, and we are confident that the jury will convict her." Hank.

"Naturally, we are happy the court ordered this defendant held for trial but not surprised." Ian.

Evan tried to breeze by but the reporters had had enough of the winners and were now ready to hear from the voice of defeat.

"Mr. Wonder. Are you disappointed with the court's decision today?"

"Not really," Evan tossed the answer off as he kept on walking. By now there were reporters all around him and a couple of cameramen backpedaling in front him as he headed for the Cadillac.

"Mr. Stonebridge believes that he has an over-whelming case. Care to comment on that?"

Through the forest of notebooks and micro-phones Evan could see Ian straining to hear his answer so he stopped walking and spoke loud enough for his voice to carry through the parking lot. "Those of us who know Mr. Stonebridge know that he is easily over-whelmed." He waited for the Fourth Estate to catch up and position itself. "Rachel wanted to be done with this flimsy prosecution today, but that hope was unrealistic and I never really expected anything different than what we got. I believe, however, that we have now heard the prosecution's case and I am impressed with the lack of any eyewitnesses, the lack of any direct evidence, and the lack of any concrete proof of my client's guilt. I also want everyone to remember that Rachel has already lost her husband, her home, and the comfortable life which she had been living. Mr. Stonebridge's theory that she traded all that for a prison cell and the speculative chance at a few dollars of life-insurance money would be too ridiculous to be taken seriously if not for the fact that he is now trying to kill her with it. Therefore, even though we have to take it very seriously indeed it is still ridiculous and the prosecution is foolishly barking up the wrong tree."

"How about you, Mr. Wonder? You had resigned from practicing law. Why did you agree to take this case? The D.A. says that your motives are personal."

Evan shook his head and looked straight at Ian. "No more personal than his are. We're both hoping that this case will hide the real truth about ourselves."

Chapter 14

The afternoon was still young when Evan reached his office and since he had neither classes nor office hours scheduled he spent some time with the arson investigation textbooks he had borrowed with interlibrary loan. He had to reacquaint himself with the characteristics of incendiary fires. The fires were fast-burning, hot, and unusually resistant to normal fire-fighting techniques, and the most successful chemical accelerants were flammable, explosive, and volatile. None of this was exactly new information for Evan, he had handled a dozen arson cases before Rachel's, but he had a gnawing sense that something was wrong with the Commonwealth's theory about the Pope fire. He kept reading and re-reading the chapters about accelerants hoping to find out what it was. He was startled when Rose knocked on his door. "Evan, if you don't need me to do anything else today I think I'll go home now." Evan checked his watch and was surprised to see that he had been reading for three hours.

"Go ahead, Rose. I'll see you tomorrow. Office hours from eleven till three."

"Good night."

He pulled closer to his desk and picked up the phone while paging through the faculty directory. It was getting late but he decided to chance a call to the Classics Department.

"This is Dr. Montgomery."

"Professor, this is Evan Wonder from Political Science." Montgomery knew who he was and when he heard his request he was gracious, indeed courtly, in his agreement.

"Well, it's an unusual request, Professor Wonder, but of course I'd love to have you audit as much of the course as you would like."

"Just one lecture, I think, will do it." He found out the time and place of the class's next meeting. Montgomery said he had heard about Evan's "pre-pedagogical distinctions." Then he added, "I'm glad that Dr. Pope's widow has such an excellent champion.

"We'll see you tomorrow, Dr. Wonder. This *is* an intermediate-level course so I hope that you already have some Homer."

"I do, and Professor Montgomery?"

"Yes?"

"Please don't call me Doctor."

Evan locked up the office and started walking home. He passed some students he knew and they exchanged waves and smiles. It was nice to see that not everybody on that campus hated his guts. The Pennsylvania autumn was in the air and the days were getting colder all the time. The sun was setting as he walked home and the sky was streaked with cobalt and scarlet, but Evan wasn't paying much attention to his environment. His mind was filled with firemen's schedules, hot air drafts, chemical bottles, and a thousand other unconnected facts about Christmas Eve. In the middle of every cloud of details there was Rachel, sitting on the roof, shivering in the orange glow from the window and wearing those damn sneakers. Before he was even aware of having left the campus, he was home.

Evan unlocked the oak front door and flicked on the foyer lights. There were still a few logs in the bin next to the fireplace so he stacked them in a crisscross pattern, stuffed newspapers in the middle and struck a long wooden match. The flames drafted up through the spaces between the crossed logs so that the superheated air could reach the chimney. The hot updraft was enough to ignite the wood, and pretty soon the fire was raging. It worked like that every time. Evan loved lighting fires.

After closing the fireplace doors, he went into the kitchen to cook dinner. The kitchen was basically just a big open room. There were no "islands" or "peninsulas" to get in the way. The open space made room for the big table which took up most of the center of the room. A sign above the kitchen door said "Welcome to the Old Country."

Evan put on a cooking apron and got some food out of the refrigerator. Eggplants and sausage. Some tomato sauce. A clove of garlic. He started slicing the eggplants and put the chunks of sausage in a pot of boiling water. He peeled and chopped the garlic and let it simmer in the tomato sauce with some pepper and oregano. The eggplant slices sautéed lightly in a little olive oil while he ground and brewed some Blue Mountain beans. His cell phone rang. It was Deborah.

"Evan. Why are you going to Montgomery's class tomorrow?"

"Well, I hope to learn something. How did you know about it?"

"I *am* a Classics major. Remember? It's a small department and I know everything that goes on around here."

"I remember. I've got some food cooking. Come on over."

"Half an hour." She hung up and Evan laid out the dishes. The living room fire was still burning. By the time Deborah got there dinner was on the table.

Deborah dug right into the sausage and eggplant and the two of them ended up eating the whole pan, sopping up the sauce with thick bread crusts and drinking a bottle of burgundy. They were too stuffed to think about desert so they just piled the dishes in the sink and took two mugs of Blue Mountain into the living room where they both stretched out on the couch in front of the fire and put their feet up on the coffee table.

"Do you mind if we talk about Dr. Pope's case?"

Non-lawyers always named cases after victims instead of defendants. "Not at all."

She took her feet down and sat up in the couch. Still looking ahead at the fire, she asked, "What does Montgomery's class have to do with any of this?"

"Probably nothing. I'm just trying to get a handle on the full cast of characters. Rachel, I know. Stonebridge and Foster, I've known them for a long time. The other Commonwealth witnesses I've either met already or I've read their statements. Ted Pope is the one I know the least about. We met at some faculty functions and I read one of his books. But that's it. I talked to Dr. Jackson about Pope's work with Homer, and he advised me to talk to Montgomery. So I'm auditing Classics 223 tomorrow."

"Well the course is Homer all right; we're just starting *The Iliad*. Tomorrow is Book 1, the plague of Apollo. Have you read *The Iliad*?"

"This may surprise you, Ms. Radcliff, but erudition is not the sole province of the young. My whole life has not been spent in law courts. I've read Book 1 of *The Iliad*, *The Odyssey*, most of Plato, enough Aristotle to get by, Sophocles, Aeschylus, and a little Euripides. In Greek."

"You have?"

"Sure. It's in the blood."

"You're Greek? But I thought, Wonder? Evan? Those are not Greek names, are they?"

"Not necessarily. But when my father came across Ellis Island his real name was 'Aporo' and some immigration officer spoke enough Greek to translate that into "Wonder," and put that name on the immigration papers. That's what we've been ever since. 'Evan' is Greek, just shortened. My full name is 'Evangelos.'"

Deborah thought back to her lexicon. "Angelos is angel, and the 'eu' prefix means 'good' or 'beneficial.' So that makes you, what? The good angel?"

"I give you a C-plus for that translation. 'Angelos' is the word you find in the Bible to refer to the heavenly spirits. But the original meaning is 'messenger,' someone who brought news. A reporter almost. And the 'eu' prefix describes the report not the reporter. The New Testament evangelists weren't 'good angels.' They were the ones who brought the good news of the Gospel. Get it?"

"So. Professor Evan Wonder. Are you here to bring us good news?"

"We'll find out how good it is when Rachel's verdict comes in." They sat silently for a while until the fire burned itself out. When the room got dark, Evan told Deborah that It was time for her to get home and then he went into the kitchen and washed the dishes.

Chapter 15

The classroom was about half filled with upper-classmen by the time Evan arrived, a few minutes before the bell. Professor Montgomery sat at a wooden desk at the front of the classroom, contentedly leaning back in an old hardback chair with a small leather-bound Greek *Iliad* propped open on a bended knee. Evan had brought a new copy of Fitzgerald's translation and after he found a seat he started thumbing through the familiar scenes of long-dead heroes struggling desperately a long way away from home. More students streamed in and sat sideways in their chairs, chatting with friends before class came to order. There was not much overlap between Political Science and Classics and Deborah told him that she planned to skip this class so he didn't expect to be recognized. He was twenty years older than the other students so his presence did raise a few eyebrows, though.

The class bell rang and Dr. Montgomery closed his book gently and stood up. The room was silent with all students now facing straight ahead. Montgomery was wearing a three-piece tweed suit with cuffed pants and a brown and tan striped necktie. A long watch chain passed from one vest pocket through a buttonhole and into the other pocket. He was about six-foot-three with the physique of a faded athlete. He had almost no hair on the top of his head, but a full grey halo around both temples. He wore a large beard, not long exactly but wide and full. Every hair and whisker was meticulously trimmed. He put down the leather-bound Homer and picked up a copy of *The Iliad* in translation, also Fitzgerald's, and started to read aloud from Book One.

His voice was deep and craggy as he walked around the classroom, up one aisle and down the other. He recited as much as read the ancient story, which he knew with the familiarity of having lived with it for fifty years, maybe more. Hector Montgomery could teach first-year Homer in his sleep. In a coma. Evan followed along as he read and found that in some places his recitation differed from the text. Not in substance but in nuance, in tone. Evan realized that while Montgomery was reading from the translation he was thinking in the original Greek and whenever he thought the translator missed the true sense of a passage he just corrected it as he read. He spoke with the easy assurance of the man whose mastery of his subject was complete. The students listened with rapt attention as he circled the room telling them about Achilles and Agamemnon and the squabble that could have destroyed the Greeks. He told them about the plague that Apollo sent down upon the generals who had offended him. Apollo, the sun god whom Homer called "Ekebolos:" the one who sends death from a distance. Montgomery read about half the first book, three hundred lines or so in translation, and then answered a few questions.

Montgomery never called the poet of *The Iliad* "Homer;" that was a term which he applied to his subject matter as a whole. Just as a biologist would say he taught biology, Montgomery said he taught Homer. But when he referred to whoever had written the words he had just read, he called him "the author of Book One" or "the author of these lines." Clint had been right, the Homer question was no idle debate for Montgomery, it was something that he held so close that it had seeped into his speech patterns.

Soon the period was over, and after the students filed out Evan remained in the classroom. Montgomery walked up to his seat and sat down in one right next to it. "Well, Professor Wonder. I hope you didn't find this excursion out of the political science department a complete waste of time."

"Hardly that, Professor. Actually I hope you won't be offended if I tell you that I came here for a bit of research on the Pope case."

"The Pope case indeed. Perhaps it's the ghost of Achilleus whom you suspect of killing Dr. Pope?"

"No. The defense isn't that desperate just yet. Maybe if things get any worse I'll figure out a way to pin the rap on some dead Greek, but I didn't come here today looking for suspects. I was just trying to get a feel for the subject to which Dr. Pope devoted his life. I can't say it will help me win an acquittal, but it's usually a good idea to understand as much as possible about the victim in a murder case."

Montgomery looked amused. "What would you like to understand about Dr. Pope?"

"I'm not quite sure, really. What kind of things did the state police want to know when they came to talk to you?"

"The state police, yes." He looked away as if he was bored with the question. "Police officers seem to feel that their profession carries with it such worldliness that they can pass themselves off as wise." He looked back at Evan confidentially now. He was disgusted. "They know nothing about Homer. They made some puns about baseball while they asked me if I ever disagreed with Pope about anything."

"And you had."

"Yes, of course I had. Our careers took different tracks from a very early stage. You may know that my father was Pollard Montgomery, the most brilliant Homerist of his generation. A colossus. A giant. He saw straight through the one-Homer fad that was running roughshod over scholarship. I was brought up in his house. I breathed his air and I followed in his footsteps.

"Pope was a fine fellow with a keen mind, but he held to another view entirely. So yes, we disagreed. But it was the disagreement of two professional friends who happen to see things differently. By the time I had explained about ten percent of that to those police detectives, they decided that it was too trivial for their consideration. They thanked me and left."

"They don't have too many classes about Homer at the state police academy," said Evan. "Mostly guns and fast cars."

"Yes, well, the two officers who came to my office spent about twenty minutes with me before deciding that I was beneath their interest," he seemed genuinely put off. Then he snapped back to the present moment, smiled at me and said, "At least you had the good manners to sit through an entire class." He stood up and went back to the front of the classroom and picked up his few books off the desk. "Why do you suppose they wanted to talk to me in the first place?"

"They talked to a lot of people, Doctor. They're still talking to people."

"Are they really? Even now that they have Mrs. Pope in jail?"

155

"They want to make their case against her as strong as they can. I expect they will be conducting interviews right up to the trial. They may even come back to see you again."

"I doubt it."

"Yeah, I doubt it too. But you never know."

"From what I understand from the gossip around town, Mrs. Pope seems in rather deep water. I never would have expected it of her, naturally, but you probably know how strange it seemed to all of us when Dr. Pope married her."

"I suppose they loved each other." Evan had suggested the same thing to Clint Jackson.

"Yes," he paused to remember, "perhaps they really did. At first. She was young and lovely and stronger men than Ted Pope have fallen for the superficial charms of beauty. My word, just look at the story of Helen of Troy. If men didn't chase after beautiful women Homer would have had nothing to write about."

"Not in these two poems anyway," said Evan.

"Yes." Evan's response seemed to have taken Montgomery by surprise but he recovered quickly. "Well, in time Ted went back to chasing after Homer. Always looking for an important find. 'Something big,' he always said. And that gave Rachel a lot of time alone," his face

156

darkened, "during which I understand she was tolerably successful at occupying herself."

"So I understand," Evan agreed. "Thank you for your help, Professor, and for letting me sit through your class. It's been a long time since I had any reason to read Homer."

Montgomery walked Evan to the door. As they shook hands Montgomery smiled in mock distress. "But Professor Wonder, simply being alive is sufficient reason for reading Homer. Good-bye."

Chapter 16

Rachel's trial was eventually placed on the court's calendar for the third week of October, ten months after the fire. A week before its starting date, Evan returned to the Dauphin County Courthouse for the pre-trial conference. Pre-trial conferences are not a routine part of Pennsylvania's criminal practice, but any judge can order one in a case which requires some preliminary discussion of ground rules or trial procedure. When Evan got an email from the court administrator announcing that Rachel's pre-trial conference would be in the chambers of courtroom nine, he suppressed a chuckle. Courtroom nine was assigned to Judge Harold "Dirty Harry" Flinchbaugh. Flinchbaugh had been a judge a year or two longer than Evan had been a lawyer so their practices never overlapped. Flinchbaugh was known to have once been a pretty fair trial lawyer who now tended to his courtroom with an advocate's flair. He was active in the conduct of the trial and treated the lawyers like players in a minor league from which he had been called up. Ian's email arrived a few minutes after the one from court administration. He was not happy with the assignment. "When it comes to trying a big case around here," he wrote, "Harry is probably the only guy in Dauphin County who can be a bigger pain in the ass than you."

Ian was already in Judge Flinchbaugh's chambers when Evan arrived. The judge and the prosecutor were sitting at a small conference table chatting conversationally. As soon as they noticed Evan, Ian waved hello without standing up and the judge pointed to an empty chair.

"Evan Wonder." The judge looked at him with a wide and sincere smile. "I can't imagine what this case has to bring you out of retirement. I was just asking Ian that question, but he says you're not talking. What do you say to a little off-the-record disclosure?"

"No mystery, Judge. I wanted to do what I could to help Ian's campaign and I figured that the only chance he had of winning this dogshit case was if it was defended by some over-the-hill, out-of-practice bum like me." He turned to face Ian. "I hope you're grateful, Stonebridge I'm putting off a week of grading term papers for you."

"And don't think for a moment that I don't appreciate it, Professor. It's refreshing to hear for once that you're not doing it because you think your client is innocent."

160

"Innocent? Never. Not guilty? Maybe. But I don't think Judge Flinchbaugh called us here to rub my nose in this foolish decision."

The judge nodded. "I suppose the jury will tell us how foolish a decision it turns out to be, Evan. But you're right; I didn't order this pre-trial conference to gossip. I want to get a feel for this case and to find out if you two anticipate any unusual problems at trial. Ian, suppose I start with you. I know you're asking for the death penalty. Do you really think that's appropriate in this case?"

"Yes I do, Your Honor," he answered to no one's surprise. "This defendant intentionally murdered her husband for a million dollars in life insurance money." At Ian's mention of the amount the judge whistled through his teeth in mock surprise, although that fact was prominent in the court file which he had just finished pouring over. Ian nodded to acknowledge the judicial amazement and continued. "And murder by arson is one of the statutory aggravating circumstances. So yes, we think that this is clearly a capital case."

"What about you, Evan. I guess you disagree with that."

"Not at all, judge." Ian and Flinchbaugh looked at each other with exaggerated wide-eyed surprise. "I understand the Commonwealth's theory and I agree with most of it. If Mrs. Pope set the fire with the specific intent to kill Dr. Pope then it's first-degree murder. If she's convicted of that, then the jury will have already found an aggravating circumstance that warrants the death penalty. Maybe they will also decide that there are mitigating circumstances and she doesn't deserve to die, but Ian is right. If she were guilty, this would be a death penalty case. But she isn't."

"Isn't what?" asked Harry.

"Isn't guilty. That's our defense. She didn't do it."

Ian and Flinchbaugh both paused at such candor from a defense lawyer. "Well okay, Evan. That's simple enough. You say she didn't kill her husband and that's your defense."

"We say she didn't set the fire, that's right."

"But you don't deny that it was arson?"

"Not at all. Everything I've learned about this fire convinces me that it was indeed arson and I'll probably tell the jury that before the trial's over."

"You know, Evan," Ian was speaking now. "If it was arson, and you say your client didn't do it, the jury is probably going to want to know who did. Do you have any answers for them?"

"I have an answer, and it's the same answer that the court is going to give them. It doesn't matter who did it. If it wasn't Rachel then she gets acquitted, and the jury doesn't have to worry about whether the real killer ever sees the inside of a courtroom."

"Don't worry, Evan. I will tell the jury exactly that." Flinchbaugh knew his business. "All the same though, juries like nice neat endings. If they can't finger anyone else for this murder, then that million dollars that Ian was talking about is going to look an awful lot like a motive. Ian, is that the only motive you'll be proving?"

"Not sure yet, Judge. We know that the defendant had been unfaithful, we just don't know if she had any other lovers at the time she killed her husband. The state police are still chasing down leads."

Flinchbaugh shook his head. "I don't have to tell you this, Evan, but all of this can look pretty goddamn bad for your client. Maybe you and Ian should have a heart-to-heart about working this out."

"A plea bargain? No, I never have liked playing for a draw. And anyway, Judge, we all know that there are no perfect cases."

Ian leaned forward just a little. "This one comes pretty close, though. At least as far as I'm concerned."

Evan smiled at him. "I meant perfect from a legal standpoint, Ian. Not a political one."

Once the banter was over, they got down to business. The lawyers agreed that the Commonwealth's case would take three or four days. The judge said he would allow a week for jury selection. Ian handed out a non-binding list of his witnesses. Hank Foster, Mike Morrow, the insurance agent, a doctor who examined Rachel after the fire, Gladys Reynolds, some forensic scientists to talk about the shoes and some other scientific evidence, maybe a few neighbors and some firefighters. That would be about it. At the bottom of the list was a footnote reserving the right to call witnesses about "the defendant's amorous interests," which probably meant Clint Jackson. Evan said if he put on a defense he would need a minimum of three days more. The judge gave both lawyers the judicial equivalent of "go to your corners and come out fighting" and they shook hands all around.

Evan and Ian left the room and went their separate ways without saying goodbye. The next time they saw one another Rachel's life would be on the line.

PART THREE

The Trial

In chess, as it is played by masters,
chance is practically eliminated.

Emanuel Lasker

Chapter 17

J ury selection took five solid days and ended late
on Friday afternoon with the seating of the two
alternates. The alternates would sit through the
trial and be dismissed before deliberations started unless they had to fill in for dying, disqualified or disap-
pearing jurors. Court was adjourned till Monday at 9:00
am, so Evan decided to preside over the Saturday tournaments at the Lasker to clear his head.

The grand prize went to Stella the sixth-grader
who pinned her opponent's bishop to force a checkmate.
It was her first Saturday tournament win and her parents took about a hundred cellphone pictures of Evan
handing her the check. Brenda the psychiatrist was
there too, her first time since the night of Rachel's arrest.
After the awards ceremony she asked Evan if he had time
for a drink. "Sure," he said. He was planning to take the
night off from trial prep anyway.

They drove in separate cars to Stay Tuned,
Evan's favorite bar. The name referred to its motif of

1950s and '60s TV sitcoms. *The Honeymooners, Ernie Bilko, Car 54, Get Smart, Gilligan's Island,* the posters were all over the walls and videos played on a dozen television monitors. Nostalgia aside, the tavern was a beautiful combination of oak paneling and furniture, brass fixtures, leaded mirrors, and oriental pattern carpeting. It had the unpretentious eclecticism of a place that was simply filled with whatever its owner happened to like. In his previous life, Evan had gotten the owner out of a tight spot with the IRS so he was treated like royalty there and his money was no good. He always tipped big though, and in cash. The wait staff didn't owe him any favors.

Evan ordered fish and chips and a bottle of St. Pauli and Brenda got a reuben and a chardonnay. While they waited for the food, they sipped their drinks and watched *The Honeymooners* on one of the TV screens. It was the classic "$99,000 Question" episode where Jackie Gleason as Ralph Kramden tries to beat a game show by identifying the names of popular songs. He prepares by having his best friend Ed Norton, the brilliant Art Carney, play songs for him all day and all night on a rented piano. The gag of the show is that every time Norton begins playing a new song, he warms up with a few bars of "Swanee River" which drives Ralph crazy. Finally, it's show time and Ralph has to start the game by answering the fifty-dollar question: "Who wrote 'Swanee River?'" He gasps, he chokes, he sweats, he pulls at his collar, he's out of time, and finally just at the bell he gasps out his desperate guess: "Ed Norton?" A great moment in American humor.

The food arrived just as the typical 1950s beautiful stage girl is leading Ralph off stage. Evan ordered another round of drinks. Brenda leaned forward in her chair. "You know, Evan, ever since those two state troopers walked into the chess club the members have been even more curious about you than before. Not everyone knew that you were a lawyer, or are a lawyer, or whatever. Now the news is full of reports about your defense of Rachel Pope and people are trying to guess why the once-great Evan Wonder has returned from oblivion."

Evan smiled. "What do you think?"

"I'm more interested in human nature than I am in mysteries. I'm curious about why you decided to give up your practice in the first place. I've heard that you were the best lawyer around."

"Have you ever heard of the Ronnie Porter case?" Brenda shook her head.

Evan put his fork down and took sip of beer. "The Porter case is why I'm now a college professor. In a way, I guess the Porter case is why I'm representing Rachel Pope." Brenda nodded her head slightly, therapeutically, and waited for Evan to continue.

"Ronnie Porter was seventeen years old when he was arrested for murder. A clerk was shot to death during a convenience store robbery in Ronnie's neighborhood and two customers identified Ronnie as the shooter. It was a death penalty case just like Rachel's, first-degree murder during the commission of a felony. Hank Foster had been transferred to criminal investigations from patrol and it was his first big case. Ian Stonebridge was an assistant D.A. then and he got assigned the case. Ronnie's family hired me to defend him.

"Ronnie swore up and down that he didn't do it, and he had a defense. Alibi. He was home with a bunch of family members the night of the killing, and although family alibis aren't the greatest, these were all decent, solid, hardworking citizens, and they were certain of the date and the time and Ronnie's presence. The family had all gotten together to watch a football game. Steelers against the Ravens. Like most football fans around here, Ronnie's family was rooting for the Steelers and they all remembered that Ronnie was there, in the living room with his brothers and parents and a couple of cousins when the Steelers' kicker scored the go-ahead field goal. I got the game tapes and that kick went off at exactly 7:12 p.m. All of the witnesses to the shooting remembered that *60 Minutes* had just started on the store television. That meant that I had Ronnie accounted for within twelve minutes after the crime. Alibis don't get much better than that.

"The trial went great for the defense. The eyewitnesses wavered, no one new claimed to be able to identify the shooter, Ronnie was primed to testify and I had a room full of alibi witnesses ready to go. When Ian wrapped up with the last eyewitness, everybody expected me to pull off another miracle."

Evan looked down at his hands. "Until."

Brenda stayed quiet. Years of listening to the misery of her patients had taught her how to let the silence work for her. Eventually Evan started talking again.

"So the eyewitnesses are on and off the stand and the judge asks Ian if he has anything else. Everyone waited for him to say 'No, Your Honor,' so I could start my case. But he didn't say 'No, Your Honor.' he said he wanted to recall Hank for additional testimony. Foster steps up. He had already testified about the crime scene, the recovery of the bullets, Ronnie's arrest. I didn't think he had anything more to say.

"But then Ian asks him how many times he's been to Ronnie's house, the house he shared with his family. The house where he was alibied for the shooting.

"'I've been there twice,' he answered calmly. 'The first time was the day I arrested him.' He struggled not to smirk at me. 'The second time was yesterday.' Ian had a roadmap on the video monitors and Hank had a stopwatch in his hand, and I got sick all of a sudden.

"Foster turns to face the jury and tells them that yesterday at 7:00 p.m. he had driven the distance between the crime scene and Ronnie's house. I could mouth the next question along with the D.A. 'How long did it take you to get from the scene of the crime to the defendant's home where he admits he was on the night in question at 7:12 p.m.?'

"'Four minutes,' says Foster. He traces the route on the video map and explains that he used a calibrated stopwatch to time the trip. Then the Commonwealth rested.

"I stand up to call my first alibi witness and the D.A. asks for a recess to discuss an important evidentiary matter with the court in private. So we all go into the judge's chambers and the D.A. tells the judge that my alibi isn't an alibi at all. The crime is at 7:00, the defendant is unaccounted for until 7:12, and it only takes four minutes to get home. There is still enough time, 'plenty of time' Ian says to the judge, for the defendant to commit the crime, get home, and watch the game. The fact that he was home at 7:12 is not an alibi at all, says Ian, in fact it's irrelevant and none of my witnesses should be allowed to testify.

"I pour my heart out arguing against that objection. 'Twelve minus four leaves eight minutes,' I argue. 'What kind of person could murder an innocent man, drive home, and sit to watch a football game like nothing happened?'

"But before I can get another word out, the judge says, 'Maybe the same kind of person who would shoot down an innocent man in cold blood in the first place.' And he tells me to send my witnesses home, the Commonwealth's objection is sustained.

"I don't remember the walk back into the courtroom but I do remember Ronnie's face when he asked me if everything was alright. I told him what the judge had just done and I told him that it was devastating to our case. Ronnie could still testify and I didn't think that the judge's ruling would stand up on appeal; so, thinking like a lawyer, I figured that even if the worst happened, we'd get a new trial and I'd win that one.

"Ronnie testified and did a great job on direct. On cross he got eaten alive.

"'How can two eyewitnesses be mistaken?'

"'I don't know, sir.'

"'You admit that you live only four minutes from the scene of the murder?'

"'I suppose so, sir.'

"And it got worse with every question. Here was Ronnie, seventeen years old and all alone in a strange place, being perfectly polite to the man who was using all of his professional skill and power to kill him. 'Yes, sir.' 'No, sir.' A perfect gentleman. Just like I told him.

"Well, the cross went on for an hour or so and Ronnie left the witness stand shaking like a leaf and looking, even I had to admit it, like he was guilty.

"We went right into closings and I uncorked a beauty. I spoke for ninety minutes and tore the prosecution apart. How can anyone believe the eyewitnesses? How come the police never found a gun when they searched Ronnie's house? How come they didn't find Ronnie's fingerprints at the store? How come, how come, how come. When I sat down, I thought we still had a chance.

"Then the prosecutor stood up and ignored all of my 'how comes,' reminded the jury that he had two eyewitnesses who saw Ronnie do it, and all I had was a pile of questions that really didn't need to be answered in order to convict. And then he talked about Ronnie on the stand. "'Ladies and gentlemen, you all saw the defendant testify. He was nervous and scared and evasive. Those are signs of guilt and if you disbelieve his claims of innocence, that disbelief is enough all by itself to convict him.'"

Evan shook his head at the memory. "The jury was out for two hours and then brought back the first-degree murder conviction. The judge asks me if I'm ready for the penalty phase and reminds the jury that they must set the penalty at life or death. Now I can put on the family members but they can't talk about the alibi. All they can say is that Ronnie is a good kid, never in trouble, loves his family, they love him. Please don't kill our son, our brother, our friend.

"You have to close again after the penalty phase, and I stood up with a big lump in my throat and a mouth full of cotton. But I spoke. About life and youth. I lied about the faith that I had in the jury to do the right thing. And I talked about redemption and the terrible tragedy that it would be to throw this kid away at seventeen, even though they had already decided that he had made one horrible mistake. I don't remember what else I said, but it must have been enough because after the longest ten hours of my life the jury came back with a life sentence."

Brenda was neither smiling nor frowning. "That doesn't explain why you're a college professor now, Evan." She waited again.

"It gets worse. I started working on the appeal and studied the law on alibi defenses. I was convinced that I could get Ronnie a new trial. When I told him that, he just nodded and said that he appreciated everything I had done.

"After four months, in a decision that even sur-prised me, the trial judge reversed himself on post-trial motions and ordered a new trial. I ran back to the office to call Ronnie's family with the great news. I did it, I would tell them. Next time will be different, I would tell them. But before I could say any of that, Ronnie's mother had some news for me. Ronnie had gotten tired of waiting, tired of thinking that he was going to live out his life in that stone cage." Evan drained his beer glass. "The night before he had ripped up some bedsheets, made a rope and hung himself from the top bunk in his cell. He was dead. 'We don't blame you, Mr. Wonder. We know you did everything you could.' And that was it. The judge was sorry, though not remorseful. Ian and Hank told the reporters that Ronnie had acted out of guilt.

"That was the Porter case. After I hung up on Ronnie's mother, I spent the afternoon and most of the night right here getting drunk. I slept out in the parking lot in the Cadillac. The next morning I sat in my office for a while, and then called my staff into the law library and told them to wrap things up. Sell the furniture, refer out all the cases, and cancel the lease.

"That was the Porter case."

Brenda's eyes had never left Evan. "That's a sad story, Evan. Suicide is always tragic. But let's talk about you. Why do you think that story explains why you're a college professor now?"

"Oh come on, Brenda. No psychiatry bullshit now please. Ronnie was my client. I was responsible for him. He trusted me with his life and now he's dead."

176

"And you blame yourself?"

"Damn right I blame myself." Evan had raised his voice and had to remind himself that they were in a crowed public place. "Who should I blame? Ronnie?"

"No, not Ronnie." Brenda was in her element now. "Suicidal people leave behind a big hole and the survivors are always hurt and often angry. But the dead rarely deserve that anger. Suicide is an act of desperation and hopelessness. Almost never an aggressive act."

"Right. Hopelessness. And why was he hopeless? Because I fucked up. I lost that case because I got cocky. I never drove from the store to the house. I had my lawyer tricks and my lawyer act and my lawyer attitude and I thought I could make everything better. Big fucking mistake."

"Maybe he was hopeless for another reason." Brenda gave him her therapist gaze.

"Another reason? Besides spending his life in prison?"

"Yes."

Evan didn't get it. "What could have been worse than that?"

"Well, Evan. You have described a close-knit family unit. Gathering to watch football games. Rooting for the same team. Supporting a family member when he gets in trouble. Willing to come to court and testify. I assume they collected the money for your fee?"

"Yeah, they called on everyone they knew. They had a bake sale. A dance at the community center. They passed the hat in church."

"Don't you see that Ronnie must have felt terrible about bringing such heartache to his family? People in that situation often fear that their loved ones will never recover from the pain they have caused. It can make a person hopeless."

"But Ronnie didn't cause anything. It was me. And Ian. And Hank and the judge. It was all of us."

"Unless."

"Unless?"

"Evan, maybe he really was guilty."

Evan stood up so violently that his chair crashed over backward. "Guilty? Don't give me that shit. What do you know about any of this? Have you ever even been in a courtroom?"

"Pick up your chair and sit down, Evan." He did as she asked. "You always criticize your chess opponents for not watching the whole board. What have you been doing? You turned your whole life upside down because

178

of a fact that you have assumed was true. That Ronnie was innocent."

"Of course he was innocent."

"Evan, you were a faithful guardian and you believed he was innocent because he told you so. But he told the same thing to other people too. Twelve jurors for example. And they believed something different. Are you sure they were all wrong?"

"Yes."

"Because you have some special insight into the secrets of the past? Divine omniscience maybe?"

"Brenda, I asked you to stop with the psycho ..."

"Don't you see, Evan? You have spent these past years convincing yourself that you, Evan Wonder, chess master, courtroom mastermind, Prince of Darkness and all-around perfect genius, can pierce every illusion to see what is true and what is false. You have transformed the inexplicable tragedy of Ronnie's suicide into a condemnation of yourself because it was easier to think of yourself as a failure than to believe something even worse. That you are just human, and that being human you are fallible.

"You say that you were too cocky to measure the drive time from the house to the store. What if you had done that and known all along that it was only four minutes? What could you have done differently? Maybe the judge did make a legal error by not letting you present the alibi evidence, but what if you had done everything you have blamed yourself for not doing? Would that have moved the store farther way from Ronnie's house? Would it have made the drive longer, or the timetable less incriminating? Wasn't Ian right that Ronnie did have time to kill the clerk? And, be honest Evan, isn't that question more important than the one about whether Evan Wonder can work miracles?"

"Not to me."

"No, not to you. Two honest witnesses identified your client as having committed a terrible crime at a place where he may very well have been. And you have been beating yourself up because you weren't God Almighty, able to transform the simple reality that actually existed into the one that you liked better.

"I have to go, Evan. But please consider this: if you're planning to redeem yourself by transforming Rachel Pope's guilt into innocence, you may be headed for another terrible crash."

"She is innocent," he said.

"You don't know that."

"I'm one hundred percent sure," he said.

"Why do I believe that you once said the same thing about Ronnie Porter?"

They sat in silence for a while. Neither one of them had finished their food. "I have a patient coming in early tomorrow morning. She's in crisis so I agreed to meet her on Sunday." Brenda stood up and placed her hand on Evan's shoulder. "Will we see you when the trial's over?"

He nodded and watched her as she turned and walked out the door.

Chapter 18

On Monday morning, Courtroom One filled up with an atmosphere of crisp formality. At 9:00 a.m. sharp, Harry Flinchbaugh stepped through the door that connected the judge's bench to his private chambers and the bailiff faced a packed gallery with the expectant solemnity of a ring announcer. He loudly declared it to be time and place set for the trial in the case of the *Commonwealth of Pennsylvania vs. Rachel Pope*, Number 2918 on the Criminal Docket. Whosoever drew near and gave their attendance would, he promised, be heard. God would save the Commonwealth and this Honorable Court and the battle was joined. The judge sat down and nodded toward the prosecution table. "Are you ready to open, Mr. Stonebridge?" Ian thanked him, said that he was indeed ready, and stood up.

Ian's opening statement was direct and matter-of-fact. Everyone in the courtroom knew what his case was all about and his opening move was as predictable as pawn to queen four. Psychologists, salesmen, and prosecutors know that a person's tendency to believe an unproven something—*This car is the best, You look great in that coat, The defendant is guilty*—increases dramatically with repetition. So he used his time to good advantage and told the jury over and over again that she did it, and then he told them how she did it, followed by why she did it. He never raised his voice or looked at the defendant. He said a few nice things about Evan, whom he always called "Professor" to remind the jury that he was just some egghead whom they could safely ignore. He finished by telling the jury that although the burden of judgment was an awesome one, they could take comfort in knowing that this was a straightforward case and reaching the right verdict would not be a great chore. Then he sat down, cast a friendly smile at the defense table and it was Evan's turn.

The judge was thumbing the pages of a loose-leaf binder and casually looked up at Evan. "Do you wish to proceed now with your opening statement, Mr. Wonder, or will you reserve it until the conclusion of the Commonwealth's case." Evan stood up, a legal pad dangling from his left hand and he picked up a pencil to carry around in his right. "We will open now, Your Honor." He looked all around him, three hundred and sixty degrees, took in every face in his line of sight. He had not felt this electric thrill for many years and now for the first time he realized how much he had missed it. The buzz in his inner ear, the surge of excitement, the physical

184

awareness that the courtroom now belonged to him. He could be brilliant or he could be awful, but for as long as he stayed on his feet he was the trial. He was the point at which a thousand years of Anglo-American legal history intersected with the life of Rachel Pope. No one knew what his case would entail. No one knew what he would say. Every face was curious. Evan took a couple of steps towards the jury box, put down his pad on the corner of the clerk's rail, tapped his pencil twice against thin air, and he began his defense.

"Ladies and gentlemen of the jury. Mr. Stonebridge tells his story with such confidence and style that I am sure some of you are wondering what we all are doing here. Dr. Pope is dead, Rachel started the fire, she killed him, which makes her guilty. It's that simple. Well, if it really were that simple, the prosecutor would be right and you and I could all go home and the sheriffs here could just take Rachel Pope off to death row to wait for that last short walk to the table where an executioner waits to pour deadly poison into her veins. It would serve her right, too. But it isn't that simple, and the fact that we are all here with the judge proves it, proves that there are difficult tasks ahead of us and serious questions to answer. The answers to those questions don't come from here"—Evan put his right hand open-palmed on his chest—"or from here"—he walked to the prosecution table and pointed his finger about two inches from Ian's head—"or even from there"—he waved his outstretched right arm toward the judge. "No. The answers come only from you. We have entrusted this decision to the twelve people in our community who are the best suited for that job. We called you all to the courthouse away from your families, your jobs, your day-to-day lives. We spent day after day talking to you, but most of all listening to you. We told other folks, all good and decent people in their own ways, that they just were not good enough. They just weren't what we were looking for." He stepped up and stood two paces in front of the center of the jury box rail. "They just weren't what we were looking for. You are.

"There are some places in the world, I'm sure we've all heard about them, where a person gets arrested and automatically he's guilty and he's sentenced and punished and they haul him away. In places like that they let the police decide if citizens are guilty or not." He winked openly at Hank Foster. "That's not the way we do things in America though, is it Hank? Some places they let prosecutors condemn people to death on their own say-so. Not here. In America, we don't leave critical issues of guilt and innocence to the government to decide for us. To tell us what's right and what's wrong. We would never let twelve policemen or twelve lawyers or even twelve judges take your place in the jury box. We would not, ladies and gentlemen, allow the Supreme Court of the United States to hear the evidence in this case and render a verdict." Things were quiet in the courtroom now. Evan was getting away with a lot of drama and Ian didn't like it. The jurors were attentively basking in the glory Evan was heaping on them and starting to forget how pissed off they had been when the judge said the trial might last five days. "No. The ones we trust to do what's right, the only ones we trust to do what's right, are you twelve. Some of you may have known one another before this week began or you may all be complete strangers to one another, but today you twelve were brought together perhaps for the only time in all of your lives, assembled here by some universal fate and by the spirit of almighty justice for one purpose and one purpose only—to hear the evidence in this case, to make sense out of the horrible tragedy that took the life of Professor Theodore Pope, and then to announce to this court and to the world that Rachel Pope," Evan was behind her chair now with his hands resting lightly on her shoulders "is not guilty.

"Not guilty?" He walked up to the jury box rail. He still hadn't looked at the legal pad and the longer he was on his feet the surer he was that he wouldn't need to. He put his hands on the jury rail and spoke softly, confidentially to the jurors. "Not guilty? Who am I kidding? After all the evidence Mr. Stonebridge just laid out for us, all that testimony, doesn't that prove she's guilty? Doesn't that count for something? Well, don't ask me, ask the judge. He will tell you that nothing any prosecutor says anytime during a criminal trial is worth a hill of beans as far as evidence is concerned. It is not evidence at all, it is not testimony, it is not proof, and it doesn't count at all. The only evidence in this case or any other case in any American courtroom comes from the mouths and hearts of sworn witnesses. And even then, that evidence is worth no more than you decide. You may find that all the witnesses put together don't prove a thing. The law doesn't require that you believe a word you hear from the witness stand. But, and this is important, even if you believe everything you hear, even if you swallow it all hook, line and sinker, the law doesn't tell you what to do with it. You can decide that all the prosecution evidence does nothing more than raise a lot of questions, nothing more than make you real suspicious, that maybe, just maybe Rachel Pope really did do it.

"Well, then where are you; the judge will tell you about that, too. Let's say you are sure in your heart" I pointed to Rachel and snarled "that she probably did it, not only that, you are convinced that more likely than not she did everything the prosecution says about her. Well then, your verdict is easy, isn't it? A snap? Sure, your decision is as easy as Mr. Stonebridge suggested. A piece of cake. Not guilty." Evan spun around at the jury with a face full of mock confusion. "Not guilty? If she probably did it? And you know it? Yes, ladies and gentlemen, not guilty. The prosecutor didn't mention this of course but in America we don't convict people and send them to their death based on probabilities, nor on possibilities, or likelihoods. We don't play the averages with human lives. We demand proof, compelling, overwhelming proof that establishes guilt beyond all reasonable doubt. And if we don't get it, if the prosecutor can't serve it up to us so that no reasonable doubt remains, you are commanded by the law, bound by your oath, and required by every rule of common decency to find this defendant, any defendant, not guilty.

"That is not just your right, it is your duty, and it is the glory of American justice." A little thick, perhaps, a couple of the jurors were squirming, getting impatient, ready to get started with the trial and solve some crimes. But most of them were paying attention and Evan hoped that they might be seeing their role in a little different light than a few minutes ago. He would finish soon, but not yet. "What about the police? They have spent a lot of time, probably a lot of money too, investigating this case and they arrested her. Surely, we have to give that some weight. No we don't. We can't even let that thought enter our minds, and you can't even mention it to one another when you go into the jury room. Otherwise you would be standing the Constitution on its ear. We never assume that a person may be guilty just because someone arrested her. We don't have a presumption of guilt in this country. We have a presumption of innocence.

"And why is that? Because the police are crooked? Because prosecutors only care about headlines and convictions? Not necessarily. But there are cases, and this is one of them, where the people who should be responsible for making wise prosecutorial decisions and the ones who are supposed to take care before charging decent citizens with awful crimes, simply mess up. They jump to conclusions, they don't pay attention to details, and they overlook simple things. And they come up with a case that cannot stand up to the light of day. The kind of sloppy and reckless thinking that makes sense in the dim light of police stations at night often winds up looking just plain silly in the bright glow of common sense which illuminates our courts of justice.

"Well, that leaves one question and I'm sure this question will weigh heavily on your minds throughout this trial and even long after it is over. Who did kill Dr. Pope? If Rachel didn't do it, then who? Isn't that what we're here to find out? Isn't that what we have to know? Well, sure we would like to know. Sure we're all curious, but that is not why we're here. The sad fact of the matter is that the tragic mystery of Professor Pope's death will not be solved in this courtroom. We have not been called here to search for clues or to solve the mystery or to decide if there is more or less evidence against Rachel Pope than there is against anyone else. The truth about this crime lies outside the doors to our courtroom. The search for perfect answers, for final justice, must be left to another day and a higher authority.

"The authority which has brought us here, together, requires of us only that we keep our minds open, and that we remember that Rachel Pope's innocence of these crimes is presumed by law to be a true fact. If we do those things, then we have been faithful to our consciences and to justice.

"Thank you."

Evan walked slowly back to his chair and glanced at the wall clock. He had spoken for about fifteen minutes without saying a word about the defense. But it had been pretty good. Ian hadn't looked up yet from the pad on which he had been doodling. The advocate's practiced pose of casual disinterest. Hank, whose pride of authorship in this prosecution was more personal, was looking at one of the investigative reports with renewed interest. Looking to his friendly facts for some reassurance that the certainty of conviction had not just now become tentative.

When Evan sat down, Rachel looked at him uncertainly. Was it good? Did it help? Will we win now? Her hunger for results made her a bad critic. She naturally didn't care about style, methods, strategy, or even greatness, except as guarantors of success. She took a deep breath, smoothed some silky black hairs off her forehead, and said, "I guess this is where they start trying to kill me."

"I guess."

"Call your first witness, Mr. Stonebridge." The judge's order kept Evan from having to say more.

"Your Honor, the Commonwealth calls Mark Cornwall."

Chapter 19

Mark Cornwall was the life-insurance agent who sold the Popes their policies. It was an unusual way for the prosecution to begin and Evan thought it was unusually risky. Prosecutors typically like to set the crime scene before the jury with the first witness and that practice has a few obvious advantages. First, it puts the jury in chronological parity with the police investigators and can engender a psychological connection. The jury enters the case at the same moment as the police, with the commission of the crime or its discovery. After letting the jury reenact the case's beginning, the prosecutor can follow those witnesses with the investigators who recount the early search for clues. Then would come the witnesses who had the clues: eyewitnesses, scientists, persons to whom confessions were made. Thus, the prosecution roughly recreates the life of the investigation. Successfully told, such a story grasps the jury's attention and commits them to active listening throughout the more mundane testimony to follow. And finally, as Professor Pope himself would have appreciated, beginning with the crime scene inevitably made the narrative start *in media res,* in the middle of things, borrowing the dramatic device that poets and dramatists had been using successfully for over three thousand years. Ever since Homer.

But as Mr. Cornwall took the stand Evan appreciated Ian's strategy. During jury selection and the Commonwealth opening, the jury had already heard plenty about the fire and Professor Pope's grizzly demise. If Ian started off with evidence of blazing death the desired effect on the jurors would be blunted by recent familiarity. Furthermore, it would take three or four witnesses before the physical story of the fire pointed any fingers at Rachel. Starting with the insurance man put Rachel in the case immediately by establishing her powerful motive. With this nailed down, Rachel would be the jury's prime suspect when they later heard from the fire witnesses. Ian's approach was unorthodox but inspired. By the time the jury again heard about the gruesome murder they would be ready to be shocked all over again, and with the motive established the crime would seem all the more dastardly and cold-blooded. And the assessment of guilt would fall to Rachel as inevitably and naturally as the sunset.

Ian clipped off his questions like a meat slicer, letting each answer fall in place. "State your full name and give us your business address, please."

"My name is Mark Cornwall and I have an office at 260 Woodlawn Avenue in Harrisburg."

"What is your profession, Mr. Cornwall?"

"I'm a general agent for the Dauphin County Life Insurance and General Indemnity Company."

"Do you, as part of that business sell life insurance to customers directly, by yourself I mean?"

"Yes."

"And in the course of that business have you had occasion to meet the Defendant Rachel Pope?"

"Yes. I first met Mrs. Pope September of last year, September 12 it was, when she and her husband came to my office to ask about our various life insurance products."

"Please tell the jury about your dealings with Mrs. Pope and Professor Pope."

"Well, when they visited my office they were interested in life insurance policies for each of them. They didn't know too much about the different products, the different types of life insurance, so I tried to educate them a little. I got some information which I needed from them and I ran off a few plans which they could take home with them. We agreed that they would review what I had given them, discuss their needs with one another, and call back for an appointment. I told them I would be glad to come to their home with the applications if that would be more convenient for them."

"Did they call you back?"

"Yes, Mrs. Pope called me the very next day. She told me to stop by that evening with applications for two whole life policies, one on each spouse, and each for a $500,000.00 death benefit."

"Did you do that?"

"Yes."

"Were the policies written and fully in force at the time of Dr. Pope's death?"

"Yes. Mrs. Pope made a claim for the death benefits but that—."

Evan stood halfway up. "Objection."

"Sustained."

There was no point in letting the insurance man add his voice to the chorus of guilt by telling the jury that his company refused to pay off on a murder. Ian didn't miss a beat.

"Mr. Cornwall, is it true then that as of December 24 of last year Rachel Pope stood to benefit from her husband's death to the tune of half a million dollars?"

196

"Well, actually more than that. The policies had a double indemnity clause for accidental death."

"Such as a death in a house fire?"

"Well, yes. Any accident or violent death."

"One final question, Mr. Cornwall. During your dealings with the Popes, did they appear to be equally interested in this life insurance purchase?"

Evan knew that the question was, technically objectionable as stated because it asked for an inadmissible conclusion. But if he objected, the jury would think he was trying to hide the answer and Ian would then be able to introduce the information by any number of proper questions. Evan sat tight and Cornwall answered without hesitation. He knew this question was coming and he had his answer ready.

"No. No they weren't. Mrs. Pope seemed to be extremely anxious to get this coverage written. Extremely anxious. The professor didn't seem to care one way or the other. I got the impression that he was doing it to make his wife happy."

Ian smiled over at Evan. "You may cross-examine."

The direct examination had been short, focused, and deadly. The last answer not only put the whole impetus for getting the policies squarely on Rachel but also made poor old Ted seem like a cooperative and attentive husband. Juries always wanted to avenge a likable corpse.

"Mr. Cornwall, you said you explained the different sort of life insurance products, isn't that right?"

"Yes, that's right."

"By that I assume you mean that there are different kinds of policies available: term insurance, whole life, universal life, maybe even more than that. Is that right?"

"Yes. The life-insurance industry is always developing new kinds of life-insurance plans, some contain an investment component, some help the policyholder with financial planning, some have automatic savings features, some have tax-deferral advantages as well."

Evan cut off the sales pitch. "Yes, I see. Well, Mr. Cornwall, these policies which have investment components, what are they called?"

"Most of them are either whole-life or universal-life policies. Those kinds are what we call permanent policies because the premium never changes, the policy can be paid off after a period of years and then it provides permanent coverage at no cost to the policyholder. They have many advantages."

198

"Part of the money the customer pays for them goes into an investment plan?"

"Yes. That's how the policy accumulates cash value. After a few years the policyholder can borrow against it, reinvest the value accumulation as premium, or add the cash value to the death benefit."

"So with this policy the customer is buying more than a simple death benefit. Right? These whole-life and universal-life policies are mainly for people who want more than just a payoff at death, isn't that so?"

Ian was sitting back in his chair as bored with this insurance lesson as everyone else in the courtroom except for Evan and Cornwall. The last question got Hank's attention and he buzzed a few whispered words which launched Ian to his feet with an objection.

"Excuse me, Your Honor. Professor Wonder, I'm sure the study of life insurance is a fascinating subject but as the court knows this is a courtroom and not a classroom. The only reason life insurance is relevant to this trial is that it provides this defendant," he pointed a fist with a forefinger extended at Rachel as she sat still as a statue, "with a motive to kill her husband."

"Your Honor, I am cross-examining this witness and I intend to show that this particular kind of life-insurance policy was inconsistent, I repeat inconsistent, with an intent to kill. If I am also going to have to cross-examine Mr. Stonebridge, then let's swear him in so that he will have an incentive to tell the truth."

Rachel stiffened. Evan never looked at Ian. He didn't take my eyes off the judge. "And as for this not being a classroom, let me remind the prosecution that our sole legitimate purpose here is to obtain knowledge, knowledge concerning the truth of this case. And if the prosecution objects to ..."

"That's enough, Mr. Wonder. The Commonwealth's objection is overruled. We do, of course, seek knowledge here but not in a vacuum and not for its own sake. Our search is guided by the rules of evidence and both counsel are also bound by the requirements of courtroom decorum. The former requires that you be relevant, the latter that you be civil. It falls to me to enforce both of those sets of rules. Am I making myself clear to you, Mr. Wonder?"

"As a bell, Your Honor."

"Mr. Stonebridge?"

"Yes, sir."

"Good. Class is dismissed." The judge's smile and a few chuckles from the jury were as welcome as music to Evan's ears. Humor in a criminal trial always favors the defense. Fun is inconsistent with the nearness of evil and levity displaces the atmosphere of guilt. He turned to the jury with a big smile to make sure they knew that he also appreciated the joke. Then back to the witness.

"So then, Mr. Cornwall, whole life, universal life, these policies really are a kind of investment program, aren't they? I mean in addition to actual life insurance?"

"Yes, that's right. That's their main advantage."

Evan was still on his feet from arguing Ian's objection and he took a couple of steps away from the defense table to set up the emphasis for the next questions. He folded his arms. "That kind of insurance policy is attractive to people who are planning for the future, right?"

The witness looked over to Ian for guidance but Evan stepped in between the witness stand and the prosecution table to cut off his line of vision. He was an honest man and a conscientious witness, but as often happens he had started to get emotionally invested in the cause of the side that called him. Evan moved in. "Well, aren't they, Mr. Cornwall? That's how you market them, that's how you present them, that's what they are designed for. Isn't it?"

"Well, yes. I suppose you're right."

Evan stepped lightly towards his chair and raised his voice by about fifty percent. "Of course I am. That's how you presented these policies to Dr. and Mrs. Pope, isn't it?"

"I think so." Then, "Yes." Then, "Yes. I'm sure it was."

"There are other kinds of policies, simple term insurance, that would provide a higher death benefit for the same premium payment if a person was not interested in planning for the long term. Right?"

"Yes."

"And because you are a careful man and an ethical life insurance agent, you explained all of this to the Popes?"

"Certainly."

"And they picked the universal-life policy?"

"Yes, that's right."

"The one that means they were planning a long-term investment program?"

"Objection." Ian made this one quick and without a speech.

"Sustained." Of course. This guy couldn't know what was on their minds. But the jury now knew what was on Evan's.

"And of course, as you have told us already, Mrs. Pope was calling the shots when it came to picking the kind of policy, wasn't she? She decided on universal life, she picked out this policy which only made sense for the long term, didn't she?"

Silence.

"Come on, Mr. Cornwall, if she was interested in the biggest possible death payoff because she was planning for her husband to soon become dead, she could have loaded up on term insurance for the same premium. Couldn't she?"

"That's right."

"But she didn't do that, huh?"

"No. She didn't."

"She didn't do that at all?"

"No." Evan sat down and scribbled a few notes. One more point needed to be made. "Mr. Cornwall, as part of the application process did you find out the ages of Dr. Pope and Mrs. Pope?"

"Yes. Mrs. Pope is 36 years old and Dr. Pope was 66 years old when he died."

"And did you find out who was the breadwinner in this family?"

"Yes. Dr. Pope was. Mrs. Pope had no separate income."

"Mr. Cornwall, how long have you been in the life insurance business?"

Back on familiar ground his face relaxed and his answer came easily. "Twenty-two years."

"And you have sold hundreds, maybe thousands of policies to husbands and wives."

"Thousands, I'm sure."

"When you have a wife who has no income, no career, who is married to a man who is her sole support, and who is many years older than she is, it's not unusual for such a woman to be interested in obtaining for herself some protection on her husband. Is it?"

"No. Not at all."

"That's the way Mrs. Pope acted during her dealings with you, isn't it?"

"I guess that's a fair characterization of it."

"Nothing unusual about it at all, was there?"

There was a moment of hesitation so Evan asked another question before Cornwall could say something Evan would not want to hear. "There was nothing, absolutely nothing about this transaction which aroused even the slightest suspicion in your mind, was there?"

Evan stared directly at the witness. It was a cold stare. "Mr. Cornwall, if you had even the slightest reason to believe that this insurance policy was going to become a motive for murder you would never have let yourself be party to it, would you?"

His expression was dull and passive. He would have to become a defense witness now or else he would have to admit to selling Ted Pope's life short for a middling commission. At that moment, all Mr. Cornwall wanted was to get the hell out of that courtroom and the surest shortcut to the exit door was the answer that Evan wanted to hear. Quick and easy. Neat and tidy. And he knew it.

"Absolutely not. This was strictly a run-of-the-mill transaction. As far as I was concerned there was nothing wrong with it, nothing suspicious. Nothing at all."

"No further questions. Thank you, Your Honor." A polite nod to the judge. Cornwall came down off the witness stand, briskly walked down the aisle to the courtroom door and left. Not a word to anyone, not even a glance. The judge looked up at the courtroom clock and announced that it was time for the luncheon recess.

The judge stood up a second before the bailiff pulled himself out of repose to call court into recess. The jurors filed out of the box and Ian sat back with his arms stretched to each side and his legs stretched out straight in front to discharge some first-day-of-trial jitters. Hank was already buzzing with advice about the next witness, backing up each point by waving around pages from his police report. Rachel sat still, carefully guarded by two deputy sheriffs who were forced to stay far enough away to allow for confidential legal consultation but close enough to react promptly if she did anything forbidden by her status. Like stand up.

"Hey, Ian." Evan leaned over to close the gap of the aisle between the two tables. "Why don't we ask the judge if we can move the witness stand into the back of the courtroom?" Ian's lip curled up into the slightest hint of a smile, but Hank was true to his badge and had evidently never heard that you could joke around during a murder trial. "Sure," Evan continued, "I won't object, and it will cut fifteen yards off the distance your next witnesses have to sprint to clear the door when I blow them out of the courtroom."

"Don't worry about it, Professor." Ian looked up from Hank's sacred text. "They're all in pretty good shape. You just surprised Cornwall, that's all. We told him he didn't have anything to worry about from you, that you were out of practice. But that was actually pretty good work. Too bad there aren't any financial planners on the jury." Ian was right. The drama of Cornwall's direct testimony had been effectively neutralized, but Ian could cure most of the substantive damage in his closing argument. The Commonwealth had lost the opportunity for a blockbuster opening shot, but Rachel still had a million dollars' worth of motive and it would be naive to think that the jury grasped the different financial plans inherent in different insurance vehicles. A couple of minutes of cross-examination razzle dazzle and a few good answers were not going to wash away the fact that Ted Pope's last breath was worth a fortune to Rachel.

"He was lying, that prick." Rachel was whispering. "Ted wanted that insurance every bit as much as I did. He picked the fucking policy. That toad Cornwall. Why's he trying to fry me? Let's get him back here and make him tell the truth." Such was the sophisticated trial analysis of the accused. Every false word is a lie. Every lie is personal.

"Great idea Rachel. Let's bring him back and make him retract all the testimony that sounded as if you were expecting Ted to stay alive." Evan nodded to the deputies. They moved closer. One took out a pair of handcuffs. "I'll see you in an hour." Stand up. Hands out. Click, click. The mope of the cell-bound defendant.

"Who's next after lunch, Ian?" He didn't have to reveal the order of his witnesses but with prosecutors the belief in an open and shut case often leads to unnecessary courtesies.

"Your old pal Gladys Reynolds. She's in my office downstairs right now. She's been chomping at the bit for a shot at you."

.

Chapter 20

A t one-thirty sharp, Gladys Reynolds strode up to the witness stand with the self-assurance of an honest citizen who didn't recognize criminal justice as an adversarial system. She knew The Truth and was here to tell it and it had never occurred to her that anyone would challenge her honesty. She was a fine, upstanding pillar of the community, after all. Not like that wicked Rachel Pope who had murdered one of the finest men ever to walk the earth. Ian and his staff would have cautioned her against volunteering any personal views. Just answer whatever questions she was asked without editorializing her answers. But witnesses who carried a grudge with them to the witness stand were like time bombs. With her blue skirt and white blouse, her garden-club hairdo and the same strings of pearls she had worn during Evan's last visit to Second Street, she was immensely dangerous. She hated Rachel and had come to court today to bury her. She had no proof that Rachel set the fire, but the jury was bound to respect any spontaneous accusations, even if unfounded, of someone so connected to all of the major players in the case. If Evan gave Mrs. Reynolds the slightest opportunity on cross, if he asked a sloppy question or let her answers rattle on an instant too long, she would blurt out a potent denunciation of Rachel and the jury would remember it. She was completely convinced that Rachel was a guilty, loathsome, villain. The fire was just one part of it.

Gladys Reynolds swore her oath on the courtroom Bible, took the witness stand and looked over at the defense table. Evan had no idea how much she would have by now told Ian and Hank about Christmas Eve.

Ian led her gently through her biography. Her marriage and widowhood. Her long friendship with Dr. Pope and the first Mrs. Pope. Meeting Rachel. And then the night of the fire. Yes, she had called in the alarm. Yes, she had gone outside to watch the fire. Yes, she had feared for her own safety. She then told the story of Rachel's escape through the second-floor window and her rescue by the firefighters. Throughout all of this she didn't watch Ian, nor did she ever look over at the jury. She stared coldly at Rachel, and once or twice at Evan. Rachel, who had been so ready to challenge Cornwall on any microscopic inaccuracy, just looked down at her hands folded on her lap. As the direct examination wore on it became obvious that whoever watched this testimony would recognize the secret known to both women—that Gladys Reynolds lost more to the fire than

Rachel did. When Ian passed the witness without asking any questions about cars or strange men who drove off before the fire Evan breathed a small sigh of small relief. He would have rather not asked her any questions but there were a few things he needed. And one that he just wanted.

"Mrs. Reynolds, I need to ask you some questions about the sequence of events on the night of the fire, starting with the moment that you called the fire department."

"Very well, Professor Wonder." She answered with a thin smile and leaned on the "Professor" a little too much for accident. Ian had prepped her well and that little stunt reminded Evan how dangerous she could be. He had to keep her on track with every question or she would certainly start talking about things that would do Rachel no good whatsoever. Keeping the hostile witness under control meant asking questions which channel into very narrow yes-or-no confines. No open-ended questions, no room for explanations, and no opportunities for speeches. Yes. Or. No. At least that was the theory.

"You are positive, are you not, that you saw Rachel Pope climb out of a second-floor window onto the porch roof, and that she stayed there until the firemen arrived?"

"Yes. I had just—"

"Thank you, Mrs. Reynolds. Do you have any doubt about that whatsoever?"

"No. None whatsoever." She sat calmly and seemed comfortable in the hard-backed chair. Every once in a while she would look up at Flinchbaugh and they would exchange familiar smiles. Did they know each other?

"And you were already out of your house watching the fire when you saw her do that. Correct?"

"Yes. I was in my front yard."

"The firemen had not yet arrived?"

"No, not yet." She was biting her answers in small bits off of the big chunk of truth which she was anxious to give the court. With a witness like Gladys, one who is just dying to blurt something out that you don't want to hear, the best bet is often to waive cross-examination entirely. But there was one more fact that Evan needed to emphasize so Ian wouldn't be able to argue it away in his closing, and another one which he had to extract from her story. No one but Gladys could give him either one.

"So, Mrs. Reynolds, on the night of the fire, you did these things in this order: you saw the fire, you called the fire department, you walked out of your house into your front yard, and you saw Rachel Pope climb onto the roof of her front porch. Correct?"

There was nothing for her to say but "Yes."

"Between the moment you first discovered the fire and the moment that you saw Rachel climbing out the window, a few minutes must have gone by for you to do those things. Correct?"

"Perhaps just one minute."

"One full minute, thank you. And when Rachel Pope came out the window, the house was burning behind her. Correct?"

Gladys was clearly tired of being so accommodating. "Well, I wasn't really close enough to tell."

Evan had had enough of Gladys Reynolds and he wanted his answer. "Come on now, Mrs. Reynolds. You've already testified that you called the firemen before seeing Mrs. Pope climb onto the roof. You called them because you had already seen the fire glowing inside the Pope home and then Rachel climbed out the window after you called the firemen. Isn't that right?"

"Yes, that's right," she agreed, but that confrontation, mild though it was, had irked her badly and she was raring to talk about the person, "some cheap bum, I'm sure," who dropped Rachel off at home. It may even have been the noise of that vehicle which woke her up in time to notice the fire. There was no way around it though. He had to ask one more question, and if there was a millimeter of play in it, the jury was going to hear about Rachel's return from an adulterous rendezvous. Evan had worked on the question for two hours last night and he thought he had it perfect. He recited it verbatim from memory, locking up the witness's attention with a stare which he hoped would keep her on track with her answer.

"Before you called in the alarm, was your attention first drawn to the fire at the Pope residence by the sight of the fire, or by a sound?" Mrs. Reynolds had explained this to Evan on Second Street, but anything can happen in a courtroom. Ian and Hank looked at each other wondering where this was going, and Ian automatically started to stand to object before realizing that the question was entirely proper in spite of being unexpected. Evan kept my eyes riveted on the witness.

"It was a noise. It sounded like 'whoosh.'"

"Whoosh!" Evan repeated the word at twice her volume. "Whoosh," windmilling his arms as he called out the sound effect. And again, the peril having passed, "WHOOSH!"

Gladys sat as still as a missed heartbeat and then answered. "Yes. It was very much like that."

Evan folded into his chair, disjointed by relief and forgot to excuse the witness. "Do you have any more questions, Mr. Wonder?" the judge asked. Evan shook his head, Ian had nothing left to ask her, and Gladys

214

Reynolds stepped off stage. She held her purse with both hands, waist high in front of her as she walked down the aisle between the two tables without looking to either side. A court officer held the swinging gate for her as she passed from the well of the courtroom. Evan noticed a long pause before she pushed open the door to the hallway to leave. This was the last place she would ever again be so close to Ted Pope and she was reluctant to leave it all behind.

Evan never laid eyes on her again.

Chapter 21

After Gladys Reynolds's testimony the Commonwealth called a few more neighbors who were awakened by the fire trucks and watched the house burn. They didn't have much to say and could have just as well stayed home, but prosecutors always over-try their cases. The witnesses had been interviewed by the police, they all had their own page in Foster's report, and so they all got to testify. None of them contradicted Gladys on any material point, and Evan passed them all with very little cross-examination. During the afternoon recess he had a few words with Clint who was hanging around in the hallway waiting for Ian to decide if he would testify. Judge Flinchbaugh adjourned court for the evening around 4:30 and told everyone to be back the next day at 9:30 a.m. Evan and Deborah packed things up and carried them out to the Cadillac.

Evan drove them a few blocks to Stay Tuned. Clint was waiting for them at a table in the back. He had ordered drinks for them already. A screwdriver for himself. St. Pauli for Evan. Jack Daniels for Deborah with a cup of coffee on the side. Evan draped his suit coat on the back of an empty chair.

"So what did Ian want you to talk about, Clint?"

"He had a list, partner. And we went over every one of these questions just so he can make sure I don't forget the right answers. For starters, he wanted me to say that Rachel and I were lovers. I had to laugh at that thought. I told him that Rachel didn't have any lovers. It took a while to come up with the right word. Companions? Hobbies? Victims? We finally settled for 'sexually involved.' But he wasn't happy to hear that I hadn't been with her for almost a year."

"Doesn't Ian believe that Rachel got over her fling with you and then returned to happy marital bliss with Ted?"

"No Evan. He doesn't quite believe that, and he wants to know who came next. He wants to know that really bad. Foster's talking to all of Rachel's friends again, all of Ted's friends. Some other guy, I think his name is Piper, has a lot of questions for some of the faculty. They thought that the neighbor lady Gladys Reynolds had something for them, but she must have told them to pound sand. They've asked me for my list of suspects."

"What did you tell them?"

218

"I told them that I haven't got the slightest idea. But they said they'll ask me again under oath."

"For what? Hearsay? Gossip? The only way Flinchbaugh would let you answer that question is if Rachel herself told you who she was fucking around with. Did she?"

Clint leaned back in his chair with the kind of blank look that could mean anything and said, "Of course not."

"And is that what you'll say when you're asked that question under oath?"

"Of course it is, Counselor."

"Is that the truth?"

"The truth, the whole truth and nothing but." Clint leaned forward in his chair. "You know what always got me about this case, Evan? The police latched onto Rachel as a suspect right away. She wasn't necessarily the only one, but she was on the shortlist. Even before there was any evidence against anyone, even before there was any evidence at all. Why Rachel?"

"She was married to him."

"So what?" asked Deborah. "That always bothered me too. Even if their marriage wasn't perfect, it seemed acceptable in its own unconventional way. And if she wanted out of it anyway, she certainly didn't have to kill him. She could have divorced him, gotten a nice settlement, and gone away. Ted wouldn't have lifted a finger to stop her."

"All of that's true. But in violent death the surviving spouse is always the number one suspect. If the marriage was on the skids, then the police have an easy target. Otherwise, it's like that country song that says nobody knows what goes on behind closed doors. If it appears to have been, as you say, 'unconventionally satisfying' then its strangeness attracts attention. It's an old story. Even a classical one. Spouses have been bumping each other off forever." Evan stopped for a drink and asked for a menu when the waitress walked past.

"Sure that's true, partner. But why Rachel and Ted? So what if she's tired of him and she wants to take off with whoever? Leave him. Divorce him. Burning down the house just seems a little extreme to me, that's all."

Evan was looking at the menu while Clint was talking. He decided on a Greek salad with extra anchovies. He passed the menu to Rachel who ordered the same thing. Clint shook his head.

"Well, Clint, think back to Agamemnon. He's fighting the Trojan War; he comes home from ten years of battle and expects a hero's welcome. What happens? His wife Clytemnestra sets him up for an elaborate murder. Why? She could have left him. She could have disappeared in the years he was away at Troy. She could have gone off with some other Greek king. Why the slaughter?"

"According to Homer, she killed him to take up with a new lover," said Deborah the classics major. "A lot like Stonebridge's theory of this case."

"Well, that just goes to show that even Homer sometimes jumped to the easy conclusion," said Evan. "Whenever one spouse kills the other, everybody from Homer to Hank Foster looks for some mundane reason. Money. Insurance. Another lover. But it's usually much deeper than that, because you're right. People can just divorce each other and leave. There are some people, though, that can never leave the other one completely behind. Some people carry a piece of the other one around forever. A little piece. A little hot burning piece that sticks in a corner of their soul and keeps on burning away. These are the people who fall in love by letting down a lifetime of defenses. They let someone else into that place within ourselves which we keep private. A very secret, very solitary place. The part of ourselves which most of us never really give up, a psychic retreat where we are safe and secure, protected by all the defenses of emotional security that it takes an adult lifetime to build up. I don't know what you'd call it, but it's deep down inside. Close to our center, very close to the kernel of our personality.

"But let's say that when you fall in love you give up that place. You let down all your defenses. You invite your lover into the corner of your personality where you are the most real, where your personhood, comes from, where you are most vulnerable. Once you let them in there, it can be hard to get them out. Once the love is gone you feel betrayed, taken advantage of. You aren't possessed by a warm and comforting lover anymore; you are occupied by a hostile and excruciating presence. The pain is unremitting. You can divorce the person, but that won't exorcize the part that stays behind, embedded in your consciousness. All the time. Every day. In your blood. You can't leave that. It has to be deleted. Excised at the source." Evan stopped for a minute and thought about other killings, other killers. "The courts call them 'crimes of passion' but when you talk to the killers, it sounds very much like self-defense. Or necessity."

Clint wasn't smiling anymore. The salads arrived and they ordered some more beers. Evan speared a couple of anchovies with his fork and ate them on a cracker. The Greek dressing and the sardine saltiness and the olive oil hit his taste buds like a freight train. He chewed it real slow and then washed it down with a gulp of St. Pauli. "You know," Clint finally said, "you could be right about Homer's version of the Agamemnon story being too simplistic. He has Agamemnon's ghost tell it to Odysseus. Pretty straightforward. 'I came home after the war. My wife had a new man and they killed me in my own house.' But a few hundred years later, the playwright

Aeschylus tells the story again and this time there's a lot more to it."

Deborah nodded in agreement, "Lots more."

"Like what?"

"Well, first of all the lover, his name is Aegisthes, wasn't just some guy that Clytemnestra picked up with. He was Agamemnon's cousin. His father was named Thyestes and he and Agamemnon's father Atreus were brothers. A long time ago, Thyestes had an affair with Agamemnon's mother, Aerope. When Atreus found out he swore that Thyestes would suffer the greatest possible punishment. So, get this, he kills his brother's kids, has them butchered like sheep and cooks them in a stew which he then serves at a family dinner. Then he tells Thyestes what was on the menu. Thyestes goes wild with anguish and horror, but Atreus is still the king and so he can't be touched. Later, Thyestes has another son: Aegisthes. This was Agamemnon's cousin who becomes Clytemnestra's lover.

"When Agamemnon becomes king, his sister-in-law Helen is kidnapped and taken to the kingdom of Troy by a Trojan prince. Helen of Troy, get it? Agamemnon has to help bring her back. He assembles a huge fleet to sail into battle, but when his ships are ready to go the weather is calm and no ship can sail without wind. He consults a fortune teller who says that to get a sailing wind, the gods require that Agamemnon sacrifice his daughter Iphigenia. No problem, says Agamemnon, and he kills his own daughter for the sake of a good wind.

"Clytemnestra broods about the death of Iphigenia for as long as Agamemnon is gone, for the whole Trojan War. He comes back home ten years later expecting the Greek equivalent of a ticker-tape parade but everyone in town, except him of course, knows that Clytemnestra has been waiting to avenge Iphigenia and now she has Aegisthes to help her. Agamemnon gets to the palace where a crowd has gathered for the inevitable excitement. They don't have to wait long. Agamemnon goes strolling in, there's a lot of screaming and moaning and pretty soon Clytemnestra comes to the door covered with blood. She explains that she just chilled her old man. She fades back into the palace and no one really blames her very much. With Agamemnon dead, Clytemnestra and Aegisthes expect to live happily ever after. It doesn't work that way in Greek tragedy though and eventually Clytemnestra gets what's coming to her. But that's another story."

Clint was slowing down now. "Sometimes our actions betray us. Sometimes our guilt brings us to ruin. But Aeschylus makes a point of explaining that Agamemnon was cursed by his father's ancient sin. Something very old, very powerful, had reached through the ages to destroy him."

Evan swallowed the last piece of Greek cheese, while Clint pushed away from the table and crossed his legs. During the story he was belly up to the table, gesturing with his hands and leaning into the story so he could tell it while still keeping his voice down.

Deborah took this as her cue and she finished the story. "Most people read the Agamemnon story as a simple tale of somebody getting his just deserts. Agamemnon killed his daughter so he deserves to die. But really, it's a story about the curse. Agamemnon's father's sin corrupted the bloodline. That's what made Agamemnon so cruel that he could kill Iphigenia, that's what made Clytemnestra so unfaithful and vengeful. It was an ancient sin come back to haunt the generations."

"There," said Evan. "You see, Clint. The answer to murder might seem simple on the surface—hatred, greed, revenge—but sometimes the crime grows out of a very old seed. Older than the killing, sometimes older than the killer." Evan asked for the check and signed his name to it. He knew he would never get a bill. This was Stay Tuned, after all. He put a twenty on the table under an empty beer bottle and mumbled under his breath, "Sometimes the answer to a murder is older than anyone can possibly imagine.

"Carrying a blood grudge for years, burning away in silent rage until she can't stand it anymore and then killing the object of her hatred. Rachel? That's not the Rachel I knew.

"No. It's not Rachel at all. And the crime itself speaks against a hateful murder. Burning a house down is a pretty impersonal way of killing. You don't get to see the victim die. He never knows it was you that killed him. This was murder with a motive, but I never believed that the motive was personal."

"The D.A. says it was money," said Deborah. "Isn't that pretty impersonal?"

"Or do you think Ted was cursed?" Clint smiled. "Is that what you'll tell the jury?"

"No, not Ted. No curses. And maybe it was something as simple as money. But I haven't ruled out an ancient motive. You'll both just have to listen to my closing to find out."

"Well, I have the luxury of leaving those thoughts to you tonight, Evan," said Clint. "My immediate concern is what's in store for me tomorrow when I testify."

"Stonebridge will be friendly with you. You'll have to admit the affair with Rachel, and as to everything else just tell the truth. You are, of course, one of the possible alternate suspects so don't be surprised if I start asking you about your own motive to murder Ted."

"Is that a joke?"

"No joke, Clint." Evan stood up and put suit coat back on. "My job this week is to defend Rachel and I'll be doing that job all week long. Even while you testify. Your faculty party alibi is good but not perfect. You did have a motive to kill Ted, and a better one for killing Rachel. Maybe she was your real target. Maybe Ted was collateral damage. The cops let you go because Rachel was an easier target. I'm not bound by their decision." Clint's face got purple with anger. Evan started to tell him that it was nothing personal, that a public accusation of murder need not affect their friendship, and all the rest of that crap which makes sense to lawyers but to nobody else, but instead he just turned to Deborah and said, "Ready to go?"

Deborah nodded her head and stood up.

"How about you, Clint. Or are you going to stay here for a while and reconsider your answers to some of the D.A.'s questions?"

Chapter 22

Evan wasn't hungry after the Greek salad and he didn't feel like cooking. There were some bills and letters under the mail slot in front door. He stepped on them on the way in without picking them up. Reading, television, movies, visitors—all out of the question. They were elements of a prior life which ended with the swearing-in of the Pope jury. This week only one thing mattered. Rachel's trial. Only one place was real. Flinchbaugh's courtroom. Only a few people had any substance. Stonebridge, Foster, the jurors, the witnesses. There was nothing else. These were the only things that existed. Being home, away from them, outside of their reality, made Evan feel strange and otherworldly. Thinking about anything other than the case would be impossible and he knew it. So he went into the dining room, spread the case files out on the big table, and dug in. Deborah said that she would come over and help after she went home to feed her cat. He left the front door unlocked.

Evan had known the evidence by heart for a couple of weeks now but he still sorted out and read all of the pre-trial statements from the witnesses he expected to hear from tomorrow. There would be Mike Morrow again to talk about the heroism of the firefighters and the grisly corpse of the professor. There would be the doctor who treated Rachel at hospital. According to the medical records his name was George Deeling. There would be the state police chemist who found the diethyl ether on Rachel's shoes. Evan and Stonebridge had stipulated that Professor Pope had died in the fire: as opposed, for example, having had a coincidental heart attack an hour before the arson or being struck by an asteroid. Therefore, there wouldn't be any testimony from a cheerful pathologist about autopsy techniques, rib saws, lung cross-sections, and the like. Foster would clean up a few details of his investigation, and Ian might even find some reason to call Piper. But the star of the show would be the fire marshal, Roger Williamson, who would establish that the fire had been arson. Then Stonebridge would probably be ready to rest his case. It would be a full day, the most important day of the trial until the jury returned the verdict.

Deborah walked into the dining room as Evan finished up re-reading Williamson's arson report. She had a Starbucks carrier with two cups in one hand and a bottle of Jack Daniel's in the other.

"I know it's not Blue Mountain, but I thought you'd need some caffeine." She put one Starbucks in front of him and held up the bottle of Jack. "And this is in case you feel like getting hammered after you just accused one of your best friends of being a murderer."

Evan looked up from the case file and took the lid off the paper coffee cup. "I didn't actually accuse him." It sounded like a thin denial even to him, even as he said it. "All I said was that he had a couple of motives and that makes him a prime possible suspect. Criminal defendants are always allowed to establish a reasonable doubt of their guilt by pointing at somebody else. This isn't a faculty luncheon, it's a murder trial. Life and death. If I have to throw a little acid around to save my client that's what I'm going to do and I can't really afford to be too worried about who gets splashed."

Deborah unscrewed the whiskey and poured some in each of their coffee cups. "How do you think it's going so far? Do you really need to implicate another suspect?"

"You never know what you needed to do until the jury tells you that you didn't do it." He sipped from his cup. "How's it going? Not so great. Ian has proven that the life insurance gave Rachel a motive. He's proven that she had the opportunity to commit the crime because, so far as all the evidence suggests, she was home the whole time. And there's no way for us to get the ether off of Rachel's shoes. If she was already in bed when the arsonist doused the place her shoes wouldn't have anything on them but snow. Those shoes put her right at the fire's point of origin. Put that all together and you can almost hear Ian's closing argument. She was right there because she did it. She poured the accelerant, lit the match, and went upstairs, and then crawled out the window to wait for the firemen to save her. It was a pretty good plan. The next day she would be the sympathetic widow who had survived a harrowing experience. And a millionaire."

"So doesn't that let Professor Jackson off the hook?"

"Well, according to the prosecution theory it does. There is no reason to believe that she had an accomplice, and even if she did she's still guilty." Evan took a longer drink this time. "So what do you think? You've watched the whole trial so far and it's your first murder case. That makes you like one of the jurors. What's the verdict?"

Deborah didn't flinch. "Evan, I always thought she was guilty. At first I thought that maybe that was because I adored Dr. Pope so much, but hearing the evidence, reading the investigation reports, doing the research—I'm convinced. I mean, how can she not be guilty?"

"Because she's innocent." His voice didn't betray the slightest doubt. "I know that."

Deborah leaned forward and she almost reached out to touch Evan's hand but stopped herself. "No you don't, Evan. You don't know that at all. You want to believe it and you hope it's true but you don't know."

She ran the fingers of both hands through her hair. "Listen, Professor Jackson didn't finish the Agamemnon story. It ends with the death of Clytemnestra when she was killed by her own children. Orestes and Electra. They executed their own mother for the murder of Agamemnon. For centuries, scholars have disagreed about Clytemnestra's death. Hundreds have tried to absolve her: She was the victim of a curse, she acted with justification, she was compelled by necessity, she was crazy with grief. Hundreds more have accepted the verdict of her own children who put her on trial and found her guilty. Who's right? Who's wrong? Who knows?

"No one knows why you're trying to convince yourself that Rachel is innocent." She paused. "At least no one knows why for sure. But you don't really know whether she's guilty or not, any more than we can decide right here if Clytemnestra got what she deserved. You make fun of academia because you've always known that you don't really fit in. And you look down on people like Professor Jackson. Maybe even Dr. Pope. Maybe even me." She paused for a moment but when it was clear that no denial was forthcoming, she continued. "But lawyers are not the only people who struggle with questions that are important to them. You may find all of this pretty silly, but scholars have fought duels over the things they believed in. Hell, some have even committed suicide when one of their favorite theories was disproven. If the history of scholarship proves anything, it's that no one is infallible: not even you. And you had better accept that pretty quick or else this jury may teach you a painful fucking lesson."

Deborah left Evan's house at about 2:00 am. He thought about the things she had said to him, but in the final analysis he knew that he didn't have time for the luxury of careful self-reflection right now. Rachel was innocent and he was responsible for her life. He picked up one of the legal pads on his table and started making a list. He needed to prove a few facts to save Rachel. Gladys Reynolds had unknowingly given him one of them. He would produce the second one tomorrow while the whole courtroom was looking the other way. The third one had to come from Williamson, the fire marshal, and Evan would have to drag it out of him in full view of Ian and Hank and Flinchbaugh and the rest of the world. Evan had to read the file over and over again to convince himself that he would be able to pull off that last move, the final move in the endgame checkmate that he had been planning for months.

As for Clint, Evan didn't really think Ian would call him. But what was Evan's move if he did? Clint was an available alternate suspect, his alibi was shaky, and anyone could have found that gas can. One of the jurors might not like him, and it only took one holdout to hang a verdict. On the other hand, Clint knew a lot of things about Rachel and if he got sufficiently pissed off and defensive he might blurt out something that Evan didn't want the jury to hear.

Decisions, decisions. Evan kept drawing lists, then flow charts, and then chessboards. He was ninety percent sure how the case would go from now on. All of the isolated details which had been milling around his consciousness for months in search of each other had finally come together. He drummed his fingers on the table for half an hour counting to four over and over again, without accomplishing a damn thing except for raising his anxiety level about two hundred percent. He turned off the lights and went to bed.

Chapter 23

C ourt reconvened at 9:00 a.m. and the morning went just about as Evan had expected. The chemist explained the process he used to discover and identify the accelerant on Rachel's shoes. Check. Mike Morrow's testimony about fighting the fire and rescuing Rachel off the ledge was almost identical to his testimony at the preliminary hearing, direct and cross. A couple more firefighters testified and then the judge broke for lunch.

After lunch, Ian stood up to announce his next witness. "The Commonwealth calls George Deeling." The young emergency room resident from Harrisburg Hospital looked like he had just changed his clothes after an all-night shift. His khaki pants, blue button-down shirt and Penn State tie were all spotless and wrinkle-free, but his eyes were droopy, his hair was slicked down but unwashed, and he yawned before he took the oath. Ian must have assured him that he would be on and off the stand in a few minutes. All he wanted him to say was that Rachel had made it out of the inferno unscathed: presumably so that he could argue in his closing that she wasn't surprised in her sleep but was alert and ready to escape as soon as things got hot. Evan had his own ideas.

George Deeling was a second-year resident on the night of the fire. He had been called to the emergency room to check on Rachel precisely because she was so free of injury and didn't need a more experienced doctor. He testified with the easy comfort of a witness who knows that he has only a little bit to say, and no likely way to say it wrong. He had probably never been in a courtroom before, and Harry and Ian were treating him like he was there on a field trip. When Ian finished his direct, the judge asked Evan if he had any questions that would follow up on the direct examination.

"Only a few, your Honor. Dr. Deeling, you have testified that you performed a complete examination on Mrs. Pope. Is that right?"

"Well, as complete as the circumstances warranted. We didn't do a gynecological examination, for example. We checked her over for signs of injury from the fire."

"Thoroughly?"

Deeling looked as like he had been warned to expect sleazy lawyer tricks from Evan and he started to straighten up in his chair, as if his professionalism was under attack and he needed the leverage of his full height to ward off the blows. Evan stood up and put on the same kind, professorial smile that he would use with the slow students in class. Ian didn't know it and the judge didn't know it and Foster sure as hell didn't know it but Deeling was the most important witness of the trial and Evan was determined to get the answers he wanted if he had to tear them out of his liver. "Don't get me wrong, Doctor. We've heard about your education, your experience, the fine work you do at the hospital, your training, and I have seen the medical records which you filed. I'm not questioning the thoroughness of your examination. In fact, I just want to confirm it. So let me ask you again. In the context of the injuries which you were looking for, was your examination of Rachel Pope completely thorough?"

He relaxed a little, but he looked over at Ian for guidance. Evan wanted to break the eye contact, so he picked up his copy of Rachel's hospital chart and walked up to the witness stand, positioning himself directly between Ian and Deeling. They couldn't see each other. "Well, was it? Doctor?"

"Yes, I believe it was." Close. Very close.

"Well, Doctor, you knew that you had a patient that had just escaped from a raging fire. Surely you realized that it was necessary to rule out all of the kinds of injuries that a fire can cause. Isn't that right?"

He wasn't about to admit that he might have forgotten something obvious, so he said, "Of course."

"And I see, for example, from the report which you signed and filed with the medical records office at the hospital," Evan gave him a dangerous smile that only he could see, "and by the way, state law requires that these reports be accurate, doesn't it? There are serious consequences for filing a false report, did you know that?"

His fun was over. This day in the park had turned into a survival training session. He was lost and lonely, but Evan still didn't have the third move toward checkmate.

"Yes, I know that. And yes, that report is accurate."

"I thought so. So let me draw your attention to that part of the report where you discuss the defendant's nose."

You could almost hear Ian's lungs collapsing as he lost his breath, gasped it in again and bolted out of his chair. "Did I hear you say nose? Your Honor, what can the defendant's nose possibly have to do with this case? I object. Irrelevant. And Mr. Wonder, please stop crowding the witness. He's the only doctor in the

240

courtroom and if you scare him into having a heart attack we won't have anyone left to take care of him."

"Scare him?" Evan pretended to be indignant. "Why Mr. Stonebridge if you'd been paying attention to the cross-examination instead of thinking about the next Political Candidates Night, you would know that I have done nothing but reassure this witness that I believe he did a fine and thorough job."

Flinchbaugh figured he had better quiet this down in a hurry. "The prosecution's objection is overruled. The doctor is here to testify about his examination of the defendant and if he examined her nose Mr. Wonder can ask him about it."

"Well, what about her nose then?"

"We examined her nose and it was normal." That was the exact language of his medical report. Evan needed more.

"Normal means fine, right?"

"Normal means normal." He was bolstered by Ian's show of support, and he answered with an allegedly cute little smile.

Evan asked his question again. "Normal means fine, right?"

"Fine is not a medical term, so I guess I don't understand your question."

"The normal nose is uninjured. Correct?"

"Yes, that's correct."

"So, leaving aside four-letter, one-syllable words that you don't understand, can we agree that 'normal,' in the way that you used it in this report, means 'uninjured?'"

"Sure." He tossed off the answer with an arrogance that Evan knew the jury would not appreciate.

"Did you look inside her nose?"

"Yes."

"Did you use an instrument to examine the inside of the defendant's nose?"

"Yes. We have a standard instrument that we use for that examination. A nasal endoscope. We spray the patient's nasal passages with medicine to make them numb, and then we place a lighted tube up the patient's nose."

"And what did that examination reveal?"

"It revealed that her nose was normal."

"Uninjured?"

"Right, uninjured."

"Inside and out?"

"Yes, inside and out."

"Uninjured?"

Ian had enough nose talk. "Your Honor, that question has been asked and answered. I object to any more cross-examination about the defendant's nose."

Flinchbaugh was sympathetic to that objection. "Mr. Wonder, we have heard more about the human nose that I expected to. Move on to something else."

"I understand your Honor, but there is just a little bit more. And it's important."

"Very well."

"Dr. Deeling, why did you examine her nose in the first place?"

"Because in fire cases, we often find that the internal membranes of the patient's nose may have been burned or at least irritated by the heat from the fire. A person is in a hot and fiery place but she still has to breathe. The air she breathes in is extremely hot, and injury to the nasal membranes may result. If her nose is injured, then we have to check to see if there are other injuries as well. In her sinuses or lungs, for example."

"You would expect that sort of injury if a person had recently been right in the midst of a roaring fire, wouldn't you?"

"Yes."

"But you didn't find those injuries in Rachel Pope's case?"

"No, not in Mrs. Pope's case."

"Did you find so much as a single nasal hair seared or a single bit of smoky mucous? And getting away from her nose, did she have any burns anywhere on her body? Any singed hairs, any singed eyelashes or eyebrows?"

"There is nothing in my report to indicate that I made any such findings."

"And if you had made any such findings, you would have documented them in your report, wouldn't you?"

"Yes." He remembered the little talk about "serious consequences" and added "Yes, of course I would have."

"Thank you, Dr. Deeling. That concludes my cross-examination, and please accept my best wishes for a long and happy career." Deeling stepped off the witness stand and racewalked to the door leading out of the courtroom. One move till checkmate.

Ian rounded out the day with a few filler witnesses: crime-scene technicians who brought in and identified floor and carpet samples. Police photographers who had taken pictures of the Pope house. Evan didn't ask any of them a single question. At three o'clock when Ian announced that his next witness would be Fire Marshal Williamson and that his testimony would be lengthy, Flinchbaugh decided that it would be a good idea to quit a little early. He warned the jurors not to talk about the case, not to watch or read media reports about it, to keep an open mind, and to be back on time tomorrow. Court was adjourned.

The sheriff's deputies led Rachel away, and as Evan put his files in his briefcase Hank Foster came over to the defense table wearing an insincere, interrogative smile. "What the hell got into you with that doctor back there?"

"Nothing, Hank. Why do you ask?"

"I ask because it seemed you were ready to rip him apart and none of us can figure out why."

"Sure you can, Hank. Give it a try. Read your reports again." Evan snapped his briefcase shut. "It's been a long time since you and I were together in a real courtroom."

"A long time. I'm glad we're starting again with a simple case like this." This time his smile was sincere. "There's no way for anybody to fuck it up."

"That's what I'm counting on, Hank. That's exactly what I've been counting on." Evan patted him on the shoulder and left the courtroom.

Chapter 24

The next morning, Hank Foster was waiting on one of the benches outside the courtroom. He got up as soon as he saw Evan. "We need to talk," and walked away from the courtroom doors fully expecting that Evan would follow. He was right.

They found an empty conference room on the other side of the building. Hank locked the door when they were inside. Neither of them sat down.

"Okay, Hank. What's this all about?"

"It's Piper."

"Piper? That little twit that hassled me at the Pope house? What's he been up to that you and I have to talk about?"

"He doesn't like you, Evan." Before Evan could say anything, Hank held up his left hand to stop him. "Yeah, I know. You don't give a shit and I'm not a hundred percent crazy about him myself, but he thinks you made him look bad at the crime scene and it looks like he's decided to get even."

Evan thought that Piper was a moron, but he knew that anyone with a badge and a gun who decides that he wants to get even with you deserves your careful attention. Especially if he's a moron. "How?"

"Well, he's not going to arrest you for being in the restricted area that day, and I think I've talked him out of shooting you. But a couple days ago a local cop found him parked down the street from your house, about a half a block away. He's been tailing you, Evan. He's put you under surveillance."

"For how long?"

"He says a few weeks, off and on. He says it's been mostly on his own time. The night the local cop found him though he was on duty. When I found out about it I scared the shit out of him with a detailed description of the direction his career would be taking if I ever let it get around that he was using a state police vehicle and badge to conduct an unwarranted surveillance of a private citizen, and a defense attorney in a pending case at that. He listened, and I don't think he'll be back. But he said that he didn't think it was unwarranted. He thinks you are somehow involved in the Pope case. He's been trying to get something on you that he can use to fuck you up."

"Of course I'm involved, I represent the defendant. Didn't that boy ever read the Constitution?"

"I don't know if he has ever read the Constitution or not, but he has been talking to people about you. People at the college. He thinks you're involved in the murder."

"Now just a minute, Hank." Evan didn't think this was the slightest bit funny anymore. "Aside from that being ridiculous, I'm not even mentioned in any reports. Not by any of the witnesses, not by you, not a single word. I was never a suspect. I don't have a motive. Do I need an alibi now? What's gotten into him?"

"I don't know. I got him to admit that he has nothing on you, and that he had better never breathe a word about this to anyone else."

"And?"

"And that's not the end of it."

"What else is there?"

"Monday he got an anonymous tip, at least that's his story. Some guy called the station and said he had information about the Pope case. I was here in the courtroom so the call routed to Piper. The caller said that there would be something interesting happening at your house that night. He stayed there half the night and it seems that he saw some young girl, some young great looking girl, leaving your house at two in the morning. He took pictures, Evan. These pictures." He handed Evan a large manila envelope. Evan opened it and took out three very sharp photographs of Deborah Radcliff closing Evan's front door with a clearly identifiable half-empty bottle of Jack Daniel's in her left hand. "Isn't this the student that's been helping you with this case?"

"You already figured that out, Hank. And since she's over the age of consent why do we need to talk about what I do in my own home at night?"

"We don't. But Piper says he has a civic duty to report this to the dean of the college." He stopped talking and looked directly at Evan. "How much trouble can this be for you?"

"Enough." Evan knew that having Deborah helping with the case was not a problem. But having any female student in a professor's house in the middle of the night drinking whiskey? Johnstone would have a field day with that. Especially if the evidence came from a state trooper who also accidentally insinuated that this same professor might be a person of interest in the Pope murder. "I hope this isn't one of your tricks to distract me before Williamson's cross. Or is it something even more direct than that?"

"Like you throw the trial and we lose the pictures? Nothing like that, Evan. I still know you too well for that. But Piper is going to do something with them, and I just wanted you to be ready. Or at least as ready as you can be."

"Well, he better do it quick because the trial is almost over, and after Rachel walks anything he does is going to look like sour grapes."

"Rachel's not going to walk, Evan. We're way past the time for posturing and saber-rattling. I've got an airtight case and you've got nothing." He looked pretty sure of himself. "That's the way it is."

"Well, here's the way I see it," said Evan. "Stalking is a crime in this state and it's a court martial offense for Piper. He strikes me as the kind of guy who wants to end his career with a pound of gold braid on his shoulder, not parking cars at the Farm Show. So tell that asshole he had better not do anything until the verdict comes in. If I win, which no one really expects, then these pictures are worthless to him. If I lose, he can put them on the front page of the *Patriot-News* under a headline that says 'Stupid Lawyer Should Have Stayed Retired.' But if I hear one whisper about any of this before that, I go to your Bureau of Professional Responsibility and blow the whistle."

"You'd be blowing the whistle on yourself then, Evan. If Piper spills his guts, you're out of a job."

"Yeah, but he can do that anyway. And I've been known to make sudden career changes before."

Hank got serious all of a sudden. Evan knew it wasn't about Deborah. "The Porter case. That's what all of this is really about, isn't it? You think you have to make up for Porter."

"I don't know what you're talking about," Evan lied.

"It must be the Porter case. You closed your law office the day after he died." Hank turned and put his hand on the doorknob. "That should never have happened." He shook his head in resignation.

"Well, it's a few years too late for you to be telling me that now." Evan pushed Hank aside and opened the door to the hallway. Court started in five minutes. "Just make sure that Piper gets my message. And make sure he knows who I am. I am nobody that boy wants to be fucking around with."

"Come on, Evan, that's not a threat is it?"

"No, not a threat. Just a reminder that although I may have been away from the law for a while, I still remember how to make sure that justice gets done."

"Evan, now that does sound like a threat." Hank wasn't nearly so friendly anymore.

"Justice? Yeah, you tell Piper that I have threatened him with justice. That ought to shut him up." He put the pictures back in the envelope. "Meanwhile, I think I'll hold on to these."

There were no preambles when Evan reached the courtroom. No cute jokes, no preliminary witnesses. Ian and Hank were checking the placement of the video screens that had been installed overnight to be sure that the jurors could still see the witness stand and the judge as well as both lawyers' tables. Roger Williamson was walking around the front of the courtroom testing the range of the remote control he would use to advance and reverse the video images from the witness stand. Deborah was sitting behind the defense table in the first row of the public gallery with her binders and legal pads stacked next to her. One of the sheriff's deputies asked Evan if he was ready for the defendant. He nodded and in a few minutes the side door of the courtroom opened up and Rachel was led in by three armed guards: one in front of her and one behind with the third one on her right side pushing her along by the handcuffs that manacled her hands behind her. The third guy unchained her at counsel table and pushed her down into her seat with a hand on her shoulder. At exactly nine o'clock, the tipstaff called "Oyez, oyez, oyez" and Flinchbaugh took his seat on the bench. He sorted out the papers he would need for the day's proceedings and without looking up said "Good morning" to no one in particular, and then "Are we ready to proceed?" Ian said yes, Evan just nodded, and Flinchbaugh told the bailiff to bring in the jury. Court was in session.

Every trial has a star witness. Sometimes it's an accomplice who has made a plea bargain and agreed to testify against the defendant. Sometimes it's the eyewitness who will never forget a face. Sometimes it's the crime victim who sobs out her assurances that the defendant has ruined her life forever and should pay a high price for what he's done. Whoever the star witness is, his or her appearance on the witness stand is a moment filled with drama and fraught with danger. In this trial, Roger Williamson was that witness. Without his testimony, the Commonwealth could not prove that an arson had been committed let alone that Rachel was the one who had committed it. He was the one whose testimony would convert a routine house fire into an act of villainy. Whether Rachel started the fire or someone else did, Williamson's opinions made the death of Theodore Pope first-degree murder. And no one knew that better than Ian Stonebridge.

He started the direct examination off slow and easy. "Please give us your name for the record."

"My name is Roger Courtney Williamson."

"And what is your occupation?"

"I am attached to the criminal investigations unit of the departmental headquarters of the Pennsylvania State Police where I serve as the forensic fire marshal for the Central Pennsylvania Sector."

"How long have you been so employed?"

"I've been with the state police for twenty-one years. I've been a fire marshal for fifteen years."

"In that capacity did you conduct a forensic investigation of the cause and origin of the fire at 9152 North Second Street that claimed the life of Dr. Theodore Pope?"

"Yes. I investigated the death of Dr. Pope and then assisted the arresting officer Trooper Foster in bringing these charges against the defendant."

Next came the questions about Williamson's background with arson investigation. Ian would be offering him as an expert witness which meant he would be allowed to state his conclusions about the fire. Normal witnesses can only testify about what they have seen, heard, or experienced, but experts can express opinions and draw conclusions. Williamson didn't see the fire burn and he certainly didn't see it start, but after Flinchbaugh certified him as an expert he could tell the jury all about it. Ian had him give a detailed description of his education, his experience and training in arson investigation, the number of fires he had investigated, the many previous times he had testified, and the trials at which he had been accepted by the court as an expert arson investigation witness. Like any professional witness, Williamson looked at Ian as he listened to the questions and then turned to look at the jurors while he

255

answered them, creating the illusion that he was speaking to them directly and personally. They taught all of that at the police academy.

As Evan listened to Williamson's life story he agreed that his credentials were impressive. There was probably no one in all of Pennsylvania who knew more about suspicious fires than Roger Williamson. He had taken dozens of college courses and attended over a hundred training sessions. He had scooped his way through the debris of several hundred fires, and he had testified as an expert ninety-seven times before today. After half an hour of the Roger Williamson Testimonial Extravaganza, Ian stood up and told the judge, but mostly the jury, that "The Commonwealth offers Marshal Williamson as an expert witness in the field of arson investigation, and the causes and origins of fires." He turned to Evan with an "I dare you to open your mouth" kind of look and added, "We tender him to the defense for questions about his credentials."

Usually this would be the time to probe any inadequacies in the witness's expert credentials, any reason why he should not be allowed to testify as an expert. That would have been pointless here—Williamson's resume didn't have any holes in it and if it had, Flinchbaugh was prepared to overlook them. Instead, Evan asked what seemed to be a simple question. "Marshal Williamson, over the many years that you have investigated arsons and studied fires, have you become familiar with the physical properties of fire itself?"

It was a proper question and so Ian couldn't object to it. The question surprised the witness and he looked at Ian and Hank before he answered it. He stared at them for a few seconds before saying, "I don't quite know what you mean by physical properties."

Williamson was a mostly honest guy and he thought of himself as fair, but he carried a badge and was paid by the state police. So after telling the jury that he knew everything there was to know about fire he now told Evan that he couldn't answer that simple question.

"You don't know what I mean by physical properties?"

"No." he turned to face the jury with a little grin that told them that he was not going to let that pain-in-the-ass defense lawyer start splitting hairs and try to confuse everybody.

Evan pressed on. "Well, Marshal, one physical property of fire is that it is hot. Did you know that?"

"Yes, that's true, Counselor. Fire is hot."

"Another physical property about fire is that heat rises. Is that also true?"

"Heat does rise. Yes, it does." Juror number three was smiling back at him now.

"I suppose on that same line, another physical property of fire is that it tends to burn upwards rather than downwards."

"Yes, that's also true."

"Now do you see what I mean by 'the physical properties of fire'?"

"Yes, now I see what you mean."

"And would you agree that you have become familiar with those physical properties over the years?"

"I agree with that."

"Would you say that your experience as an arson investigator makes you an expert with respect to the physical properties of fire?"

"I think so. Yes."

"Your Honor, I agree with the Commonwealth that this witness is an expert on all aspects of fire investigation."

Flinchbaugh nodded to Ian and made a note in his book. "The court accepts this witness as an expert in fires and arson investigations. You may proceed, Mr. Stonebridge."

Ian and Williamson went through the direct testimony like a pair of master craftsmen. How his crew had shoveled out the first floor and how he had to be careful to retain samples of the debris for evidence. At every step of the narrative, Williamson brought up an image on the monitors that showed the awful devastation of an intentional catastrophe. When they got down to the floor level, Williamson told the jury all about alligator charring and flow patterns and downward burning. He had been meticulous in this investigation. He had taken photographs of the whole first floor once the debris was removed and, sure enough, the burn patterns were fluid and irregular as if liquid fire had been flowing all over the house. He had taken samples of the floorboards, and turned them over to the crime lab where they tested positive for diethyl ether.

"So," Ian asked Williamson in conclusion, "do you have an opinion based upon a reasonable degree of expert and scientific certainty as to how the fire at Pope residence was started?"

Williamson repeated the opinion he had given Dan Blasko at the preliminary hearing: "In my opinion, the December 24th fire at 9152 North Second Street, Harrisburg, Pennsylvania was started by the deliberate act of a person who distributed a liquid chemical accelerant, in this case diethyl ether, and then lit it for the purpose of igniting the structure."

"Marshall, are you familiar with the chemical properties of diethyl ether."

"Yes. Through my experience and training, I am."

Ian nodded. "Do you have an opinion as to whether a quantity of diethyl ether of approximately one quart could have resulted in the fire that destroyed 9152 North Second Street and killed Dr. Pope?"

"That would have been more than enough. Diethyl ether is a highly volatile chemical, highly flammable, and easy to ignite. Very dangerous. Once it was exposed to an ignition source, the resulting fire would have been immediate and explosive."

Williamson explained again that the fire was fast-burning and fast-spreading, and then Ian picked up the evidence bag containing Rachel's sneakers. He walked over to the witness stand with as much drama as he could muster, and it was plenty, and placed the bag on the counter in front of his witness. "Marshal Williamson, I have put before you the pair of sneakers which we have previously marked as Exhibit 22 for identification, the sneakers that the defendant was wearing on the night of the fire."

"Yes, I recognize them. Trooper Foster showed them to me after the chemistry lab concluded their analysis."

"Finding diethyl ether on both shoes." It was not really a question, but the chemical was crucial to Ian's case and he was not going to waste an opportunity to remind the jury about it.

Ian circled back to his table. As he was walking he asked Williamson whether his investigation included an inspection of the layout of the second floor of the Pope house. It had. The video screens lit up with a floor plan which the insurance adjusters had drawn up when they were still considering paying Rachel's claim. Evan had no objection.

"Did you determine where Dr. and Mrs. Pope's bedroom was?"

"Yes, I did."

"Did you determine the location of the window which led to the roof from which Mrs. Pope was rescued?"

"Yes. Mrs. Pope escaped the fire through the guest room window."

"How would one get from the master bedroom to that window?"

"A person would walk about halfway down the upstairs hallway to get from one to the other." Williamson's remote control had a laser pointer and he used it to trace Rachel's escape route.

When Ian reached his chair he stood behind it, the incriminating shoes were still in his right hand. "Was that second-floor hallway still intact when you examined this crime scene?"

"Some of it was but a lot of the second floor had collapsed onto the first floor during the fire. After we found evidence of arson on the first floor, we removed whatever floor samples we could from the second floor, from the hallway and the other rooms, looking for traces of an accelerant."

"Did you find any?"

"No. None at all."

"Not in the defendant's bedroom, or in the hallway, or in the guest room?"

"None whatsoever."

"So Mrs. Pope, while walking from her bedroom to the window, would not have walked through any sort of chemicals that may have been spilled onto the floor of the hallway or any other part of the second floor. Isn't that true?"

"That's true."

"Do you have an opinion as to where in the house Mrs. Pope could have gotten diethyl ether on her shoes on the night in question?"

262

"In my opinion there is only one place."

"Where?"

"On the first floor of the house, during or immediately after the floor was doused with accelerant. No other explanation fits the physical evidence which I discovered at the crime scene."

Ian looked over his notes, checked off a few things, crossed out some others and then looked up at the judge and said, "We have no further questions of Marshal Williamson."

Chapter 25

I t had been a virtuoso performance for both of them. Granted, they had months to put it together but they hadn't wasted a minute of that time. Williamson's testimony was clear, easy to understand, convincing, and it tied a pretty tight knot around Rachel's neck. For most of the trial, and at least since her tantrum after Cornwell's testimony, Rachel had just sat quietly next to Evan and listened to witness after witness as they all tried to put her away. Like many clients, she didn't have a clear picture of the Commonwealth's strategy and didn't know who she should be worried about. But Williamson's testimony was different. It put her right on the spot and she knew it. She was trembling involuntarily. If Evan had tried to comfort her it would have seemed like a sign of weakness. Flinchbaugh leaned forward and asked, "Mr. Wonder, do you have any questions for this witness?" Evan and Williamson were staring at each other. Neither one was smiling.

"Just a few, your Honor. Marshal Williamson, let me remind you of some testimony you gave at the preliminary hearing in this case. You remember that hearing, of course."

"Yes, I do."

"Do you remember that at that hearing you and I discussed your theory of the fire?" He said that he did.

Evan picked up his copy of the hearing transcript and turned to a dog-eared page. He handed a clean, unmarked transcript to the witness. He walked back to the defense table but did not sit down. "Turning to page fifty-four of that transcript, Marshal, do you remember giving this testimony. Question: 'So you believe that someone spread some quantity of this highly flammable and volatile chemical on the first floor of the Pope house?' Answer: 'That's my opinion. The arsonist probably hoped that the fire would be ruled accidental.' Question: 'Then?' You asked me 'Then what?' and I asked 'What did the arsonist do after walking around the first floor pouring out the ether?' You answered, 'Well, then she used a match or some other ignition source to light the fire.' I asked you if that was your expert opinion. Just read your answer from your copy of the transcript."

"My answer was, 'Well sure. Someone had to start the fire.' That's what I testified."

"Is that still your opinion?"

"Yes, of course. That is still my opinion."

Checkmate.

"Well Marshall, tell us what happened between those two events."

"When?"

"While the arsonist was spreading the ether but before he lit the match. What was going on during that period of time?"

"Well, I don't quite under—"

Evan cut him off and waved the transcript at him. "Please don't tell this jury that you don't understand the question. It's a very simple ..."

"Your Honor, I object. Mr. Wonder must let the witness ..." Ian was on his feet screaming but Evan just screamed louder.

"... question." Evan ignored Ian and shouted at the witness. "Everyone in this courtroom understands that question, including you. Now if you will just answer ..."

Flinchbaugh was banging his little-used gavel. "Both of you sit down. If this witness—" But Evan ignored him too.

"... me. What was happening during that time?"

Flinchbaugh again. Cold as a day-old corpse. "Mr. Wonder, if you interrupt me one more time in my courtroom, you will be making a very big mistake. The witness says he doesn't understand your question, so you will either restate it so that he can understand it or you will move on to something else."

During all of this Hank was stoic, at least externally. But he understood Evan's question and he knew what the answer had to be. As much as he hated it, there wasn't a damn thing for him to do. "With all due respect, Your Honor, I believe that this man understands my question very clearly. He just doesn't want to answer it because he knows it destroys this whole flimsy prosecution."

"That's strike two, Mr. Wonder. One more and you're out. Now ask another question or I'm ending your cross-examination right now."

"Very well, Your Honor." Evan sat down and turned back to Williamson. "First, the arsonist spreads the ether, right?"

"I guess so."

"You know so, don't you? He can't light the fire before spreading the ether, can he?"

Williamson was shaken now or else he would have corrected Evan's gender pronoun. "That's true."

268

"And then he walks back to the foot of the stairs, right?"

"I guess so." Evan loved it when a prosecution witness used the word "guess." It was so very inconsistent with positive proof.

"Well, while he was doing those things, what was happening to the ether that he had poured on the floor?"

"According to my investigation, it was laying on the floor, making the flow patterns I discovered."

"Yes, I suppose that some of it did exactly that. But some of it did something else, didn't it?"

Ian was standing up to object to something but no one ever found out what because Flinchbaugh, who was now interested, just waved him off. "No, Mr. Stonebridge. We'll take the answer to that question."

"Well, Marshal, what did the rest of the ether do? On direct examination you told Mr. Stonebridge that diethyl ether is highly volatile and explosive. What does any highly volatile accelerant do when it is exposed to air?"

"I suppose that some of it vaporized."

"Oh, you don't have to suppose anything. You know very well, as a matter of absolute fact, that for the entire time the arsonist was walking around the ether

269

was evaporating, turning into a highly explosive gaseous vapor. That's what happened isn't it?"

Williamson had no choice. Any high-school chemistry student in the country could answer that question and if he was going to cling to any shred of his expertise he had better answer it too. "Yes, that's what would have happened."

"And what would those volatile gases have done?"

"Some of them would have risen from the floor where the chemicals had been placed."

"Now let me remind you of some testimony given here in this courtroom by Mrs. Gladys Reynolds. Do you remember Mrs. Reynolds's testimony?"

"I remember Mrs. Reynolds."

"This was her testimony." Evan picked up a couple sheets of testimony which he had cajoled the court reporter into transcribing the day after Gladys testified. He saw from the look on Ian's face that the prosecutor didn't have it.

"My question to her was, 'Before you called in the alarm, was your attention first drawn to the fire at the Pope residence by the sight of the fire, or by a sound?' Her answer was, 'A kind of a noise. Like … whoosh.' I repeated the answer for her. 'Whoosh?' She agreed. 'Yes.

It was very much like that.' Do you remember her saying that?"

"Yes. Yes, I do."

"You have no reason to doubt her testimony, do you?"

"None whatsoever."

"That noise, that WHOOSH that Mrs. Reynolds heard was the sound of the ether vapors blazing throughout the house. Once the arsonist, whoever he was, tossed the match the flames would have spread like—well, like wildfire. Wouldn't they? It would have been, to use the word you have repeated several times during this case, explosive. Right?"

Ian was catatonic. Well, nobody anticipates a four-move checkmate. The jury was staring at Williamson and waiting for his answer. "Well, I suppose—. Yes. You're right. The ether vapors would have ignited into an immediate and explosive fire." Williamson tried to save face. "I believe I have already testified to that."

"That's true, Marshal, you have." Evan looked straight ahead, "But I wanted to emphasize that previous testimony because I don't think the district attorney understood it the first time." Ian started to stand up but then stopped. Why bother objecting now? "Mrs. Reynolds also told us that Rachel Pope was on the upper-level

271

porch roof with the house fully involved in flames behind her. Do you remember that?"

"Yes, I do."

"And you don't dispute that do you?"

"No, I don't dispute that at all."

He was done now. Finished. A fish on a hook. But Evan still had to reel him in. "Tell us again about the floor plan of the Pope house. It was a two-story house, right?"

"Right."

"And there was a staircase that connected the first and second floors, right?"

"Right."

"And you found evidence of the ether being poured close to the bottom of that staircase, right?"

"Yes, I did."

"When I was asking you questions earlier today about your knowledge of the physical properties of fire, you told me that heat rises. And that fire tends to burn upwards. Do you remember that?"

"I remember."

"Well, then. When those chemical vapors exploded into flames with an explosive WHOOSH right near the bottom of the staircase, where do you suppose the fire went?"

"Well, I—." He paused too long for Evan's liking.

"Let me tell you where it went, Marshal. It went up the staircase. The staircase became a chimney. Heat rises. Fire burns up, not down. You've told us that. That stairway vented the fire right up the steps, right up to the second floor, and right through the roof. That's why Chief Morrow saw the fire coming through the roof as soon as he got there. Isn't that what happened?" And then Evan added without a hint of sarcasm, "In your expert opinion?"

"I suppose that's what would have happened."

"That's what did happen." Evan stopped for a moment to let it all sink in. The cross examination had been pretty intense. Flinchbaugh looked down and asked, "Are you done with the witness?"

"Almost, Judge." Back to Williamson for the final move. "That leaves us with an interesting question, Marshal. How could Rachel Pope commit the arson on the first floor, and then climb to the second floor on a staircase that would have been consumed by fire? Fully involved, as the firefighters have testified. How do you think that could have happened?"

273

"She could have run up the stairs, she could have dashed through the flames. It's possible."

"Possible?" Evan had to restrain himself. "A lot of things are possible, Marshal. Some people think that anything's possible. But there is one thing, one clear and simple thing, which I suggest to you is not possible. It is not possible that Rachel Pope ran up a burning stairway, ran through a raging inferno, ran through a house that was filled with superhot flames, all without singing a single hair in her nose. Without getting any smoke in her nasal mucous. Without searing a single hair on her head. Without a blister or any other symptom would have suggested to Dr. Deeling that Rachel Pope had been anywhere closer to a fire than the upstairs hallway." Evan was feeling, perhaps, a little too cocky now, but no matter. "You don't really think that's possible, do you?"

"I don't—." I don't know."

"Yeah. Well, 'I don't know' is a long way away from proof beyond a reasonable doubt." Evan sat back in his chair. That had been the flaw in the Commonwealth's case that it had taken months of sleepless nights to put together. If Rachel set the fire on the first floor, she could never have gotten to the second floor where Gladys Reynolds and all the other neighbors saw her, on the ledge above the porch. Hank knew it too, although he would never bring himself to acknowledge it. He sat quiet and still at the prosecution table.

Williamson started to say something and before Evan could stand up to object he blurted out, "But what about the ether on her shoes?"

"You're asking me questions now? Please, Marshal Williamson. You've had month after month and all of the resources of the entire Commonwealth of Pennsylvania to try to solve this case. Now that you've failed, don't expect me to explain every little detail in five minutes."

Ian didn't even bother to object to that. Evan just looked up at the judge and said, "I have no more questions for this expert witness."

Flinchbaugh called the court into recess. Evan looked over at Rachel. She was still stiff as a board, but she was smiling. "Don't count your chickens just yet. We still have to hear the verdict, and anything can happen." She nodded, still smiling, while the deputies led her away.

Ian came over to the defense table. "That was good work, Evan. I underestimated you. I guess that's what comes from not having seen you in action for a long time."

"There was nothing to see, Ian. I haven't been in action for a long time. Is that it for your case? Are you going to rest when the judge comes back?"

"I'll be calling Hank to testify that he got the defendant's clothes from the hospital."

"Stipulated." Evan said it without hesitation.

"He will verify the accuracy of that floor plan."

"Stipulated."

"Very agreeable today, aren't you Evan? Well, in that case we just have one more witness. But don't worry. It will be short."

"Who is it?"

Ian turned away. "Don't worry. It will be short."

"What was that all about?" Deborah had walked into the well of the court while the lawyers were talking.

"I'm not sure. Walk around the courthouse and see if you can find any familiar faces."

Chapter 26

When the judge and jury came back, Ian stood up and said, "If it please the court, we have one more witness to call." Hank was nowhere to be seen. "The Commonwealth calls Dr. Clinton Jackson." Evan turned around to see Hank leading Clint into the courtroom. Hank's face bore a renewed confidence and Clint didn't look at Evan or Rachel as he took the witness stand, swore his oath, and sat down.

Deborah had found Clint waiting in the foyer of the district attorney's office, waiting his turn. Evan knew that he would still be worried that Evan would try to lay Pope's murder off on him. By the time Clint found out what Evan did or did not plan to do, it would be cross-examination and he would already have done whatever damage he was going to do on direct. Evan needed a ploy, a gambit. He calculated his next move while the witness answered Ian's first question.

"My name is Clinton Jackson, and I am employed as an associate professor of Classics at Crawford College."

"Do you know the defendant, Rachel Pope?"

"Yes."

"How long have you known her?"

"About seven years." Clint was slicing off each answer down to the fewest possible words. His face didn't give anything away.

"And during those seven years what sort of a relationship did you have with Rachel Pope?"

The witness didn't pause for an instant. "For most of that time I knew her as the wife of Dr. Pope with whom I taught Classics. I saw her at faculty events and when I was a guest at the Pope home. Then about two-and-a-half years ago, we became sexually involved." Well, at least Ian should be pleased that Clint was remembering his lines.

"How long did your sexual relationship last?"

"Until December 31st, almost a year before Dr. Pope's death."

"How is it that you can recall the exact date?"

"It was a sad day for me. And I remembered it."

"Tell us about the sort of relationship you had with this defendant."

I was on my feet. "Your Honor, I request a sidebar."

"Yes," Flinchbaugh had been frowning before I stood up all the way. Ian and I walked up to the front of the courtroom. A sidebar is a conference between the lawyers and the judge which is held right up at the side of the judge's bench. The judge will allow a sidebar when there is something for the lawyers to discuss that he doesn't want the jury to hear. Normally, everybody leans close and whispers but Evan had something different in mind. When they got to sidebar, Evan objected. "Judge, what kind of question was that?" He looked at his legal pad for emphasis, as if he was reading something. "'Tell us about your relationship with this defendant.' What does he want, positions? Frequency? The Commonwealth has gotten everything they can out of this witness: He had a relationship with the defendant, it started two-and-a-half years ago, and it ended over a year before the fire. If that gives the defendant a motive, so be it." Clint, like all witnesses during sidebars, was sitting straight in his chair straining to hear the conversation while pretending not to. Evan raised his voice loud enough to make it easy for him. "I think that the district attorney has taken this line of questioning as far as he can. I don't think any of this even makes a difference, to be honest with you." Evan turned as far toward the witness stand as possible without looking obvious. "In fact, I don't even plan to ask this man a single question on cross-examination."

Flinchbaugh looked at Ian and told him he didn't want to hear any more about the witness's love life.

"I have one other area, Your Honor."

Evan wasn't out of the woods yet, but he was sure that Clint had heard what he said about waiving cross. Did he believe it? Did it matter if he did? Evan wouldn't have to wait long to find out.

When the lawyers got back to their tables, Ian asked his next question. "Dr. Jackson, do you know whether or not the defendant was involved in any other adulterous affairs after that day, New Year's Eve?"

Evan stood up to remind the judge and the witness that this question could only be answered based upon the witnesses' first-hand observations or admissions from the defendant, not rumors or gossip. Flinchbaugh agreed and said so.

Clint took the instructions with perfect patience and courtesy and then said, "No."

"No?" Ian didn't like that answer, but Clint gave it right back to him.

"No. Mrs. Pope no longer discussed her personal life with me. In fact, I never saw her again. Until today."

"Do you mean to tell us, Dr. Jackson," Ian was mad now. Hank must have led him to expect something better than this, "that when your relationship with this defendant ended she didn't give you any reason, any explanation? A new lover perhaps?"

"Objection. That's a leading question." Was it ever.

Flinchbaugh. "It is a leading question. Mr. Stonebridge, there won't be any more of those will there? I didn't think so. Do you have any proper questions for this witness?"

"During the time you and the defendant were sexually involved, was knowledge of your relationship the subject of gossip in the college community? Did you become aware that other people knew about it?"

"I'm suppose some people knew about it, or at least suspected."

Ian kept fishing and Flinchbaugh would have disallowed any question Evan objected to, but he knew the pond was barren and he wanted the jury to watch Ian keep casting out bait and reeling back empty hooks. "How could an affair between two well-known members of a small college community go on for so long and no one else know about it?"

Spero T. Lappas

"Well, I wasn't about to say anything," Clint answered. "And Rachel swore to me that she wouldn't tell anyone about our love affair." This was the first time anyone had used that word to describe Clint and Rachel.

"She gave you that promise?"

"She did."

"And what did you have to give her in return?"

Clint looked at his lap and then directly at Rachel for the first time, and she seemed a little surprised by the intensity of his gaze. There was a long pause before he answered Ian's last question, but not even Flinchbaugh would try to hurry this one along. He turned away from Rachel and faced Ian directly. "I had to sacrifice a very great deal for Rachel. It may be a long time before I understand exactly how much."

Ian wasn't going to touch that so he passed the witness to Evan who, true to his completely inappropriate and totally improperly communicated promise, said "No questions." The judge told Clint that he was excused, and he left without a word, without a glance.

Ian asked the judge for a few minutes of indulgence and he and Hank huddled together over their table. A few more of the prosecutorial entourage joined in from time to time, even the crew-cutted Piper showed up. Every cop had an idea that would salvage the prosecution, but since Ian wasn't paying attention to any of them

282

they were talking mostly to each other. Hank was gesturing with both hands and complaining in loud whispers. Every once in a while he would rip a page out of his report and show it to Ian. Ian just sat still except for every few seconds when he would shake his head. After a moment or two of this Hank settled down and Ian stood up and said, "Your Honor, we move for the admission of all Commonwealth exhibits."

Evan said, "No objection." Flinchbaugh said "They're admitted."

"With that, your Honor, the Commonwealth rests."

Ian looked at Evan expectantly, the judge was looking curiously. Evan slid his chair back, stood up, and said, "Your Honor, the defense rests."

The packed courtroom buzzed with all the people who wanted to know what had just happened and those who wondered why it happened and those who said they had seen it coming since jury selection. Flinchbaugh told his tipstaff to adjourn court until the next morning at 9:30 when counsel would make their closing arguments.

"Well, Teach, how did we do today?" Rachel was now completely optimistic and almost back to her old self. When the deputy put a hand on her shoulder, Rachel didn't react as if it weighed a thousand pounds and was made of hot lava. When she stood up to go back down to the cells, Evan stood up with her.

"Well, I don't think they jury believes that you set fire to that house. Is that what you mean?"

"Of course," she smiled. "That's what I'm trial for isn't it?"

"Yeah, that's what the paperwork says. I just hope the jury doesn't convict you for murdering Clint Jackson."

PART FOUR

Closing Arguments

The laws of chess do not permit a free choice:
you have to move whether you like it or not.

Emanuel Lasker

Chapter 27

Deborah asked if she could help Evan prepare his closing, so a few hours after court the two of them were sitting around his dining room table. The file boxes were stacked against the wall and Evan had a bottle of St. Pauli. Deborah had brought her bottle of Jack Daniel's and a Starbucks. She shook her head in amazement.

"How did you do that?" she asked.

"Simple. I knew she was innocent." He took a sip straight from the bottle. "It was obvious."

"No. No it wasn't. It wasn't obvious to the police, they thought she was guilty. It wasn't obvious to the district attorney; he thought she was guilty. The judge seemed to think she was guilty. Everybody in town thought she was guilty. You were the only one who believed she was innocent. How?" She was genuinely curious and Evan had invited her to his house to hear the answer.

"I had a couple of advantages that no one else had."

"Such as?"

He walked over to the sideboard and brought back one of his chess boards and the box of pieces. He took out a few of the pieces and set them up in an end-game configuration that he knew by heart. "First, the prosecution made the common rookie chess-player's mistake, playing against the last move." He moved the white queen to the rook's seven square and captured it with black's king. "Their game was always reactive to whatever had happened most recently.

"Ted Pope died. In a fire. Look for arson.

"Find arson. Look for suspects.

"Find a suspect. Put her on trial."

He moved white's knight to capture a bishop and check the black king who had to move one square ahead.

"I didn't look for suspects. I looked at the whole board. In a chess game the location of the pieces is all-important. The origin point for the Pope fire was on the first floor of the house and Rachel was out on the ledge. Those were the positions of the major pieces and their locations were indisputable. They did not depend on guesses or theories or speculations. They didn't rely on

288

the honesty of any witnesses or on any conjecture about who did what. They were the facts of the case.

"The prosecution theory tried to put those facts on the same square. They wanted Rachel and the chemicals and the fire all to be at the same place at the same time. But there was no evidence of that ever being true. They were always playing against the board position they wanted to exist, without noticing the position that really did exist. The one that was right there in front of them the whole time."

White's other knight checked black's king and forced it to move diagonally toward the center of the board. "Once I recognized the position of the pieces, it wasn't hard to understand how the game would play out."

Deborah looked at the chessboard. The black king was exposed in the middle of the board. The white king was still on his starting square.

"I'm impressed. But you said you had a couple of advantages, what was the other one?"

"Why, the other one was you, Miss Reynolds." She almost blushed.

"Me? But I didn't really do anything that helped very much. I was just trying to learn something. Mostly what I did was sit around in the courtroom and listen."

"Don't be so dismissive of your contributions, Deborah. You cracked the case wide open."

She was grinning widely now. "Really? And how did I do that exactly?"

"You just said it. You were sitting in the court-room, this afternoon. You saved Rachel's ass."

Now she was confused. "I don't get it, how did I save her ass just by sitting in the courtroom."

Evan reached for the white king rook pawn and moved it up two squares. Black's king moved one more diagonal square.

"We haven't reached that move yet, Deborah. Let's go back to the police report, that big file that Ian gave me the day after Rachel was arrested. One of Fos-ter's first reports told me that Clint had actually been an early suspect. A lot of people knew that Clint was in-volved with Rachel. Hell, I even knew it and you know how out-of-touch I was. The only way that suspicion made sense to me was if the cops thought that Rachel dumped Clint to return to Ted. If that's what had hap-pened then maybe Clint saw an opening if Ted wasn't around any longer. Ted dies in tragedy. Rachel is griev-ing and lonely. Maybe she feels a little guilty. Clint is familiar, sympathetic, comfortable. They could live hap-pily ever after."

Deborah's face got a little bit darker. "The police never really, I mean really and truly, suspected Clint— uh, Dr. Jackson, did they?"

"Yep, they really did. He had an alibi, of course, but his alibi had the same holes that alibis always have. Lots of people saw him someplace else but none of them could swear that they had their eyes on him the whole evening." Evan thought of Ronnie Porter again and Hank Foster's second trip to his house. "Ted and Rachel lived a five-minute drive away from campus. Drive to their house, pour the ether, light the match. Twenty minutes, tops. That's a bathroom break at a crowded party. A couple of cigarettes on the veranda. A phone call you step outside to answer. Nobody would have missed him and every other guest would have been sure he was there the whole time. But if those alibi witnesses had ever had to plant their asses on the witness stand, they would all have had to admit that they weren't really certain. Clint's alibi would have been worthless if Foster decided to move against him." Evan picked up the white king bishop pawn and pushed it forward one square, again checking black's king.

"The luckiest day of Clint Jackson's life was the day that the police chemist found ether on Rachel's shoes. That made her an easier target." Evan pointed to the center board. Clint's defense was not impenetrable," he moved Black's king one square forward it to escape the check of white's pawn. "But he thought he was relatively safe."

"But me? This afternoon? Saving Rachel's ass?"

"Don't rush the game, Deborah. We're not there yet." Evan pushed one of white's bishops. Check again. He moved the black king further into enemy territory. "Clint was obviously relieved when Rachel was arrested. He had nothing to do with setting that fire, of course, but he knows that innocent people get arrested. If the case against Rachel collapsed, or if I made it too hard on the prosecution, Ian might abandon the Rachel theory and return to the Clint Jackson option. It was important to him that he keep track of what was happening with this case. The police were not going to tell him, and I had a duty of confidentiality to my client." Deborah was on her feet now pacing back and forth behind her chair. "That's right, Deborah. That's where you came in isn't it?"

"When did you find out?" She reached for her drink. She had to hold it with two hands to get it to her lip.

"It wasn't like that. 'Finding out,' as if the answer landed in my lap all at once." Evan sat back and looked up at her. "I started getting suspicious that first day you came to my office to talk about the case. Rose Miller, the department secretary, got all flustered that you were calling the office so much. And then she accidentally mentioned the fact that I have fifty-seven students. Fifty-seven. A lot of them are pre-law. A lot of them are criminal justice majors. These are kids whom I would have expected to think of a murder case as a thrilling adventure. But not one of them approached me. Maybe it's just not the kind of thing that college students want to do nowadays. But you did approach me and that never made much sense. You're a Classics major. Ted was your faculty advisor. There was no reason for you to want to help the woman that was accused of murdering him. I started to wonder what you were really doing."

Evan moved the white rook one square. Black's king only had one move. "Then there was this." Evan pointed at the bottle of Jack Daniel's and the Starbucks cup. Not many people drink Jack Daniel's and coffee. In fact, you're the only one I know. When we went to Stay Tuned that night to meet Clint, he already had our drinks set up when we got there." Evan raised his bottle of St. Pauli. "My usual brand for me. A shot of Jack and a cup of coffee for you. I know that you drink Jack and coffee because you brought it to my house when you came over here to talk about the trial. How would Clint know? He wouldn't. Not unless you used to drink it with him.

"And then, of course, there was the time you left my house at two in the morning and posed for Piper's pictures by the front door." Deborah grimaced. "Yes, I figured that one out too. An anonymous tip? Some guy? Clint must have been one of the people that Piper was talking to on campus. He knew that moron was looking for dirt on me and the two of you arranged for him to find some. Anything to distract me from the trial so that Rachel's conviction would immunize your boyfriend, right?" Evan shook his head in disgust. "You and Clint have no talent for crime.

"But the third piece of the puzzle was the fact that you believed the same thing that the police believed about Clint and Rachel. When I mentioned to you that Foster had looked at other suspects before Rachel, you didn't seem shocked that Clint was having an affair with the widow of your murdered classics advisor. Very strange. And you and the police all jumped to the same conclusion. The police thought that she dumped him. You thought that she dumped him. You always figured that you got him on the rebound from a bad breakup."

"Of course that's what it was. I'm not proud of it, I'm not proud of myself. He's a professor. He's *my* professor. But he was miserable. She broke his heart."

Deborah was back in her seat and her voice was quavering. "At first it was just that he was lonely and sad and needed somebody to talk to. But then it grew into something more and later, when he needed someone to protect him, the obvious thing for me to do was to volunteer to help you. So that's what I did. It was my idea. Clint didn't even know I was going to do it. And I don't regret it. I'm not ashamed of it. That woman broke his heart and it would have been grossly unfair for him to take the blame for something that she did."

"Yeah. Everybody has a theory about this case." Evan studied the board for a moment. "It's just that there are two things wrong with yours." He moved the black king a square to the right. "Rachel didn't really do either of those things."

Deborah face was painted with bewilderment. "What things?"

"She didn't start the fire, and she didn't break his heart."

Evan liked the board position. White would have to move soon, but for the moment he let it stand. "That was third puzzle piece, Deborah. Rachel never broke Clint's heart. Rachel didn't dump him. Clint dumped Rachel."

"That's ridiculous." Deborah had recovered from her shock. She felt that she was on solid ground again. "Of course she dumped him. He told me all about it."

"I'm sure he did." It was time for white to move his king. One square ahead, exposing the queen's rook. Checkmate. "I admit that he may not have wanted the relationship to end. And he may have been reluctant to terminate it. But their relationship had become too obvious. There were too many people who might have known about it, and one who actually did know. Ted. Ted might not have been a perfect husband and maybe it's true that their marriage had cooled to a matter of convenience. But he was still Ted Pope and he couldn't afford to be a laughingstock in his own department. Not to mention in his own home. So he had a little talk with Clint and reminded him that he was in a position to make things go very, very badly for him. If Ted dropped a few hints at the next classicists' conference, Clint would be lucky to get his work published in *Mad* magazine. Worse yet, if Ted went to the dean of the college to complain about Clint Jackson's moral turpitude Clint would be out in the street. Clint wanted to be a full professor. He wanted to keep his job and his tenure and he wanted to stay a rising star in the Classics universe. The next Hector Montgomery, maybe. Maybe even the next Ted Pope.

"After Ted had his talk with Clint, Clint had a talk with Rachel. She wasn't happy but what could she do? As for Clint, with Rachel out of the picture he needed a new girlfriend. Someone naive. Someone available. Someone ... protective. Sound familiar?"

"You can't possibly know any of this for certain." Deborah was shaking her head so hard her glasses almost fell off. "That woman lies all the time. You can't prove a thing."

A few days in a courtroom, thought Evan, and she thought that she was an expert on the burden of proof. "Oh I think I can," he said. "You see, Ted had also been worried about proof. College faculties are notorious rumor mills. That's why you knew you could use Piper to get me in trouble. If Ted tried to start a scandal in his department with nothing more than gossip on his side, Clint would have just denied the accusations. Ted needed proof." Evan reached down into one of his file boxes and pulled out a small leather-bound journal. "So he looked for this. Rachel kept a diary. This diary. Every time she and Clint were together, every time they spoke. Right in this book. I found it in Ted's office when I cleared out his books and papers. He kept it in a file marked 'Aphrodite.'"

Deborah had to smile at that one. "The Greek goddess of love and beauty. Married to Hephaestus the master craftsman. Frequently unfaithful. Notoriously untrustworthy." She shrugged. "So you've known about this all along."

"Pretty much," said Evan.

"Then why didn't you just tell me to go to hell? Why did you let me keep working on the case?"

"Well, Deborah, you were right about one thing. You really didn't contribute anything substantial to the defense. You were an available sounding board, and some of your ideas were not bad. But I never let you get too close to the board, to the real facts. When I sprung the truth on the jury and the prosecution in the courtroom today, you were as surprised as anybody. If I had trusted you I would have told you about our defense when I formulated it, weeks ago."

"Then why did you let me hang around at all?"

"You really should play more chess." Evan gestured to the board between them. "The game you and Clint were playing, or trying to play, is a classic maneuver called the King Hunt. In a King Hunt, your opponent uses her pieces to chase your king into a position where he can be checkmated. One move at a time, one square at a time. The two of you tried to corner me so my defeat would keep Clint out of trouble. The way to defeat a King Hunt is to stay in the middle of the board and fend off the attack, and that's what I did. I let Ian take every shot he could at me. I let Hank take his best shot at me. I even let that idiot Piper suspect me of this murder. I was fully exposed to every attack. That was my defense.

"But I did have one problem. And it was a big one. If Clint got too nervous about his own vulnerability, he could get up on the witness stand and tell the whole truth about Rachel and their breakup. If he testified that Ted Pope had gotten in the middle of their beautiful love affair," Deborah shuddered, "that would have given Rachel one more motive for the murder. I was much better off if everyone kept believing that Rachel dumped Clint a year before the fire and that she spent that year minding her own business.

298

"Now do you see where you came in?"

Deborah's world was racing away from her and she hadn't caught up to it yet. "Clint didn't want you to know that he dumped Rachel. He's been lying to you for months. Part of his appeal was that you saw him as Rachel's martyr. The innocent and injured victim of Aphrodite. He wouldn't want you to know that he was a conniving bastard who throws women away when they become inconvenient to his career prospects. You might have decided that he would do the same thing to you. After all, the college still objects to faculty members fucking their students."

"It wasn't like that!" she shouted.

"Of course not. But even so he couldn't afford to have you see him as the rat bastard he really is. You'd lose all respect for him. You might even hate him. You might even hate him enough to report him to the dean. No. He had to make sure you stayed happy and I had to make sure he stayed away from the truth about Rachel. That's why you were in the courtroom today. Clint was never going to tell the true story about his breakup with Rachel with you sitting ten feet away, hanging on his every word."

"So you mean he lied? Under oath?"

"Close. But he was actually pretty cagey for a first-time perjurer. Clint didn't actually have to testify falsely. He might have had to if Ian had known enough to ask him the right questions, but the ones he asked got answers that were mostly truthful. And I helped out with some well-timed objections, and by promising not to cross-examine him. He said the relationship ended and that she never told him why, and both of those things were true. She didn't have to tell him why. He told her why. He said that others knew about their affair. And he said that it cost him a lot. True and true."

Deborah's phone started to ring. She took it out of her pocket. "That will be Clint," said Evan. "He's waiting for your surveillance report."

Deborah put the phone back in her pocket, finished her spiked cup of Starbucks and tossed the empty cup on the floor. "What should I tell him? That you've been playing us all along?"

"Tell him that chess is a complicated game and that my strategy was better than yours. And tell him that by the end of the game I simply had the better moves."

Chapter 28

The next morning, when Evan walked into the unlit courtroom, he could feel his pulse beating against his eardrums. Every nerve in his body was stretched as tight as a piano wire. He was aware of every breath. He was alert to the slightest movement or sound around him and hypervigilant to the peril that lurked in every corner of the room where Rachel's life would be saved or lost today. Closing arguments began in three hours.

"Are you sure this is okay, Counselor?" The night security guard didn't remember Evan from the old days but he had orders to let lawyers into the building at any hour. Courtrooms were a different matter, but for the duration of the trial Evan enjoyed the role of temporary celebrity and honorary big-shot.

"Perfectly okay. That's all I need. Thanks." The guard ambled away and Evan found the electrical panel and flooded the courtroom with artificial light. *An appropriate metaphor for the day's proceedings,* he thought.

Evan had stayed up all night after Deborah left, looking for the right words to put a wrapper on this trial. He had a thousand thoughts, a few good ideas, and he knew the case inside out. But that would not, of course, be enough. Closing from the hip in this case would guarantee nothing but a good seat for the execution. All the facts of the case were struggling for attention within his head. Who had said this? What witness had seen that? Who paused before answering? Which juror smiled at what answer? He had two hours and fifty minutes and an empty courtroom.

Before opening any folders or checking any notes, he walked over to the jury box and stroked the rail. Then he turned around and paced off the steps that would take him back to the defense table. Seven steps. The big standing blackboard that he had ordered from the maintenance staff was in the back corner of the courtroom. He wheeled it up front to a spot directly across the courtroom from the jury box. It was low-tech and he could have used the video displays instead, but the blackboard had its advantages. He made sure that it didn't block any of the seats that the sheriff's deputies and court personnel would be using, and then sat in each juror's chair to be sure that they would all be able to see the entire writing surface. He had stopped at an all-night drug store on the way to court and bought a new box of chalk in the school supplies section. He took it out of his briefcase and put two long pieces in each of his jacket pockets. He paced the distance from the blackboard to the defense table, to the jury box, and to the corner of the rail which separated the well of the court from the public gallery. Four steps, twelve and ten. He paced off the courtroom some more, picked his spots for the best eye contact with the jurors, with the judge, with Stonebridge. All the while, the facts of Rachel's case were bouncing around inside his head. He had two hours exactly, so he sat down and began to write.

No spectators are allowed to enter or leave the courtroom during closing arguments. So, especially in a big case, the people who want to see the closings get there early. By eight thirty, the courtroom was packed and the sheriff's deputies were turning people away at the door. Ian and Hank hadn't arrived, and when the matron asked Evan if he was ready for his client he said, "Not yet." Every once in a while the judge would peek out through the door that connected his chambers to the courtroom, just to check on things. Closing arguments in a big trial, where the stakes are high, the contest tumultuous, and the result uncertain, are drama of the highest sort. The excitement is electric and no one is immune. Evan was jotting down some final notes at 8:50 when Ian and Hank showed up. Ian walked over to Evan's table and asked him to step out into the hallway. As the two of them passed through the door, Evan told the sheriffs that he was ready to have Rachel brought up to the courtroom.

Ian didn't waste any time. "Evan, Hank and I and just about everyone in the courthouse all agree on one thing: you have done a hell of a job. A great job. Really terrific. But that's the only thing everybody agrees on. Half the county thinks she's innocent, the other half thinks she's guilty. A lot of them think she's going down no matter if she's guilty or not. Have you been watching the jury? A cold-blooded bunch of bastards if I ever saw one. Some of them look like they'd convict their own mother and then vote for death."

It was 8:55, Rachel was in the courtroom, and Evan knew where Ian was headed. "Ian, I haven't been away from this game long enough to forget that the next thing out of your mouth is going to be a plea bargain offer. I don't know what you've got in mind but ..."

Ian interrupted him. "Just hear me out then."

"No, Ian. The answer's no. No to murder one and life instead of death. No to murder three and twenty years. No to voluntary manslaughter and one to ten years. No to double parking and a fine. My answer is No. Period. Let's get back in the courtroom; I've got a trial to win."

"Evan, it's not that cut and dried. She can still go down, and if she does she's getting the needle. You'd better think this over. You'd better discuss it with your client. I mean, ethically. You have to talk to her about it."

"Think it over? I always knew we'd get to this conversation, Ian. I've had months to think it over and if you think I need an ethics lecture from you, then you are crazier than I remembered. Now, if you don't hurry up and get inside the courtroom you'll have to wait out here until I finish my closing."

"How are we doing?" Rachel opened with the trial defendant's standard greeting.

Evan hesitated, but the trial was near done. There was no cause to counsel against optimism now. The jury would be watching her while the lawyers argued their cases and if she looked sad and worried that wouldn't be good. "We are doing great. Terrific. Just wait till my closing is over. They'll need the paramedics for those comedians," pointing at Ian and Hank.

"What did the D.A. want to talk about?" She had seen the two lawyers walking back into the courtroom together.

"Loose ends," said Evan. "He wants you to plead guilty."

"Plead guilty? Really? But I'm not. You know that. Why would they ask me to ..."

Evan leaned over closer to her. "Rachel, you're not pleading guilty to a goddamned thing. I know that and you know that." He was about to say more but the tipstaff called for order in the court and Harry

305

Flinchbaugh took the bench. He said a few words to the jury about what the closing arguments were all about, and then he asked Evan if he was ready to proceed. It was more a stage direction than a question. He didn't expect an answer and Evan didn't give him one. He just stood up, walked seven paces to the jury rail and began.

"Members of the jury, we began this trial several days by talking to you. Each and every one of you. One at a time. Selecting you for service on this jury. And we end the trial the same way: talking to you, to each and every one of you about what that service means. You remember that I told you in my opening that we don't convict people in America based on suspicions or guessing games or gut feelings or hunches. We don't convict people in America unless the prosecution's evidence proves that the defendant has committed the crime and proves it beyond a reasonable doubt. Otherwise, we find her not guilty. And we don't care what others may think of our verdict. We just concern ourselves with the case that's before us and then do the job that we all swore to God we would do when we entered this courtroom several days ago. And what is that job that we swore to do? 'To well and truly try the case that has been joined between the Commonwealth and this defendant.'"

He walked over to the defense table. Seven steps. "So here she is. The defendant. Rachel Pope. Did she do it? Have they proven that she did it," waving to his right. "Did they prove it beyond a reasonable doubt? That is

306

the only question you need to worry about. Did they prove beyond a reasonable doubt that the person who set fire to the Pope residence was none other than Rachel Pope?" He looked right at juror number one. "If you have a reasonable doubt about it, then you find her not guilty." He looked at juror number two. "If you have a reasonable doubt about it then you find her not guilty." A pause. A quizzical, uncertain look. "What if it's not the same doubt? What if you," to juror number one, "have a reasonable doubt about part of the prosecution case, and you," to juror number two, "have a doubt about something different? Can you bring back a verdict then? Is that allowed? Sure. Sure, it's allowed. The only thing you have to be unanimous about is your verdict. Each and every one of you can get to that verdict by a different path and that's perfectly all right. In fact, I wouldn't be at all surprised if that happened in this case. Because, while in some cases there may be one reasonable doubt to make a juror think that the defendant is not guilty, this case doesn't have just one. And it doesn't have two reasonable doubts, and it doesn't have three or even four reasonable doubts. It has five." Evan held up his right hand, palm out, with all fingers extended. "Five reasonable doubts, any one of which by itself would require you to find Rachel Pope not guilty. All together, they establish beyond all doubt that she is innocent. And let me tell you what they are."

All eyes were on Evan. Ian was pushed back away from his table and waiting for something to make a note about. Hank was watching with that 'Here comes another typical defense lawyer raft of shit' look of his; but he was listening. Flinchbaugh was paying close attention. And Rachel, well Rachel was hanging on every word.

Twelve steps to the blackboard. Evan took out one of the long pieces of chalk from his right-hand pocket and wrote in big letters at the top of the blackboard "REASONABLE DOUBTS."

The beauty of using the blackboard instead of video presentation slides was that while he was writing everybody wondered what the next letter would be, the next word. The dramatic tension was palpable and the effect of the handwritten words made Evan's presentation seem more personal, as if he was directly invested and vouching for the truth of every word he wrote. Under "REASONABLE DOUBTS" he wrote "Reasonable Doubt Number One, NO EYEWITNESSES."

Four steps back to the defense table for a drink of water, and then he continued.

"You know, it isn't really all that unusual in a criminal case for there to be no eyewitnesses to the crime. Sometimes crimes are solved with fingerprints, or someone confesses, or you have scientific evidence, or something else that takes the place of direct eyewitness testimony. But in this case we have no eyewitness testimony from anybody who claims to have seen Rachel

Pope do anything. No one claims to have ever seen her with diethyl ether; nobody claims she ever went to a chemical supplier to buy any; nobody says that they saw her with the match. Nobody saw her do a thing.

"Well, the prosecution may say to you that the lack of eyewitnesses doesn't matter. 'No eyewitnesses, so what?' They will say. 'This crime was committed at night, everyone was asleep. Of course nobody saw anything.' Fair enough. But if they don't have any eyewitnesses, they should at least bring us something. How about a confession to the crime? Nope. Rachel Pope has proclaimed her innocence to this crime, she has pleaded not guilty, she hasn't admitted to a single thing. So what is there?" Evan slowly walked the length of the jury box and made eye contact with one juror after another. "What is there? Rachel Pope is here, members of the jury, for two reasons and only two. One, she is like almost every other American wife in that her husband planned to provide for her after his death by buying some life insurance. And two, because at some point during that evening, in some way that no one can explain she got chemicals on her shoes. Insurance and dirty shoes. That's the Commonwealth's case. And That's Reasonable Doubt Number One."

Twelve steps from the jury to the blackboard. "Reasonable Doubt Number Two, NO MOTIVE." Ian had an amused look on his face as he scribbled a note on his pad. Motive was the heart of his case and it took a lot of nerve for Evan to tell the jury that she didn't have one. A million dollars was a powerful incentive to do anything and there was no point denying that, but if the insurance meant that Rachel had a motive then so did every life insurance beneficiary in the country, including the ones on the jury who had revealed themselves during jury selection. If Ted's insurance was a motive for murder then the courtroom, and even the jury box, were filled with potential murderers. "Just remember, ladies and gentlemen, that the knock at the door after your own family tragedy might not be a friendly visit from your pastor or the funeral director. It may very well be Hank Foster here coming to lock you up in your grief." Then Evan reminded them of Mark Cornwall's testimony that if Rachel was planning to kill Ted she had bought the wrong kind of insurance. And anyway, why not just divorce him for the fat settlement that she would have certainly gotten.

"You know, we have heard some talk about Mrs. Pope being unfaithful to her husband at some point long before last Christmas. Well, I don't abide with that sort of conduct any more than you do. But even if that's true, ask yourself this: What was she waiting for?" Any adulterous motive had expired. So far as the evidence was concerned, Ted and Rachel were a perfectly loving couple on the night he died. After all, they had even taken out insurance policies.

"Reasonable Doubt Number Three, NO ESCAPE." Evan told the jury that if in fact Rachel had started the fire, how could she have known that it would wake up Gladys Reynolds, that someone would call the fire department right away, that the firefighters would be right there, that they could get her down off the roof before she burned to death? How? How? How? If this was arson, Evan told the jury, it was the worst-planned case ever. The arsonist trapping herself on the second floor of a burning building with no escape and no certainty of rescue. The undisputed facts of the crime argued against Rachel committing it.

Evan brushed some chalk dust off his jacket and wrote "Reasonable Doubt Number Four. NO BURNS." He spoke briefly about the unlikelihood that Rachel could have lit the kind of fire that erupted around her like a volcano and be completely uninjured. But he passed over this point quickly, not wanting to take any thunder away from the *coup de grace* he had administered during Williamson's cross. "Reasonable Doubt Number Five, IT'S IMPOSSIBLE!"

This was the defense case and Evan had one more opportunity to drive it home. He turned to face the jury and addressed them from the blackboard. "You know, ladies and gentlemen, when you and I spoke during my opening statement, I told you that you would have to acquit Rachel Pope even if you thought that she might be guilty, that she was possibly guilty, or even if you thought that she was probably guilty. All of that is still true, but none of it matters any more. Because the

Commonwealth's case has not only failed to prove that she might be guilty, it has proven that she can't be guilty." Evan pointed to the words that he had written on the blackboard. "It's impossible. Of all the people in the world that might have started that fire there are two, and only two, that we can exclude beyond a reasonable doubt. There are only two people on the face of the Earth that we know, with absolute certainty, did not start that fire. One of them is in the cemetery, Dr. Pope himself, and the other one is right here." He walked to a spot behind Rachel and put his hands on her shoulders. She was as steady as a rock.

"Because you see, what the Commonwealth seems to have overlooked for all their fancy investigation and argument is that when the fire was started on the first floor of that house, Rachel Pope was already upstairs. She was already on the second floor. She had to be, because anyone who was on the first floor of that house when the fire started would never have made it to the second floor. There was no way up there. The staircase itself was on fire, it was blazing; it would have been like climbing up a chimney with a fire roaring in the fireplace. Heat rises, folks. Fire burns upwards, and in this case, upstairs.

"Is it possible? That someone can climb a chimney in a fire? Maybe. Maybe someone's actually done it once upon a time. I don't know and neither does anyone else in this courtroom. But now that we have all heard

312

the evidence in this trial, there is one thing that we must all agree on. If Rachel Pope did climb up that blazing staircase after Mrs. Reynolds heard the fire explode with a WHOOSH, the proof of her guilt would be written all over her body in the language of burns and blisters. Burns on the skin, hair burned off, nasal scarring from inhaling superheated air. But when Dr. Deeling examined Rachel within an hour of her rescue, he didn't find any of those things. In fact, he didn't find anything at all. In fact, she was fine."

The jury was paying very close attention to this. Some of them were leaning forward in interest, two nodded their heads unconsciously at all the right times. Evan wasn't taking any chances that any of them missed the full force of this argument. "Friends, if Rachel Pope had set that fire on the first floor, she would have still had to get to the second floor where Chief Murrow found her and the only way for her to have gotten there was to climb the burning staircase. If she did that, she would have gotten burned. And if she had gotten burned, the doctor would have told us." He stopped for a moment to let this all sink in nice and deep. "She wasn't burned because she wasn't in the fire because she wasn't on the staircase because she wasn't on the first floor because she didn't set the fire. And there is nothing," Evan stopped for a second, turned to sweep the prosecution table with a wave of his left arm, and shouted out the next word, "NOTHING that they can do that will change any of those facts. Oh, I suppose we'll hear a theory or two when Mr. Stonebridge makes his closing argument. I'm sure that we'll hear some speculation, and I'm sure we'll find out what he thinks is or isn't possible. That's okay. Let him theorize and hypothesize and conjecture and guess until the cows come home because there is one thing he cannot do. He can't change the facts. He can't change the facts of his own case or the testimony of his own witnesses.

"Just as the simple laws of nature and of fire left the Pope house a ruined, worthless wreck, those same physical laws have done the same thing to the prosecution's case. All that remains of the exoneration of Rachel Pope is for you twelve honest citizens to stand up and say so." Evan's closing was about over, but at 7:30 this morning he had remembered something that he used to like to say at the end of a trial, so having no new ideas he trotted it out.

"A long time ago, a very wise old judge called our American courtrooms the laboratories of justice. 'The laboratories of justice.' I've always liked that term because it fits the way I feel at this part of the trial. The part when I must soon sit down and leave my client's fate in your hands.

"I've done all I can do to help you see this case for what it really is: a spark of suspicion that got out of hand and threatened to consume this innocent woman's life.

314

"I've tried my best to help you all to understand that your duty in this case is a sacred one, this duty you have to find Rachel not guilty unless you are sure that the case against her has been proven beyond a reasonable doubt. I've done my best.

"Pretty soon the case will be yours and you will go back to the jury room to deliberate your verdict. Those of us, the judge and the lawyers who practice in these courts will have conducted another experiment in this laboratory of justice. An experiment that one more jury, just one more group of twelve people who have come in here from all over and swear to do what's right will do it. That's all we ask. Do what's right. If you search the facts of this case, search your conscience, remember the things I've said here this morning and just do what's right, we can all walk away from this trial with pride of the justice that we have done together.

"You see, ladies and gentlemen, it's easy to think that this case is just about Rachel Pope. She is the one sitting at the defense table and she is the one we call the defendant and it's natural for people to consider this trial to be her day in court. But for all of you," Evan pointed at a juror, "You," at another, "and you," at another, "and for all of us who care for justice, this has been our day in court as well. We may all judge Rachel Pope. But with the verdict that you return today, you will be judging yourselves as well."

Even remembered to walk over to the blackboard and erase the five reasonable doubts, thereby depriving Ian of the dramatic opportunity to cross them off one by one during his own closing. Evan's part of the trial was finished, and he sat down. Hank tapped him on the shoulder and handed him a note from Ian. There were only seven words. "Hey Prince. Please stay retired next time." Ian looked over at him with a smile, a sincere one with what Evan took to be a hint of resignation. He stood up and started to close.

PART FIVE

Post-Trial Litigation

*Truth derives its strength not so much from it-
self as from the brilliant contrast
it makes with what is only apparently true.*

Emanuel Lasker

Chapter 29

It was ten degrees outside on Christmas Eve, one year to the day since the fire that killed Ted Pope. The Cadillac's windows were fogged white in the five minutes since Evan turned off the engine. He used the palm of his glove to clear a spot of glass and look at the house. Heavy drapes covered the windows but he knew that there would be someone inside. He grabbed the bulging canvas briefcase off the passenger seat, got out of the car, walked to the front door and knocked twice.

Rachel had left Harrisburg right after the trial. After the acquittal, the insurance company paid her a million dollars and she and her money just disappeared. "Consciousness of guilt. Flight from the scene of the crime." Ian railed on in the press against clever defense lawyers and foolish juries. He promised vigilance and stern prevention from the bench, and won his election in a landslide. The state police, naturally, ignored the verdict and forgot all about the search for Professor Pope's killer. They had marked the case "closed" before the first witness testified, and it would take more than the voice of the people to change their minds. Evan had not gone near a courtroom again.

"Professor Thomas. Evan. What …"

"Hello, Professor. Can I come in?"

"Yes. But. It's, well it's so late."

"Yes, it is very late." He stepped back from the door and Evan walked past him.

The room was warm from the fireplace. In another house this large front room would be the living room but here it was a scholar's study. The walls were lined with walnut shelves from which stacks of books overflowed onto the floor. Pages of manuscript notes lay scattered on a writing table and two ancient leather armchairs faced each other in front of the fire. Evan sat down in one of them and rested the canvas bag on his lap.

"Evan, I can't imagine what brings you here tonight. Usually, I'd be in bed by this hour but I was doing some writing." He waved at the paper-covered desk for emphasis. He walked over to the other leather chair and sat down. Evan got up and knelt down by the hearth and pushed the logs around with a poker, keeping his back to Montgomery.

"Do you remember how cold it was the night that Dr. Pope died?" Sparks jumped as he stabbed at the charred hardwood. "The cold made the fire hoses stiff and hard to roll out. The cold weather probably contributed to Rachel's arrest, too. If it had been warmer she might not have put on her shoes before climbing out that window. The most incriminating evidence against her would gotten burned up.

"Such a detail. The cold. The difference between guilt and innocence."

"Now, Evan. Perhaps you feel that you have some reason for this visit, but I want you to leave now." Montgomery stood up and started for the door expecting his visitor to follow. "I suppose Rachel's case was a feather in your cap but I don't care to discuss its fine points with you. And certainly not in the middle of the night. Have you been drinking? At the faculty Christmas Eve party perhaps?"

"No, Professor. Neither one of us went to the party this year. Or last year either, did we?"

"Come on now, Evan. You really are starting to worry me. Perhaps I can call someone to come for you."

Evan tossed him the briefcase. He didn't open it.

"What's this?"

"I was impressed by your lecture, Professor. Especially when you discussed the plague that Homer describes in the first book of *The Iliad*. Apollo shoots arrows of death at the Greeks from far away. Homer has a nickname for him, right?"

"Ekebolos. The distant archer." Montgomery forgot his outrage long enough to answer a question of classical scholarship. "The Greeks never see Apollo personally; they only feel the force of his wrath."

"That still happens of course." Evan faced him. "Remote circumstances still kill people who don't see it coming and who have no idea that they have done anything to bring it upon themselves. Death from a distance, sometimes a distance of centuries. Professor Pope knew all about Ekebolos, but when his own death approached him from three thousand years away he never saw it coming."

The peaceful look on Montgomery's face now required effort and the friendliness was gone. The briefcase rested on his lap. "Death from three feet away is more like it, don't you think? Rachel left their bed, doused the first floor, and lit it. That mumbo jumbo about racing with the flames never convinced me that she was innocent."

"I'm not surprised that you followed the case so closely, Professor. No, that's not the thing that convinced me either. That was just the proof. Most of Harrisburg still believes that Rachel killed her husband, that she beat the system and that I helped her. Proof to the contrary won't convince anybody. Why, if you polled the jurors today they probably would vote to convict. Now that she's gone I don't think you could find three people in Harrisburg who believe that she wasn't guilty." Evan looked straight at him. "Just two."

Montgomery was right when he opened the door, it was very late. Too late for any further denials but he didn't know what else to do. It had become a habit and he couldn't afford to break it now. "I doubt very much that you would find anyone other than yourself. Aside from her infidelities and the insurance there are still the shoes, which you never did explain, and the fact that she failed that lie detector test which the jury never knew about." Evan was momentarily surprised that Montgomery knew about the polygraph. He must have gotten that nugget from Clint who got it from Deborah.

"The shoes were a tactical problem at trial but as a fact, they were irrelevant unless she did start the fire. The polygraph test was a different matter. The interesting thing about that is the individual question for which she showed deception."

Montgomery thought that this point favored his case and he jumped on it. "The question was whether or not she killed her husband. I agree that it is very interesting that her denial was a lie."

"Actually, the question was, 'Were you in any way responsible for the death of Dr. Pope in the fire at 9152 North Second Street?' She said no, and the examiner concluded that she displayed deception with that answer. He couldn't read her mind and all the machine could do was measure physiological symptoms of stress and Rachel had good reasons to be stressed by that question. But you and I know something that the polygrapher didn't know. Her stress was not caused by any guilt for murdering her husband. She didn't set that fire. You did."

No reaction. Well, maybe a slight involuntary exhalation, a slight lowering of the eyes. But very slight. And fleeting. "Really? Do you really believe that? Then why did you not reveal that brilliant deduction at Rachel's trial?"

"Lots of reasons. First, the appearances would have been all wrong. After the prosecution ended, I didn't present any defense evidence. Whenever the defense rests without calling a single witness that tells the jury that we don't think any of the prosecution evidence deserves an answer. If that's the desired message, then putting on any evidence at all is foolish. Whatever is introduced will seem to the jury to be the real defense, and they will balance it against the whole of the prosecution's case. Unless the defense has something really powerful, the best strategy is just to keep your mouth shut until the closing.

"My defense was that not only had the prosecution not convicted Rachel, but their proof had actually established her innocence. It all came in very nicely during the case in chief and I would have been crazy to dilute its effect with a courtroom search for the real killer. Anyway, I had no real evidence to convict you with. An accusation against you would have diverted the jury's attention away from the weakness of the prosecution case. If the jury went back to deliberate whether you or Rachel were the more likely suspect, Rachel was dead. The prosecution had plenty of evidence against her, and I didn't have a thing against you. The district attorney would have ushered you into the witness box on rebuttal to have you tell the jury that Dr. Pope was a fine man, a great scholar and your longtime friend whose death you deeply mourn and had no part in whatsoever, notwithstanding the scurrilous lies of that shyster defense lawyer. I would have been made out a slanderer who was brought to desperation by the weakness of his case.

"And anyway, I didn't need you. The case may have been close going into the trial but by the time the cross-examination of the fire marshal was over, everyone in the courtroom knew the defendant was going home. The closing was window dressing and the verdict a formality."

"You know, Evan, you tell this fairy tale with a genuine delight in the recollection of all this courtroom intrigue. But if Rachel is indeed innocent as you suggest, then the system quite properly worked true justice."

"Not really. Trying cases has an intoxicating fun which I've never denied. But for me to have a few days of fun with this one required an innocent person being at risk of execution, and the true murderer going free and unpunished, maybe even permanently immunized. The official search for Dr. Pope's killer is over. Unless some striking new evidence is delivered to the police they will never acknowledge their past failure by making a new arrest. That's not justice.

"But even more than strategy, evidence, and tactics, Professor, I didn't point to you in the trial because I didn't want to. Rachel had no idea that you killed her husband. I suppose if she did it would have made a certain kind of sense to her and she would have wanted me to prove it. You know of course that before the police hit on Rachel they looked at every possible suspect. They eliminated you because nothing pointed to you and there was no motive. Academic rivalry perhaps, but even there you and Pope didn't compete. You were in different scholastic camps weren't you?"

"Yes. As you well know, we had different views of the authorship of the Homeric poems. Professor Pope was a unitarian. He believed the fairy tale of an ancient blind poet who composed both *The Iliad* and *The Odyssey*. It's a romantic notion and one that has quite a following. But take away romance and tradition and it is nothing but a fantasy."

"And you, Hector. You are what the profession calls a separatist, aren't you?"

"More like a realist. The diction, the subject matters, the treatments of the gods, those poems are as different as they could possibly be. My father spent his life proving those things and I have carried on where he left off. The unitarians ignore all of this so that they can cling to their folklore of a singular Homer. Charming, but impossible."

"Well, they don't actually ignore those differences do they? They simply believe that those differences are deliberate variations composed into two distinct works by a master stylist."

"Rubbish. There is nothing in the archeological record to support unitarianism. Not until Aristotle, centuries later, do we hear anything about this celebrity rhapsode and his two great poems."

"No." The conversation had concluded, the friendly visit was over. Now it was cross-examination. "Aristotle doesn't mention Homer's two great poems, does he? Aristotle tells us that there are more, doesn't he?"

Montgomery looked at Evan with a hint of a smile. His grip tightened on the briefcase and Evan's heartbeat returned to its normal rhythm. He knew now. He was sure. It was almost over. Montgomery opened the bag and removed the contents. It was a folio-sized leather-bound volume. Old and plain. The pages crinkled to his gentle touch. On the front cover, embossed into the leather though obscured by centuries of wear were two words. *MARGITES* in large letters and below it, in letters just a little smaller, *OMEROS*. He cradled the book on his lap and looked at it as if it were a newborn baby. His adoration knew no language except for the mixed awe and reverence which had taken over his entire aspect. "So far as I know, Professor, that is the only copy anywhere on Earth. *The Margites*. Homer's lost third epic."

"Where did you get this?"

"Why, from Professor Pope, of course. Where else? Pope discovered it, he was planning to reveal it, so you killed him."

Montgomery couldn't take his eyes off the book. "When he started talking about *The Margites* about a year before his death, I took it for idle scholarly chit-chat. 'What do you think about Aristotle's mention?' he would ask. 'What would you expect the missing poem to look like if it ever surfaced?' Then, he told me confidentially that he had it. I didn't believe him at first. If such a thing ever existed, the centuries would have wiped it off the face of the Earth. Scholars and archeologists have searched for thousands of years and come up empty. The debate about Aristotle's allusion continued from time to time, and both sides claimed the missing epics as their trump. The separatists said a third poem attributed to Homer would prove that the ancients were quick to attach that name to all oral masterpieces. The unitarians predicted that a third authenticated poem would be a sort of stylistic bridge between *The Iliad* and *The Odyssey* with enough similarities to the other poems to prove once and for all the vastness of Homer's range and the depth of his genius.

"When Pope said he had it I thought he had probably found something old and irrelevant on one of his excursions to a library or monastery. But he told me more and more about it, and it seemed horribly plausible that his text was authentic and that it came from Homer. The one Homer. The one Homer whom I had spent my life disbelieving and rejecting. Once I started to believe that Pope's find might truly be authentic it was no longer a nice point of scholastic disagreement, as you called it." He stood up, still holding the book, and walked over to his desk. He waved his hand over the papers like a magician at his tricks. "All of my life's work would have become worthless overnight. Worse than that. It would have become ridiculous. That's what it was, you see. Not only was I going to be wrong, bad enough, but I would look," he grimaced as his mind searched for and then found the right word, "stupid."

Evan walked over to him and, gently, took the book from his hands. He didn't resist, but he looked up with mingled amazement and contempt. "Ted Pope would have never given you that book," he said.

"No. Rachel gave it to me. It was my fee."

"Your fee?" He spat out the word. *The Margites* is the greatest classical find in two thousand years. It belongs to the world."

"It belongs to me, Professor. It was the property of Ted Pope. Rachel inherited it and she gave it to me. It's mine and I've spent months reading it. So far as I know, Dr. Pope and I are the only ones to have read for hundreds of years. Probably for much longer than that." Evan bent over and stoked the fire.

"Rachel didn't exactly know what it was, she didn't know much about Aristotle. When I found it among Ted's papers I realized that the police had left it behind as just another old book. They didn't know Aristotle either. I'm a little surprised that Ted told you as much as he did, but you knew what was coming when Ted published his book."

His face bore an icy stare now. "You tell me, Professor Wonder. You're the one who's read the damn thing. If you have in fact read it. It's in Greek." He gave Evan what he thought was a clever smile. "Do you read Greek?"

"I am Greek, Professor. And although I'm not in your league academically I've had a long time to work my way through it. I think you were right to be afraid of it. It's Homer, all right. The Homer of *The Iliad*, the Homer of *The Odyssey*. The Homer of Aristotle. The one and only." I had *The Margites* securely under my arm. "But that is just my layman's opinion. I may have to give it to Clint Jackson for his confirmation."

"No!" He came out of his chair and lurched for Evan. The emotion quickly passed and he was back in his chair in a moment. "No. Don't do that. What purpose would that serve? Jackson's opinion wouldn't convince the professorial community and Ted is dead." He was calmer now. "There really aren't too many professionals who could authenticate that text." Montgomery thought that he could save himself in the endgame and he had started feeling more secure.

"That's why Pope had to die, isn't it?" asked Evan. "His word would have been golden. Clint told me that no one would have ever doubted Pope on a question of Homeric authenticity."

"Yes, damn it, that's why he had to die. He wouldn't listen to me. 'Go slow' I told him. 'Let's be sure before you publish' I begged him. But he was sure. So damn sure." He spent a few long minutes looking into the fire. "You don't think, surely, that it was easy for me? To kill my friend, my colleague, my—"

"No. I don't think it was easy. In fact for a while I didn't believe that you could actually have done it, but then one day I thought about a long talk that Clint Jackson and I had about Agamemnon. Do you remember how that story turned out?"

"Of course I remember. After the murder of Agamemnon, the task fell to his son Orestes to avenge the murder. But the murderer was his own mother. He was caught in a grievous conflict. To kill his own mother was a horrible sin, but he could never allow his father's killer to go free. So, finally, he returned to the palace and made his decision."

"There is a thing which must be done, and I must do it." Evan recited the dramatic line.

"Yes, Evan. That's the correct quote indeed. You really have read your Greek. Orestes killed Clytemnestra, and I killed Ted Pope. It was a thing that had to be done and I did it." He looked down at the floor, and sighed.

"Now, now, Professor. Don't be so easy on yourself. Orestes acted out of ancient duty, divine compulsion, and tragic inevitability. You murdered an innocent man in cold blood, risked killing his wife, and then left her to face execution just so you wouldn't look foolish. I don't think anyone will be writing any heroic poems about you."

He looked up at Evan without fear or remorse. "Now what? When do the police come for me?"

"You misunderstand me, Professor Montgomery. I'm not going to the police. I didn't come here to forgive you for Ted's death, but I didn't come here to indict you either. I have something else in mind. A deal."

"A deal?" He was lost now. Captured by events which were racing on a twisted path far too fast for him to keep up with.

"Yes, a deal. You see, you're right. There are not too many people left alive whose word would positively establish *The Margites* as Homer's work. But there is one."

"Who?"

"You."

"Me? No, you're not serious. I killed Ted Pope to keep this work from being accepted as Homer's. Do you really think that I would now be the one who proves it?"

"Sure I do, Hector." Montgomery blanched at the familiarity. "I didn't come here to make trouble for you. In fact, I came here to bring you some good news. And to make you a gift." Evan got up and placed the book on Montgomery's lap. "There. It's yours now. All I expect in return is for an article to be published in some prestigious journal describing how you found it in a foreign monastery, how you concluded that it had survived destruction, and how you have after long and careful study concluded without doubt that it is authentically Homeric."

He held the book in both hands and looked at Evan with a strange smile. "And why, pray tell, would I do any of that. Why wouldn't I just throw it in the fire?"

"Maybe you'll do what I ask to expiate your guilt over Ted's death. Maybe you'll do it because it's the right thing to do. Maybe you'll do it because if you don't then I really will go to the police with what I know. The justice of this situation is that the authentication of this work will be so destructive to your reputation, that no one will ever believe that you would falsely declare it authentic. The world will believe you simply because your admission does you such incalculable harm."

He was as white as a ghost now, but Evan went on talking. "And you won't just destroy it because while that is the only actual physical copy of *The Margites* I have very good and very complete high-resolution digital photographs of every page, every word of that. And I have also cut out several pages of the book, the whole last chapter. About twelve hundred lines. With the photographs I can recreate the text of the poem, and I can have the pages carbon-dated to establish their age. That's not as good as having the original, I grant you, but it will be more than enough to stir up an academic debate that will leave you and your father in the ashes. And then of course, there would still be the police."

They sat silently for a while. Montgomery had the book open and was reading it. He was lost in the ages now, and the look of contentment on his face belied his knowledge of the doom which surrounded him. At last, he looked up and spoke.

"You know very well that I won't do what you ask."

"Maybe not, Hector, but our chess game hasn't ended yet. You are going to have to make a move. Some move." Evan leaned forward. "Do you know the German word Zugzwang?"

"My German is quite good, Evan. Zugzwang means 'compulsion to act.'"

"Right. It's also a chess term. It refers to a position in a chess game where a player would rather not move any of his pieces. Every possible decision leads to an unfortunate result."

"Is that where we are now, Maestro?" Montgomery was not so worried that he couldn't be sarcastic. "A juncture of hopelessness in this little game you've been playing?"

"Justice must be served, Hector. You allowed an innocent woman to stand trial for your crime. She could easily have been executed in your place." Evan's voice got very cold and formal. "You have two possible moves and they both lead to unfortunate results. You can allow my discovery of *The Margites* to make you and your father the laughingstocks of your profession. Or you can allow it to vanish once again, leaving nothing behind but the memory that you and the great Pollard Montgomery had once lived lives of genius and accomplishment."

"I see." Montgomery nodded. "Well then. Perhaps before you leave, you will do me the favor of answering one last question."

"Anything."

"Why did you really defend Rachel Pope? Why did you come out of retirement after so long, to return to a life on which you had so deliberately turned your back, to take on a case which seemed so unlikely to provide you with any success or reward? Surely, at the time you didn't yet know the truth about Ted's death."

"I didn't know the whole truth, that's true. But I knew that Rachel didn't kill Ted Pope, and from the night of his death I was always pretty sure that you did."

"Even then?" He was stammering now. "How?"

Evan stood up and paced around as if he were back in class. "Sometimes it's easy to overlook the obvious facts of a murder while you are concentrating on every minute detail of the case. Take the date, for example. There was no reason for Rachel to pick Christmas Eve to kill Ted. Whoever picked that date must have had a reason and the most logical reason was that he wanted the good people of Harrisburg to be safe at home wrapping presents or waiting for Santa. There is usually not much traffic on Christmas Eve, Professor. Hardly any. And murder needs privacy. But that night a vehicle did drive down Second Street. Mine."

"Now you've gone too far, Evan. That red Cadillac of yours stands out like a sore thumb. If you had driven by that night I would have recognized you."

"I don't drive the Cadillac in the snow, Professor. That night I had my Subaru. Very inconspicuous. But still terribly frightening to a man who was about to commit murder. You had already been in the house, the Popes left their doors unlocked just like most of their neighbors did. But then you saw a car on the street and you couldn't risk having the driver see you setting the house on fire. So you walked away. An innocent citizen out for a late-night stroll. I was pretty sure that I recognized you from around campus, but I needed a more extensive observation to be sure."

"So you sat in on my class."

"So I sat in on your class. I was still not sure enough to make an identification that would stand up in court, and even if I had been certain I never actually saw you do anything wrong." Evan took a small digital recorder out of his pocket. "I may not have been positive that you started the fire until tonight but I was suspicious enough to drive here tonight and accuse you of murder. I needed you to confirm my suspicions. Thank you."

Montgomery ignored Evan's last move and considered the whole board. "But what would you be doing in that neighborhood that night?"

Evan ignored the question. "You asked me why I would come out of retirement to defend Rachel Pope. It's really very simple. I've always known that Rachel was innocent and I was not about to allow another innocent defendant die a prisoner's death when I knew for sure that she couldn't have started the fire."

"But of course she could. She was home the whole time."

"No she wasn't."

"Where else could she have been?"

"She was at my house. In bed. With me."

Montgomery gasped. "With you?"

"Yes, with me. That's how I knew that Rachel didn't start the fire. I had just dropped her off at home when I saw you walking away from the Pope house. She went inside, locked the door behind her, and climbed the stairs to her bedroom. The reason she had the chemicals on her shoes was that she got there after your first visit and she walked through the ether on her way upstairs.

She started to get undressed, you returned when you thought the coast was clear, and BOOM. The delay that your caution caused, the time you spent walking back and forth, gave the ether lots of time to vaporize. Thus the explosion that Gladys heard from next door. After you lit the match, the house erupted, and Rachel rushed to escape through the window." Evan paused. "I was the recent lover that the police have been looking for. I knew she didn't set the fire, and I made it my business to save her."

"But you could have saved her by testifying. You could have been her alibi."

"Alibi? Ha! I would have been her motive. A current lover. A tryst the very night of the murder. No, I couldn't save her by testifying. The first thing I told Rachel about this case was that it couldn't be won with friendly witnesses. We needed a flaw in the Commonwealth's case, and I finally found one. Even assuming that I was wrong about everything else, I knew for a fact that the jury would ignore the alibi testimony of an adulterous lover. If I was going to save Rachel, I had to do it from the defense table. Not from the witness stand."

"But what if someone had seen you? What if someone knew about you?"

"Someone did see me. The neighbor, Gladys Reynolds. That did give me some sleepless nights, but I was banking on her fidelity to Ted's memory. She recognized me the day I spoke to her at the crime scene. I wasn't sure what she would do or say but I was sure of one thing. She was honestly and truly in love with Ted Pope, probably more than Rachel ever was, and she wasn't going to make his death any more sordid than it had to be. Clint Jackson may have known about us, I was never sure about that, but that was just another chance I had to take. There are no perfect cases, after all. Courtrooms are always dangerous places."

Montgomery was staring into the fire now, reviewing the facts, silently critiquing Evan's story. Then he looked up with curiosity. "What about the lie detector test? How did she fail the test?"

"She failed the test because she was lying and the machine, contrary to my opinion of it, found her out."

"Impossible. She didn't kill Ted, I—"

"You did. Yes, I know that, you lit the fire. But don't forget that Rachel had just gotten home. She was awake when the flames rushed up the staircase. Ted, however, was asleep. Sound asleep."

"And she left him to burn?"

"The polygraph question was 'Were you in any way responsible for the death of Dr. Theodore Pope?' She said no, and that was a lie. Maybe she wasn't as responsible as you were, but maybe she was. I never tried to figure out exactly what she felt toward her husband. But when she realized that the house was on fire and Ted sound asleep, she knew that she could walk out of a life that didn't really suit her. And, by happy coincidence, there was the insurance. She didn't expect to be arrested of course, but—"

"But there are no perfect cases," he chuckled as he finished Evan's thought.

There was nothing left for either of them to say. The fire was dying but still warm. Montgomery gone back to reading *The Margites*. It was a time for reflection for both of them. Evan thought back to the beginning of the case, but then realized that he couldn't say for sure when it had started. Last year with the fire? The day that Rachel sent the state police to the Lasker? Or three thousand years ago, on some sunny plain in Smyrna, when Homer first sang the poem about Margites, the itinerant simpleton whom the Greeks all loved but who had been wiped off of the face of the Earth till now. Maybe it was true that death had waited for Ted Pope throughout the ages, hidden in the pages of an ancient, unknown book.

Evan's thoughts turned to a day six months before the fire, when Rachel Pope showed up at his office and sat in the student's chair and said nothing. She just sizzled in her physical perfection, and waited. When Evan started to say something, she stopped him with a smile and said, "I already know." Maybe that was the day that killed Ted Pope.

The room was filled with enough guilt to supply a hundred Greek tragedies. No matter when the case had begun, it would soon be over. Evan took a deep breath and stood up to put his coat on. Hector Montgomery stayed in his chair, and looked up from the book. His book. There was a peaceful look on his face. "You will forgive me, I hope, if I don't walk you to the door."

Evan nodded and held out his hand. Montgomery's hand was already cold, even though he was close to the fire.

They stared at each other across the abyss. Montgomery spoke first. "Have I your word?"

"My word."

When Evan opened the front door, the sun was starting to come up. He fired up the big Cadillac V-8 and roared up the empty street like a teenager.

Chapter 30

Two weeks later Evan was back in class for the second half of Great Moments in Courtroom History. Spring semester had started and he was handing out the reading lists and returning the Fall semester final exams.

"I'm sure you have all heard the Dean's announcement that there will be a memorial service this afternoon in honor of Professor Hector Montgomery, who as you all know died in his sleep a few days ago. The fire department has ruled it an accidental fire, it seems that he was a little careless with his fireplace." The class sat silently for a decent interval. "Professor Montgomery was a towering figure in classical scholarship and deeply devoted to Crawford College. I'm dismissing class early so you can all head over to the chapel and pay your respects." They all ran for the exits. All but Deborah Radcliff.

"Strange coincidence," she said.

"It's been a strange year."

"Yeah. I suppose you know things about Professor Montgomery that you won't tell me."

"Not much really," he said and sat down in one of the student chairs. Deborah started to say something but Evan waved her off. "You'll be graduating this year, Ms. Radcliff. What then?"

"I've applied to some law schools. If I get accepted I'll take a year off and start next September."

"Law schools? Your advisor can't approve of that very strongly." She laughed. "What happened to Classics?"

"I've given up on literature. It's too much like real life. Plus, it's getting pretty dangerous. Clint was at the hardware store this morning stocking up on smoke detectors."

"I don't think he has too much to worry about." Evan got up and walked to the door. "Now that I have a free afternoon, I guess I'll go downtown and play some chess."

"Aren't you going to Professor Montgomery's memorial?"

"No, I don't think so. I've just about had my fill of dead classicists."

The Lasker was never very busy on a weekday. There were only two boards underway when Evan walked into the game room that afternoon. One game was between two regulars, a real estate agent who always played the Two Knights opening and a sous chef who loved to trade bishops. The surprise was at the other table. Brenda Taylor was playing her usual technical game, but across the table was someone who had never before been in the Lasker.

"Judge Flinchbaugh," Evan grinned. "This is a private club. Should I get you a membership application?"

Flinchbaugh smiled back. "That won't be necessary, Evan. Actually I've been meaning to talk to you and I stopped by to find out when I might find you. I asked Dr. Taylor here if she knew your schedule, and she was good enough to offer me a game."

Evan looked at the board. Flinchbaugh was in a hopeless situation. Two pawns down and he had brought out his queen way too early. Plus he had already moved his king to avoid a check so he wouldn't be able to castle out of danger. "You're in a tough spot, Judge. You should ask Brenda if she'll accept a plea bargain."

"Too late," she was adamant as she moved a bishop to reveal a checkmate.

Flinchbaugh sat back and looked at the board. He shrugged. "I must be out of practice. Maybe I should take that membership application after all, Evan. Do you think any of the members here would vouch for me?"

"Sure, Judge. Follow me."

Evan led Flinchbaugh down to the first floor to the conference room where the club officers held their meetings. As the judge made himself comfortable at the antique walnut table, Evan found a membership application. "Just sign here. And next time you play Brenda, don't let her trap you on the back rank like that."

"Yes, that's good advice, Evan." He signed the form. "Would you mind if I gave you some?"

"Not at all, Judge. But I've seen you play."

"Not about chess, Evan. The courthouse is still buzzing about that acquittal of yours. Ian hoped to leave the District Attorney's Office on a high note before he took the bench. Hank Foster was expecting a promotion that didn't come through, and some ambitious young detective named Piper is now patrolling logging roads up in Moose County. It seems that you spoiled a lot of ambitions with that one verdict. But what I want to know about is you. How have you been doing?"

Evan knew that sooner or later they would circle around to the real purpose of this visit. He just said, "I'm fine Harry. Couldn't be better."

Flinchbaugh nodded. "Word is that you've become pretty unpopular on your campus now that you rescued the murderer of one of the college's most beloved professors."

"No kidding. Tell me this, Harry: You've been around a while. Where exactly does someone go to get popular for representing murder defendants? Even innocent ones? I've gotten used to the general population thinking that I'm the scum of the earth. I can live with it."

The judge nodded. "That Dr. Taylor, the psychiatrist? She thinks pretty highly of you. We had a nice friendly chat before she crushed my ego with that uncovered mate."

"Really? What could the two of you have to talk about? Do you need some anti-depressants? The seat of judgment starting to wear you down?"

"Oh, sometimes it can be a burden to exercise godlike power over total strangers," he said with a chuckle. "But no. We were actually talking about you. I told her that I never understood you staying away from the law for so long, and she recounted your conversation about Porter."

Evan stiffened. "I didn't think psychiatrists were allowed to have such big mouths. I should revoke her membership right now." He started to turn toward the stairs.

"You'll do no such thing, Evan. She spoke out of concern and she thought I might be able to help you. She was right."

"Ronnie Porter has been dead a long time, Judge, and there's nothing you can do about that. Don't let the black robe go to your head."

"No, I can't turn back the hands of time and make that boy not kill himself but I can tell you about the note."

"What are you talking about? What note?"

"Porter was not my trial, of course. Judge Washburn, wasn't it? But I was the chairman of the County Prison Board when he hung himself and I had to lead the investigation into his death. Some of these prison hangings turn out to be murders, botched attempts to resemble suicide, but Porter was an easy determination. The correctional staff found a note in his cell when they discovered him hanging. We tested the handwriting against some court papers he had signed during his case. It was definitely written by Porter, plus it had his fingerprints all over it. Very conclusive. It explained that he could no longer live with the guilt he felt for killing that clerk, for leaving the man's children fatherless, for disgracing his own family. He even mentioned how bad he felt for having lied to you. He always intended to take his own life, almost since the night of the murder. After he was convicted his opportunities narrowed but eventually he found a way.

"He would have done it even if he had been acquitted. It was all right there in black and white."

Evan was wide-eyed. And pissed. "That's what Ian told the press right after Porter's death but I thought he was grandstanding. That bastard must have known the truth right from the start."

"He did. Our report was confidential and we never released it to the public, not even to the family. But the D.A.'s office assisted in our investigation. Ian saw the note the day after Porter's body was discovered."

"And for all these years he let me suffer, thinking that my mistakes made an innocent boy kill himself?"

"Of course he did, Evan. Why wouldn't he? Have you really been away from the practice of law so long that you forgot how adversarial and self-serving it is? As long as you were traumatized with guilt you stayed away from criminal defense. That's what Ian wanted. That's what every prosecutor wanted. None of them wanted you to come back. The Triumphant Return of the Prince of Darkness? No way."

Evan was shell-shocked. "What do I do now, Harry? If you're so smart, you tell me. What do I do now?"

"Before we get to that, Evan, let me tell you another thing that Dr. Taylor and I discussed before you got here. The same question that a great many people have been puzzling over: why you returned to the courtroom for this particular case. There have been a lot of murders while you were gone. You could probably have had your pick."

"Oh really? What does Brenda think?"

"She has no idea. Not even a guess." Flinchbaugh rested his elbows on the table and steepled his fingers together as if he were getting ready to render judgment on an important point of law. "But, then again, she didn't watch the trial. She didn't see how positive you were that your client was innocent. I see lawyers trying to fake that attitude all the time, but you weren't faking. Absolute certainty was written all over your face. I saw it. So did the jury. After the verdict, some of the jurors told me that they were impressed with how confident you were that Mrs. Pope hadn't committed the murder. It influenced their votes. The jury foreman said that he suspected that there was something about the case that only you and the defendant knew." Harry paused. "I have to admit that the same idea crossed my mind once or twice."

Evan raised his eyebrows as if bewildered. "Really? I thought we just decided that the Porter case proves I can never tell who is guilty and who is innocent."

"Oh, it may not be as bad as all that, Evan. Anyway, back to your original question. What you should do now. Your semester will be over in a few months and our chief public defender Ben Monk resigned suddenly yesterday. It hasn't made the news yet. Something about a teenaged girl and a few ill-advised text messages."

Evan had to smile. He never liked Ben Monk. The guy let his lawyers get too chummy with the prosecutors. If Ben had ever known how to be a real defense lawyer he had forgotten it a long time ago. "Good riddance to him," said Evan. "But so what?"

"The county commissioners want the judges to recommend a replacement. Someone with experience. Someone who knows that there are no perfect cases but fights like hell anyway. Someone who knows how to play the whole board."

Evan was smiling now. Harry, he thought to himself, you may not be much of a chess player but you are one cagey old son of a bitch.

"So what do you think, Evan? Have any ideas?"

"I may know of someone," he said. "But first I have to revoke Brenda's membership. Or take her out to dinner. I haven't decided yet."

Epilogue

It was cold again that night, so when Evan got home after dinner with Brenda Taylor he built a roaring fire in the living room fireplace. He sat in front of it with a few dozen pages of crinkly old paper and an eight-gigabyte thumb drive. He tossed everything into the fire and the flames ate them in about ten seconds. The only thing left in his hand was an envelope, still unopened, that had arrived at his home in the afternoon mail. The engraved return address was "Crawford College, Department of Classics" and under that the initials "H.M." The postmark showed that it had been mailed the day before Hector Montgomery's house burned down. Evan opened it carefully. It was just a few lines. Handwritten. Evan recognized the paraphrase from the end of *The Iliad*.

> *On the tenth day with the sun shining the*
> *earth below, the Trojans took the man*
> *whom vengeance killed and burned him*
> *in a great fire.*

It was the funeral of Hector.

Who once had been heroic.

The Prince of Darkness tossed the envelope and the note into the fire, and sat there very still until the last flicker died away. He never heard a word about any rare old books being found among the ashes of Hector Montgomery's life.

THE END

Acknowledgments

M any friends and colleagues read the drafts of *The Widow on the Ledge* and improved the book greatly with their wise suggestions. These include, in no particular order, Attorneys Joshua Lock and William Costopoulos, retired State Police Major Diane Stackhouse, Professors Don Hummer and Charles Kupfer, retired Common Pleas Court Judge Jeannine Turgeon and my daughter Attorney Alexandria Lappas. My son, Dr. Thom Lappas, also saved Evan from the virtual scrap heap and thus is largely responsible for the story you have just read.

When, several years ago, I decided to become the published author I had always wanted to be, I had desire and drive—but not the slightest idea how to make it happen. Enter Jason Liller: bookman extraordinaire who has been my guide, guru and editor, but mostly my friend. Thanks Jason: I literally couldn't have done it without you.

None of this would matter one whit were it not for the love and devotion of my family. Thom, Ali, Shane, and Anne, and of course my two Chief Youthfulness Advisors, Spero and Stella who make it easy to believe that anything is possible.

COMING SOON

The Third Bullet

A teenager is accused of killing one of Harrisburg's most beloved citizens. Politics, ambition, and an obsessive thirst for blind vengeance threaten to put him on death row.

If Evan stands any chance of saving his client's life, he must first unravel the twisted maze of murder and solve the mystery of

The Third Bullet.

Turn the page to read a preview of
Spero T. Lappas's
next suspenseful
Evan Wonder legal thriller.

Chapter 1

Not knowing that it would be the last day of his life, Randy Samuels, Sr. started December 7 the same way he had started every other day for the last forty-seven years: Opening up the tiny, one-room, backwoods tavern which the state registry knew as The Susquehanna Steelman's Pub but which everyone in the neighborhood just called Randy's. It was the kind of place where old men showed up every morning to start drinking early and ended up sitting around drunk all day. December 7 started as no exception.

When Randy pulled his 1985 Mercury Grand Marquis over the loose gravel in the parking lot a little after 9:00 a.m., Ray Yoder and Paul Zurek were already waiting for him by the front door. Ray and Paul had retired from the steel mill about fifteen years ago and had spent most of those years sitting at the northwest corner of Randy's horseshoe bar.

"Didn't think you was going to open up today," said Ray as Randy unlocked the door. "Paul here was saying that you'da probably gone south already. To see Mickey."

Paul nodded as if to corroborate Ray's account. "And Minnie," he added. "Goofy too." The three of them guffawed obligingly for a few seconds until the two patrons took their seats and their host reached into the beer cooler and brought out a couple of cans of Pabst Blue Ribbon. PBR: the champion beer of the 1893 Colombian Exposition and the preferred breakfast of central Pennsylvania's hard-drinking inebriates.

Ray was on his fourth PBR by 10:30 and Paul was still nursing his third. Randy Samuels was behind the bar washing beer mugs, or at least rinsing them off before putting them back on the clean-glass rack. He shook his head every now and then as he realized that he wouldn't be washing those mugs too much longer. He had just turned seventy-five the week after last Thanksgiving and his son Randy, Jr. had finally talked him into retiring. They listed the tavern with a business broker who assured him that although the real estate was worth next to nothing, the Dauphin County liquor license would fetch him a pretty penny. Enough, Randy hoped, to start a college fund for the grandchildren. Next month, Randy, Jr. was taking him to Florida to celebrate. Disney World with the whole family. All of his regular customers

2

teased him about traveling south to visit a bunch of cartoon characters but Randy was actually looking forward to his first real vacation since he and his wife spent their honeymoon in Ocean City, New Jersey. That was fifty-three years ago and Disney World with all the kids sounded like it would be a lot of fun.

At least that was the plan until December 7 when the barroom door swung open at 10:37 a.m. Paul was able to tell the cops the exact moment because he was watching Fox News on the television set mounted above the bar and there was a screen clock in the corner. The two intruders entered with the bright winter-morning sun behind them. They were covered from head to foot in black clothing. Hooded sweatshirts. Ski masks. Black jeans. Black sneakers. Gloves. When the police later asked Ray and Paul if they could make an identification, neither one could even be sure of age, race, or sex. They were sure about the guns, though. "One of them had big cannon," remembered Ray. "Like Dirty Harry. The other gun was smaller. Lots smaller." Paul demonstrated how the intruders held them low at their waists, like gunfighters in a cowboy movie.

In the first few seconds of the robbery, neither Ray nor Paul paid much attention to the door opening. A few other regulars would typically wander in throughout the morning. They didn't look up until Randy hobbled out from behind the bar with a half-full bottle of

3

Seagram's 7 in one hand and a dripping beer mug in the other. "This is a stick-up," one of the robbers yelled needlessly, prompting Randy to wind up with the Seagram's and yell back, "The hell it is, you no good sons-of-bitches. You get the hell out of my bar." He got off a clean, though ineffectual, shot with the whiskey bottle but then died with the beer mug in his other hand and a single bullet hole in his heart.

By now, Paul and Ray were paralyzed with fear. They had both turned away from the action when the robbers announced their intention and they were too scared even to watch Randy take his last breath. They did testify that, while they were staring straight ahead at the television screen, they heard two shots. One louder than the other, probably because one gun was bigger than the other one. One of the robbers reached over the bar and grabbed a few dollars from the till and then they ran out. Both old men heard the revving getaway car scatter the parking lot's dry gravel. They finally looked over at Randy, bleeding from the chest wound and obviously beyond help. They finished their beers and then one of them, they didn't really remember which one it was, walked around the bar and put in the call to 911 on the house phone. Then they helped themselves to another PBR from the cooler while they waited for the cops. I mean, why the hell not? Within hours, Randy Samuels's murder became the Big Crime Story of that season. Randy, Jr. told every news outlet within a hundred miles about his father's imminent retirement. Over and over again the dead man's friends and neighbors told an army of reporters that Randy was the salt of the earth, a friend to all, quick with a joke, always smiling, not an enemy in the world. "What's this world coming to?" one of them asked. "Who would do such a thing?" another one wondered, "Why can't the police protect a harmless old man who just wants to make an honest living and then go to Disney World?"

* * * *

It was a cold Sunday night in February and Evan Wonder had been sitting in his library staring at a chessboard for most of the day. Over the course of the last week he had been helping a Swiss grandmaster prepare for next month's European championship. He pushed his knight to the F3 square just as the doorbell chimed. Making a mental note to email the move to his opponent, he carried his coffee mug over to the window were Andromeda was barking at something in the front yard. It could have been a burglar or a squirrel, maybe a gust of wind. At that time of winter it was unlikely to be a butterfly or a blue jay but in springtime any of those things would be enough to set off the alarm for a short-haired border collie who had been genetically engineered to warn her flock about even the slightest peril. She sensed danger and she wanted Evan to know it.

Evan couldn't see the steps outside his front door but he did see the grill of an unknown Honda Civic in his driveway. He didn't usually admit unexpected visitors but this one was persistent. The bell rang again and Andromeda barked louder. Whoever it was showed no signs of backing off.

"Yes?" Evan swung the door open to see a middle-aged African American man wearing what might have been a caftan along with a black skull cap and a long gray beard. Rimless glasses, baggy tan pants that looked to be made of canvas or burlap. He was standing a discreet, socially distant six feet from the door. He must have backed away after the last blast of the doorbell.

"Mr. Wonder? I'm Sean Miller. I deliver your newspaper. The New York Times?" He proved his credentials by pointing to the place on the sidewalk where the Sunday edition usually landed. "Jane Watson? Up the street?" His vocal intonation placed question marks after every phrase so as not to sound too aggressive. It was a common, sometimes unintentional, verbal manipulation.

"Jane told me about you. About you was once a famous lawyer? You see, it's my nephew Anthony. He's a good boy. Only seventeen and never in any trouble before, I mean no bad trouble. A little drugs, you know, like a lot of kids nowadays. But nothing like this. It's just not like him. No way."

A long career of hearing sad stories had taught Evan how to listen quietly while people began the most important conversations of their lives saying nothing important. Sean looked down at his folded hands until he was ready to say whatever it was that he had driven to Evan's house on a cold Sunday night to say.

Silence.

"Anthony's been arrested."

Sean held up some sheets of paper that he carried in his right hand. "I brought some of this paperwork with me in case you wanted to see what I'm talking about." Sean looked down at his feet as if eye-to-eye contact would give credence to what he was about to say.

"They say he shot that old man. The bartender. They say he murdered him. It's been in all over the news, Mr. Wonder. Maybe you heard about it."

Evan had heard about it, alright. He took the papers from his visitor and stepped out of the doorway. "Come on in, Sean. Let's take a look at this." They walked toward the kitchen while Andromeda let out a low growl, still guarding the threshold. "Let's see what you have here." He unfolded a criminal complaint charging one

Anthony Miller with the murder of Randy Samuels, as well as burglary, robbery, conspiracy, and unlawful possession of a firearm.

Sean stopped halfway down the hallway that led to Evan's kitchen. "Anthony's in jail and the police say they have a witness. The DA is sayin' he's gonna try an' give Anthony the death penalty and the police say they got a witness. But I don't see how that's possible though, 'cause Anthony says he didn't do it. His mother is like to die from her nerves and I ain't doin' so good myself."

"We need help, Mr. Wonder. Anthony and the family. We need somebody to save us."

"Well then, I'm glad you came here." His visitor smiled at the welcoming remark, never knowing that Evan was thinking that he needed that very same thing.

About Spero T. Lappas

Spero T. Lappas has practiced criminal defense at the highest levels for over four decades. He has served as lead counsel in hundreds of major cases, including some of Central Pennsylvania's most important trials.

He earned a PhD in American Studies from The Pennsylvania State University where he researched the relationship between American law and culture and a Juris Doctor degree with honors from the Dickinson School of Law where he was on the Editorial Board of the *Dickinson Law Review,* a member and faculty adviser of the National Trial Moot Court Team, and the winner of two American Jurisprudence Awards.

Dr. Lappas served as an inaugural member of the Pennsylvania Senate Advisory Committee to Study the Causes of Wrongful Convictions and the Pennsylvania Legislative Advisory Committee to Study the Death Penalty. He was a Commissioner of the Pennsylvania State Citizens Law Enforcement Advisory Commission where he served as Chair of the Critical Incident Review Committee and a member of the Rules Committee. He was among the youngest lawyers to be honored in the first and second editions of *The Best Lawyers in America* and has since been recognized in *Who's Who in American Law, Who's Who in the World, Who's Who in America, America's Leading Lawyers,* and *The Bar Register of Pre-Eminent Lawyers.* He received an AV rating, the highest possible recognition, from the Lexis/Nexus Peer Reviewed rating system. He is also a prize-winning photographer, a tournament Scrabble champion, and a former nationally competitive three-weapon fencer.

Lappas is headquartered in Harrisburg, Pennsylvania where he is the father of two grown children and their spouses and grandfather to two wonderful grandchildren. He often speaks to academic, civic, and community organizations about matters of public importance and frequently teaches as a substitute teacher in public schools throughout Central Pennsylvania.

He continues to review legal cases for possible incidents of wrongful conviction.

www.ingramcontent.com/pod-product-compliance
Lightning Source LLC
Chambersburg PA
CBHW061327050726
47504CB00013B/749